DEDICATION

Marta and many other characters were inspired by those noted below, to whom I dedicate this book.

To the artist of the portrait that gave me the idea of Marta's appearance. Although Marta should appear to readers as they see her in their own imagination, it was an inspiration.

To the young lady at the Olive Café in Mission Beach who I happened to observe skateboarding to work one day. She became the character of Marta.

To Sabrina Jensen. To me, you are the epitome of why each and every one of us has someone who comes into a life for a purpose or reason, whether for a lifetime or just a moment. One morning, when I sat down to write, I just stared at the computer screen, stuck in my thought process of where to go with this story. I went to work that day and a butterfly came to my jobsite early on and for some reason, it remained there all day, flying from one spot to another but never leaving the yard. At the end of the day, I said goodbye to my newfound friend. When I arrived home, your story came across my feed on Facebook. Sadly, tragic as it may have ended, your mother's loving words regarding your brief but full life on Earth and how you lived it up to that fateful day really resonated with me, especially her mentioning what the symbol of a butterfly would forever mean to her. The very next day, while I was at work, I was visited by what I assumed was the same butterfly. It clicked in my head that this was not a coincidence, but a sign. It not only touched my heart, but made it that much more inspiring to me that somehow, I could share some of your life experiences in the character of Marta. Someday, soon I hope, your story will be told to inspire other young adults to do the same as you before the world takes over; I know it would be a much happier place. Your life lives on continuously because of all the hearts and souls you touched with your love in one way or another along the way. Each time we see a single butterfly in our presence is a reminder that angels do exist. Thank you.

To my lovely daughter, Chelsea, on whom many of Marta's personality traits are based, and of course a personal experience or two or three or four. Ha, ha. Life doesn't always go as we necessarily plan it to go, but just the same, miracles do exist and occur as such as they have in your life. As life can be taken away unexpectedly, life can be created when it's unexpected as in yourself and your daughter, Cali. Your continued fight to survive through the adversity presented to you and your determination to not let any of it defeat you is why I am so proud to be your father, and in essence, what I tried to present through the character of Marta. More important is your understanding of compassion of others' souls, minds and bodies, no matter their disability, for you know there are disabilities in all of us, some more than others, and they should be looked at as a strength instead of a weakness. I don't know how this is even possible after fighting for you so many years, but I appreciate you even more now and the love I missed for so many years in not having you around has grown tenfold now that you are and even a hundred times more for my granddaughter.

To the young man who was and is the inspiration for Cap. I have seen you many times walking the streets of San Diego and have tried many times to chase you down, only to have you disappear after I turn the corner. I hope and pray wherever you are that help finds you as it did for Cap.

To all those who are homeless and fighting issues that lead to homelessness who shared their stories with me, bits and pieces of which I used in the book. My hope for you and the many others throughout the homeless community due to issues like trouble assimilating post-military, mental illness, home shortages, and more is that your journey ends in happiness—with a solution we as a community, nation, and world can create now and prevent this from occurring again.

To my uncle, Steven D. Fairchild, who served in Vietnam, and all the military who have served in the past during peace and war. I am grateful not only for their service, but also for all their stories, parts of which I used to represent some of the characters' backgrounds. I hope those in Washington and locally will do a better job responding to our veterans' needs when they come home from war. They should be held at a much higher level of concern than they currently are.

To the surfing, business, and residential communities all over the world, but particularly those of San Diego and Orange counties, from Imperial Beach up the coast to Huntington Beach, and inland from Joshua Tree down to the Cleveland National Forest areas of Palomar, Julian, and Pine Valley and the desert of Anza Borrego to Jacumba. These two counties are as diversified as their people, making them such enjoyable places to live and learn about all aspects of life and be able to share it in my words.

Finally, to my family. Support has been unconditional in our family, from honesty in criticism to encouragement. That is where respect comes from, as well as love. This is a lesson we probably all learned from various relatives throughout the years, but no one taught us as well as our own parents. Mom was the number one supporter of the arts. Dad was number one in encouraging us to focus on whatever we decided to do and be disciplined in our goals. Both didn't care what we were to be; they wanted us to be dedicated to it and love doing it. Every time I've called home to speak with you, Dad, your life experience always comes through with a new quote of encouragement. Mom, each time I run into an issue and feel deflated, a slight breeze crosses my brow or a single rose appears where it's not supposed to be. Much, much love for the everlasting support in life and in spirit!

"You are never too old to
set another goal or to dream a new dream."

—C.S. Lewis

IL PRESENTE

(Present Day)

Marta stood at the side of her bed, naked, curling her toes against the chilled hardwood flooring. The early morning air caused the partially open blinds to click against the window sill, creating a rhythm that seemed to be consistent with her deliberate, slow breathing. The cool air caused her nipples to become erect as she stood there, motionless, her eyes closed with her arms alongside her tall, slender body, outlined only by the nightlight plugged into the wall outlet just to side of the bed, which cast a shadow of her along the floor and up the wall and ceiling. Slowly, with her shadow following, she tilted her head up toward the ceiling, with her arms following, seemingly trying to touch it with her open palms. Again, slowly, she tilted both her head and arms toward the floor, this time with her young ample breasts following. Bending at the waist, with her legs locked, she grabbed the back of each ankle and held that position for a few more seconds before repeating the whole routine. Each time, her long brown hair, braided in dreadlocks with several different colors of small ribbons, a couple small feathers, and a piece of jewelry woven in it intermittently, touched the floor like the head of a mop. When she stood up, she reached for the ceiling with her palms one more time, holding still for a few seconds, then once again bent over toward the floor, this time with her palms touching the surface, holding that position a few seconds before standing back straight with her arms to her side and her eyes closed.

The only sounds were the blinds still hitting the window sill and her faint breathing in through her nose and out through her mouth. Marta was tall in stature, just shy of five foot ten, thin but shapely, long legged with long arms and thin, long fingers. Her skin was darkly tanned without one tan line on her body because of her occasionally lying naked on the roof of her apartment in the sun. She was a young woman—twenty-three years old—with a vibrant smile that glistened against the darkness of her skin.

After a few minutes of standing there, she slowly opened her eyes and walked over to the front door of her apartment, opened it, then pushed the screen door open while stepping out onto a small balcony. She let the screen door shut quietly behind her, not wanting it to slam and wake her neighbors. The balcony was dimly lit from the only light of a streetlamp on the corner down the alley from her place. She leaned against the railing with her bare butt and looked up into the still dark morning sky. The cold automatically caused her nipples to stand to attention again. She rubbed her arms and breasts with her hands for a few seconds to warm her body as she took in the morning air through her nose.

Adjacent to her was her wetsuit, which had been hanging over the railing to dry from the previous day's use. She grabbed it and began to slowly ease on the one-piece, black neoprene suit, with short leggings and arm sleeves, slipping one leg in then the other while she wiggled and shimmied her body, so it would slip up over her hips and ass. When she got it up to her waist, she adjusted the leggings some over her knees, then took one arm and reached into one sleeve and stretched her free arm back, bending it tightly to slide her other arm through the second sleeve. She raised up her shoulders to pull the back up along her neck and flipped her hair out from underneath the suit with both hands. She adjusted each breast to get them comfortably inside, as she only zipped the suit up to just about halfway, not totally covering her breasts. Getting into a wetsuit isn't an easy task, but Marta had her routine down pat.

She opened the screen door and grabbed the handle to the main door, slowly closing it and the screen door as well. She reached for a hairband that she kept wrapped around the screen door handle, grabbed her hair in a bunch and wrapped the band around it so it laid in a single ponytail over her right shoulder. She slipped on a pair of flip flops she'd stowed at the top of the stairs, then headed down the single flight into the alley. With each step she took, the sole of her flip flops would slap against her heel. She walked kitty-corner across the alley to the back door of a building, stopping briefly to look up and see that the light was either burned out or had not been turned on the night before. She opened the door, reached around the inside to where she felt the light switch and flipped it up. The light turned on. She walked inside and let the door close behind her. Upon entering, the aroma of bacon cooking immediately hit her nostrils. She followed a short hallway that led to a brightly lit kitchen where two men in white coats, approximate in age to Marta, stood working. She could feel the warmth of the hot water Carlos was using to wash dishes and the heat from the cooktop where Johnny was prepping some food. They were brothers of Mexican heritage who could both speak not only Spanish, but English very well.

"Buenos dias, Senorita Marta," Carlos said.

"Buenos dias, Carlos," Marta replied. "Buenos dias, Johnny boy," she said to the cook as she stopped beside him and stole a piece of bacon off the griddle.

"Hola," Johnny said. He slapped her hand with the spatula he was holding, as he did every morning. Together, Marta and Johnny said, "Some things never change, young lady," and they both smiled.

She continued out through the kitchen and into the dining area, toward the front entrance of the café, where the owner was sitting at a table by the door, reading the morning paper.

"Morning, Boss," Marta said to Emanuel, a middle-aged man, the father of Carlos and Johnny. He had very black hair slight greying on the sides where he kept it short. Marta thought and told him many times that it made him look distinguished and handsome. When she did, he would run a hand along the side of his head slowly, bowing in almost embarrassment and then raising his chin with a great big smile of gratitude for her compliment.

"Morning, my dear Marta." He lifted his head from the paper and smiled. He pointed to the bag on the side of the table with his nose and said, "In there is a new type of cannoli Johnny is experimenting with. Let me know what he thinks."

Marta put the last piece of bacon in her mouth, picked up the bag and headed toward the door looking at Emanuel. "Thanks, Boss." She grabbed a skateboard at the base of the front door, pushed the door open and walked out. In one motion, she dropped the skateboard, hopped on with both feet and started gliding past the front window, which she tapped. Emanuel turned and looked and as he did, Marta gave him a two-finger kiss from her lips and he responded in return as they did every morning.

She gave herself another kick on the skateboard and maneuvered down the sidewalk. The skateboard made a "putanka," "putanka" sound every time the wheels went over a seam or crack in the sidewalk or when she transitioned from the sidewalk to the street and then back onto the sidewalk at each intersection she crossed. She followed the sidewalk from the corner of Haines Street down along Garnett Street in the Pacific Beach area of San Diego. Along the way, the sun was starting to crest above the east; slowly dawn was breaking. The streetlamps began to shut off one at a time as the morning light crept slowly into the sky and down the street. The traffic lights stopped flashing yellow for caution to functioning normally because traffic would soon pick up. Marta knew it was getting close to 6:00 a.m.

As she continued to skate down the sidewalk, she could the see the sun chasing her along the way in the reflections from the storefront windows she passed as its rising light glistened off the glass. She skated across every intersection and past each establishment with ease, only occasionally dodging a shopkeeper or store owner preparing to open for the day and many a homeless person moving from their seemingly safe refuge for the night to another for their day. She continued her journey all the way down to just before the entrance of Crystal Pier and Cottages. Upon arriving, she eased her weight on the back of her skateboard till the front end went in the air and she braked herself to stop. She hopped off and allowed it to hit the curb and as it popped in the air, she went to grab it, missed, and it landed upside down on the boardwalk.

"Shit!" she said, loud enough for the couple of seagulls that sat perched on the boardwalk seawall to be startled and fly off. She bent over, picked up the skateboard, and continued walking over to the stairs, not far from the pier, that led down to the beach. As she started her descent down the old wooden stairs, she sort of skipped down each step and couple of landings, her flip-flops clicking in rhythm until her feet hit the sand.

With the skateboard and bag in hand, she darted across the cool sand to disappear under the pier. There, she came upon a makeshift little shelter made of some cardboard and towels that were strategically hung and built around the pier's pylons and against the seawall like a lean-to. At one end of the shelter, she saw a pair of bare feet and legs half covered with a blanket that had USMC printed on it.

Marta stood there and spoke softly. "Cap, you awake?" She waited for a response and when there was none, she asked again. "Cap?"

This time, the legs moved slowly in the sand and then there was a slight cough followed by, "Yes, darlin', I'm awake."

The blanket along with the legs slowly disappeared into the makeshift lean-to and then just as slowly, Cap crawled out from under the shelter and stood up. He stood tall, six foot three at least, and presented a body of a well-built but thin young man, thirty years of age. However, appearance wise, he presented himself in sad shape; he had messy long sandy blonde hair down to his shoulders and just as long of a beard that seemed groomed, but only from what appeared to be from him pulling at it all the time as he spoke.

"Sorry, darlin', had a long night arguing with some young punks who seemed to want to just give a homeless man some grief." He coughed again, but this time hacked up a bunch of saliva and turned his head to spit it a distance away into the sand. "Excuse me, darlin'. Sorry about that."

Cap was wearing a pair of green camouflage military fatigue pants with the knee area torn, rolled up to just above his ankles, and a dark green tattered tank top that tightly followed his thin but chiseled torso. Both were kind of filthy, but Cap didn't have an odor to him other than the smell of his sweat. The dirt and sand probably hid anything else. Cap turned from Marta and began to pull the towels off the top of the shelter. As he did, it revealed a surfboard. Marta just stood there. She knew this was his space and had learned a few months back, from the first time they met, to respect it.

"No problem, Cap. Sorry to hear about the punks," she said.

She could tell he was in a bad mood from lack of sleep, so she set down the bag next to one of the cardboard walls Cap had constructed and kicked off her flip-flops. Cap reached over the shelter, grabbed the surfboard, turned, and then handed it over to Marta. She took it, turned, tucked it under one arm while balancing it with her other hand, and began to walk toward the water.

"Thanks, Cap!"

She headed down toward where the beach meets the surf. She was about halfway when she turned and shouted out to Cap.

"Johnny tried something new and threw it in there for you to sample. Enjoy!"

Cap grunted to himself. "Ugh, I hate being guinea pig for his goddamn experiments!"

Cap crossed his feet as he stood and then slowly sat down in the sand all in one motion. He reached behind him, grabbed the blanket and draped it over his shoulders, leaned over, and grabbed the small paper bag. Opening it up, he took a whiff of the sweet smell, waved it in toward his nose with one of his hands, reached in, and pulled out the wrapped cannoli. He reached in again and grabbed a Styrofoam cup of hot coffee. He twisted it down into the sand, making a natural cupholder for himself. He then meticulously unwrapped the cannoli and took a bite as he watched Marta. She ran and dove into the water with the board and began to paddle through the low surf out to where the other surfers where waiting for the next big swell. Some were just arriving with her, while others were already out into the early morning waves.

FAMILIA DI ALFARO E MARINELLO

(Family of Alfaro and Marinello)

Marta's father, Silvano Marinello, was of Italian descent. His family came from the very small town of Abetone in the Tuscany region of Italy, high in the mountains where snow-skiing was popular. He had moved to the States as a young man searching for adventure, heading for Los Angeles for the warmer weather and the chance for stardom in the music industry. When he wasn't writing music and auditioning. he would play piano in various clubs, doing his best to become the next Billy Joel.

Marta's mother was of Hispanic descent; Alfaro was her surname. Her family spoke Spanish fluently and English with a hint of a Spanish accent, as they'd been Americans for many generations. Their ancestry was more of Spain then Mexico; they were direct descendants of the Spanish Conquistadors who had come to the Americas to explore. The dark color of Marta's skin was a combo of her father's and mother's. Her parents met when her father was doing a gig in a bar off Sunset Boulevard in Hollywood and her mother was working as a cocktail waitress. Her mother also could sing very well in both languages and her father could play anything requested of him. They soon started dating, combined their talents, began to book gigs around the area, and quickly started doing studio work across the country until her mother found out she was pregnant.

Her father stopped the touring and they got married right away. He continued to play in studio gigs and bars close to home. They were living a good life in a small place in the nearby winding roads of the Hollywood Hills area that he had rented before they had met. When the time came for the baby to arrive, it was the middle of the night; her father helped his very pregnant wife into the car and off they went to the hospital. They didn't get more than two blocks away from home when—after stopping at a four-way stop and looking both ways—he pulled out into the intersection, where their car was broadsided. Her father was killed instantly, but her mother held on until the ambulance could get her to the hospital, where she died before she made it to the emergency room. The doctors, however, were able do an emergency C-section, so Marta was born without ever meeting or knowing her parents.

Her grandparents on both sides of the family were notified. Her mother's family lived in San Diego and her father's family still lived in Italy. It was determined that she would stay with her grandparents in San Diego, as her Italian grandparents did not have the means to come get her or even take care of her, but they stayed in contact throughout the years. Marta was already named before she was born; her parents had mentioned it would be Marty if a boy and Marta if a girl because of their love for the music and lyrics of many of the songs of an old country western singer, Marty Robbins.

Marta grew up in the Old Town area of San Diego in her grandparent's home. There, she learned English and Spanish, although English was stressed more. Her grandmother made it clear that though they had four generations of Spanish-Americans heritage, English is what they would speak. There was a mixture of other nationalities through the whole neighborhood, but it was primarily filled with families of Spanish descent. As Marta got older and learned more about her parents, she also learned to speak Italian in hopes of being able to meet her father's family. She wanted to surprise them some day by knowing their language.

Music came naturally to Marta; she started singing along with her grandmother one day while her grandmother was cooking in the kitchen and Marta was sitting in a highchair. Marta would hum and make strange noises from her mouth, but they were in tune with her grandmother. As she grew, she proceeded to learn music from various family members, even learning how to play the guitar from her great-uncle Pietro. She learned a lot of the musical ways of the Mexican cantinas and classic love songs, but he also taught her all sorts of other music from The Beatles to Gwen Stefani. She really loved and treasured the latter, and thus was thrilled when her uncle surprised her with tickets to a concert in nearby Anaheim, Stefani's home turf.

Marta continued to learn to play other instruments as well. She studied and played music so much that her grandmother said she needed to find another outlet, so she could walk away from the music and breathe occasionally, or she feared she would burn herself out. So, one day her grandfather started taking her to the pier in Imperial Beach to go fishing with him—a request from her grandmother. It was her grandfather's own stress relief, after working long days as a cement contractor. He would go home, eat, and listen to Marta's practicing, and then usually fall asleep in whatever chair he was sitting in at the time. But every morning, like clockwork, he would be up early and off to the pier.

Marta didn't care for the fishing as much as she enjoyed all the old men's stories. Of course, everyone tried to outdo one another, with stories that were sometimes fishy, but there were those that were true, too, like one she witnessed one morning as a fisherman caught a big thresher shark off the end of the pier. It was a big pageant of celebration when he did. To the local Hispanic community, the thresher shark is considered a very tasty fish and it provides enough meat for a few families. A crowd gathered quickly after the catch, as they all wanted to get a picture with the shark. When they were all done, someone clubbed the shark on the head and then another cut off the tail fin and handed it to a young man who proceeded to throw it up on the roof of the bait shop at the end of the pier. When Marta looked up to see where it landed, she saw a flock of seagulls descend on it—flying in almost immediately after the fin hit the roof to fight over the pickings. She also saw a bunch of skeletons of previous fins that had dried out in the Southern California sun after being eaten down to the bone by the seagulls. A couple of the fishermen then proceeded to cut and gut out the shark. When she saw the innards plop out onto the pier and got a whiff of the pungent odor, Marta almost hurled. She turned, bent over, and dry heaved, then went quickly around to the side of the building, where her grandfather was still fishing.

Marta soon realized she was not interested in the fishing, but she found she was very amused by all the surfers on the south side of the pier. She watched intently and saw how they waited for the waves. She paid attention to their timing and it was like music to her ears. She listened to the waves like she listened to her music, feeling a rhythm go through her body as it did when she played music. Before long, she was counting the swells as they broke and trying to figure out the ocean's song. Day after day she did this, observing and learning.

One day, while her grandfather was fishing and telling her a story, he turned his head and found she was gone. He stood there looking for her and figured she had gone off to the end of the pier or the other side of the bait house, as she had done several times before. After about an hour or so of fishing, he and others near him heard some yelling coming from the other side of the pier. He reeled in his pole, picked up the tackle box, and walked over to ask people what all the commotion was about. They pointed to the surfers down below. He looked and all he saw was one surfer who had just finished riding out a wave and a bunch of guys yelling and cheering. He asked what was so fantastic and they all said it was because a girl had done that last ride.

It wasn't so unusual for a girl to surf—they had been for years—but down in Imperial Beach, it was a big deal for someone of Marta's background to do it, as most girls of Hispanic descent were doing what was considered "womanly things," such as cooking and cleaning. Her grandfather said, "Good for her. What an accomplishment for that young lady." He then turned and walked down the pier toward the shore, totally expecting Marta to have fallen asleep on the bench as she had many times in the past, but this time he didn't find her there. So, he walked along the beach boardwalk, thinking she was probably there listening to one of the old men playing music for money. She was not there, either. He then walked around the boardwalk seawall and stepped off the concrete onto the sand, slowly walking onto the beach looking for her. He started walking down toward the water's edge, looking inland along the sand and yelling her name.

"Marta!"

There was no response or sign of her, so he shouted again and again. He did this a number of times when he finally heard Marta shout back.

"Papa!" And again, she shouted, "Papa!"

He turned around, confused as to what direction her voice was coming from, and could not see her.

"Papa!" Marta shouted again.

This time he turned toward the water and saw her coming out with a surfboard in hand. Her shorts were wet and her t-shirt was soaked through, and though you could not see through it, it was obvious that her nipples were poking through the material. "Good God, my dear," he said as he made a gesture toward her breasts. Marta looked and laughed and placed her free arm across her chest.

As she approached him, he soon realized it was she who he had seen earlier from the pier, being cheered on. That was verified when he heard some of the other surfers yelling for her to come back out in the water.

"You mean you were the young girl I saw from the pier who everyone was cheering for?" he asked.

"I kind of guess so, Papa," she responded. "Can I stay longer? I can get a ride back home later, Papa."

He considered his granddaughter's young and excited eyes and could not deny her happiness. "Yes, my dear, you may," he responded.

Marta reached over and kissed him on the cheek. "Thanks, Papa. Love you!"

She turned and ran back into the surf with the board and started swimming back out to the others. Her grandfather stood there and watched her swim out. When she had reached the others, she saw he was still standing there, and she waved enthusiastically to him and threw him a kiss. He waved back and threw back a kiss. He then walked back up to the boardwalk seawall, set down his tackle box on the wall, and set the end of his fishing pole in the sand, leaning it against the wall. He then leaned against the wall as well and crossed his arms, squinting to search for Marta out in the surf until he found her, refocused his eyes, and watched her surf.

This would be their morning routine for the next several years: up at the break of dawn and off to the beach, where he would fish and she would surf. Occasionally, he would give her advice, though it was not so much advice on her surfing as much as it was advice of thought, process, strategy, and patience. Marta understood where he was coming from, would smile, say "thank you, Papa" with a kiss on his cheek, then run to the water. This always put a smile on his face, just as Marta's music always made her grandmother smile.

During Marta's senior year of high school, she planned a trip to cross the coastlines of Spain and Italy after she graduated in the spring. She would "hike it or hitch it" she would say to her grandmother whenever asked how she would get around—and she planned on surfing every chance she could get. She worked out the whole trip to the minute and the cost right down to the penny. The goal was to meet her father's side of the family in Italy and some of her mother's side in Spain. She would stay with family when she could, and the rest of the trip would involve camping or hostels. Other than her initial goals of discovering family and surfing, she wanted to study the various styles of music in the small towns she would come across.

Soon spring and graduation came and went, and with her backpack and her guitar in hand, she flew from Lindbergh Field in San Diego to Seville, Spain, with a layover in New York. There, she hitched a ride south to a small town called Las Cabezas de San Rueben, where she stayed with distant family of her grandfather Alfaro. She spent a few days, which included visiting the Donana Natural Park, where she was in awe of the many birds and flowers—from eagles, flamingos, sparrows, and finches to cacti blooms, roses, and sunflowers.

Though she was raised in the Catholic religion, Marta felt free now to view her faith on her own terms. While not fond of her Catholic upbringing and the constraints she felt it put on her as a woman, she still planned on visiting various churches on the trip, such as the Baroque church of San Rueben Bautista. The visit was mainly to view the amazing architecture of the period, but once inside she found herself alone, something she had never experienced while in church. She walked slowly forward down the center aisle, turning her head upward and her body around as she looked at all the paintings, colors, and shapes of the building. She stopped about halfway down, slowly side-stepped into a pew and sat down. She stared ahead at the statues that stood under the arch of the altar, realizing just how quiet and serene it was. She felt more at peace and in tune now than she did whenever she was inside a church filled with people. She felt a presence upon her heart and soul that she never felt before. She leaned back in the pew, clasped her hands, tilted her head back toward the magnificent ceiling, closed her eyes, and prayed. Soon, tears began to trickle and a huge smile appeared on her face as she felt full in her heart. Everything was "right."

Marta finished her stay with family in Las Cabezas de San Rueben. She headed out south on the road, hiking for a while until her feet began to get sore. She caught a ride to Gibraltar, where she stayed the night in a hostel before making her way along the southern coast of Spain the next morning.

She began by hiking again until she got to the town of El Faro, not far up the coast from Gibraltar. Marta took a short path down to the beach and stood there watching the locals surfing in the North Mediterranean Sea. The water looked so blue and clear and it sparkled from the sun like one gigantic diamond from where she was standing. It looked magical to her. She knew she had to surf right here and now.

She continued down the path until she came across a small community and found a shop near the beach. She asked the shopkeeper where she could keep her things and rent a surfboard. Even though she spoke to him in Spanish, the shopkeeper could recognize she was not from around there; he responded in broken English that he would return shortly and told her to wait right there. Marta stood there thinking he must have realized she was a tourist and just blew her off.

Just as she was about to leave, the shopkeeper came back and called out to her. Marta turned and saw him coming toward her with a surfboard. He stood it at her feet and told her she could use it. He told her she could keep her things in the back room, where they would be safe, and she could change there as well. For some odd reason, Marta trusted him and took him up on his offer. It wasn't long before she grabbed the surfboard and started to head out.

"Agradecido," she said to the shopkeeper.

"Disfruta," he shouted, as she left the shop.

Marta reached the shore running, then stopped dead in her tracks. She followed the water as it came up to her toes and over her feet and ankles and receded. It felt warm, warmer than the water in San Diego. She took in the air with her nose. Though there was the smell of salt, the scent was different than back home. Fresher, she thought. Then she took the air in again, this time through her mouth. She could now taste the salt. This time she thought it was the same; salt is salt. She could feel her heart race with emotion and then she felt it slow to the speed of her breath. Then water came across her feet again and she felt in tune. She kicked it in gear and ran out into the surf with the board under her arm. When she got about waist deep, she hopped atop the board and paddled out toward the other surfers.

Marta surfed for the remainder of that afternoon, being patient for her turn to ensure she was not disrespectful to the locals. She soon found there were many others like her, not from around there or from another country. She made many new friends while waiting for the next swell that would be hers to surf. She felt that was the backbone of surfing—the camaraderie that developed between people who in other situations might remain strangers.

When she finished for the day, she went back to the shop to find the shopkeeper was nowhere to be found. She was surprised at first, then a bit of panic set in as she thought for sure all her things would be gone, but she found he had left her a note pinned to the curtain leading to the back room. It stated there was a room with a shower and bath down the street if she wished to stay the night, gave the address of the place, and asked her to just lock the door behind her when she left. She leaned the surfboard against a wall, gathered her things, locked the door, and headed to the address he had written.

There, she showered and dressed, and then grabbed her guitar and followed another path down to the shore, where she met some of the others she had surfed with earlier in the day. They spent the evening down on the beach around a fire eating, drinking, talking, laughing, and singing songs. When she finally got the nerve to say goodbye, they didn't want her to leave. She didn't want to go either, but she knew she had to stay the course of her trip, thus she hugged and kissed almost everyone there before making her way back to her accommodations. She quietly went up to her room, laid her guitar against the wall, and lay down on the bed. She thought about what a wonderful journey she had been on thus far and this was just the beginning. She fell peacefully asleep.

Marta awoke the next morning to the smell of food. She was still in her clothes from the night before, so all she had to do was pack her backpack and she'd be on her way. She met the host at the bottom of the stairs and joined her and her family for breakfast, where they talked about her adventures and journey ahead. She asked how much she owed, and they said nothing; it was an honor to have a visitor from another country in their home. They wrapped up some food for to take with her and then Marta hoisted her backpack on her back, along with her guitar, said her thank yous and goodbyes, and went off down the road.

She didn't get far when she realized how tired her legs were already, which was obviously the result of her surfing the previous day. She was already a bit concerned about her schedule, for this was the 5th unexpected stop she had made along the way. She really had not planned or allowed for time for such things and yet it was all so worth it, as she was not only learning so much about the people and her surroundings, but also learning a lot about herself. Realizing that, she started not to worry as much about the schedule. She came to understand that maybe she was too much of a regimented person—as her grandmother had tried to explain so many times—and she just needed to go with the flow, as her great-uncle Pietro would say.

She still wanted to make sure she had time for the things she had scheduled. So, she got back onto the main road and decided to thumb a ride. A small car eventually pulled up alongside her. Although most vehicles in Europe were small, this one was really tiny. When she reached the car, she saw it was driven by one of the guys she had met the night before.

"Hola," she said.

"Hallo," he said to her. "Marta, correct?" Marta nodded her head yes.

"I'm sorry, but I met so many people last night that I have forgotten your name."

"Some first impression I must have made." He responded with a smile. Then Marta put two and two together from his accent and realized who he was.

"Hugh!" she shouted. "Hugh from Scotland."

"Well are ya going to get in or not?" he asked.

Marta walked around to the car and opened the passenger door. She went to place her things in the back when she saw he was packed for travel as well. She carefully laid down her things, with the guitar on top, and then pushed the seat back, sat down, and buckled herself in.

"Wow," she said.

"What would that be?" Hugh asked.

"This is the first time I have sat on the driver's side of a car and there isn't a steering wheel."

Hugh looked at her strangely. "I'm on the driver's side of the car," he said.

"Never mind," she responded, with a laugh, figuring it might be too difficult to explain. Hugh put the car into gear, slowly pulled out onto the road, and off they went.

Together, Marta and Hugh traveled along the coast of Spain. They stopped and surfed at Balcon de Europe Point and Galua, and finally just north of Barcelona at La Fosca. These were all places Marta had on her wish list of surfing the Mediterranean—along with visiting the little country towns inland and along the sea. Though it wasn't in either one of their plans, they shared the experience together, surfing and sightseeing during the day, music and partying at night. There was never anything sexual between them, but there was a friendship built along the way that would last them both for a lifetime.

They continued into France until they arrived in Tamaris. There, they would surf together one more time before Hugh would make the turn north to head home to Scotland and Marta would head south into Italy. At the end of a perfect day of surfing and meeting new friends, Hugh and Marta sat alone on the beach near a campfire and talked through the night about their amazing time together and how they were going to miss each other. The next morning, they exchanged gifts. She gave him an earring he had said he liked on her and he gave her the keyring that dangled from his set of keys, which featured a Celtic saying. She never asked him what it meant—the small rectangle piece made of silver had the words, "An lamb a bhier's i a gheibh" on it. When she looked up after he had given it to her, he had already gotten in the car and started it up. She looked at him and he smiled and started to drive away, and she stood there dumbfounded. He only drove a few yards when he stopped the car, got out, came over, kissed her on the cheek, and held her hand while whispering in her ear: "The hand that gives is the hand that gets." He backed away and smiled, and just before he got into the car again, he yelled, "God be with you my lovely friend!" and with that he jumped in the car and drove away. While watching him leave, she stood still in silence with tears streaming down her face.

Marta started walking down the road that followed the southern coast of France. She made the journey through Monaco and then across into the northern part of Italy, where she stayed the night in a hostel she had found through the locals outside of Varazze. Although she had stuck to her plan for the most part through her early days in Spain, she improvised when she surfed for the first time and met Hugh. Something he brought up from time to time ran through her mind.

"You know the Irish meaning of the American saying, 'No worries!'? You go as you will and you go as you may and it be as it will be!"

And then Hugh would remind her that he was Scottish, but it was okay because they all looked the same. She would always laugh, but she also felt the freedom of those words and found the past few weeks had released an inner part of her soul that was so regimented, so she wasn't so tightly wound anymore.

Tears began to flow as she sat on the edge of the bed. She looked down on her iPad and thumbed through all the pictures and selfies she took on her trip. She trashed some and others she kept to post on her Facebook page and send to all her friends and family back home, Hugh, and the other new friends she met along the way. There was much more to come on her journey and she looked forward to the next stage—meeting her father's side of the family, including her grandparents, whom she had never met in person; they had exchanged a few letters and pictures, and more recently communicated via FaceTime. Marta yawned, lay back on the bed, set the iPad aside, and fell asleep dreaming of tomorrow's plans and what they would bring.

She awoke the next morning and began her day thinking of surfing right there in Verazze before heading south, but when she hiked down to the beach, she saw a lot more people on the shore and only a handful out on the surf. Even she could tell this surf was out of her league. Apparently, a storm further off the coast, along with the regular winds, brought in unusual surf conditions that only occur once in a lifetime. She watched for a while, went back to get her things, and then started hiking to her next stop. The hiking left a lot of time to observe the beautiful scenery, much more than if traveling by some sort of vehicle, as a vision seen up close lasts much longer in the mind. It also leads to more thinking—wondering about life and its beauty as well as some of its dangers and ugliness.

Marta stopped about three hours into her hike to take a break, sitting on a large boulder, seemly put in place for a perfect bench to rest and watch over the horizon of the sea to one side of the road and the rise of the land to distant mountains to the other. The grandeur of both views was like a godsend to her soul and her heart filled with love of the spiritual awareness she felt present around her. For whatever reason, how or why, that she was this person at this point and time—able to exist to see and experience all she was taking in—was surely a divine blessing.

There and then she decided on scheduling a longer stay with family. She got up from the boulder, hoisted her gear on her back, and hiked to the next seaside village. There, she planned with her Italian family to meet up sooner. She caught a bus that would take her along the northern coast down to Lucca, where she would meet family members. It would be about a four- to five-hour trip with all the stops along the way, but it was a relaxing one for her. She was able to sit back and give her feet and legs time to recuperate and her mind time to relax, just enjoying the scenery and occasionally playing her guitar and singing, much to the delights of the other passengers.

Marta saw parts of the coast where the country just met the sea, where animals roamed without a care, and where it seemed there was a never-ending line of fishing boats. There were high cliffs overlooking the shores, many with what seemed like homes built right on them, from the top of the cliff down to the sea's edge. At times, there was nothing but lonely surf and then some areas where there was an abundance of surfing.

Though Marta was by no means a great surfer, she was a good surfer. And, she was just as good surfing the internet in researching the waves of the world and the industry. On the trip along the coast of Spain, if someone asked if she knew Kelly Slater, she would respond that she knew of him, but had only seen him surf once and that was from a distance, in a huge crowd watching off the pier in Huntington Beach, California. From her experience, it was true what Slater said—the surfing community was like the mafia; once in, you found it very hard to get out of it. Marta found it more like a religion, based on how the spiritualism grabbed you, and the best part was it wasn't defined like most organized religions. Just like the waves themselves, it is always different and the experience of riding them is just as exhilarating and spiritually free. It grabbed Marta on that summer day off the Imperial Beach pier and it had not let go of her since. As her great-uncle Pietro said to her many times, "It defines her beauty of not only on what is on the outside, but what is on her inside and it keeps her humble."

Marta loved those words, which not only defined her love for the water, but defined her as well. Surfing was a very humbling endeavor as well and being humbled built character.

The bus arrived on schedule into the city of Lucca. Marta looked out the window and could recognize a couple of her cousins from conversations on FaceTime; she waved to catch their attention as she rose from her seat with her guitar. She headed down the aisle and down the steps to open arms that came to greet her. Hugs and kisses on the cheek were shared and then time was spent waiting to get her backpack from the storage area under the bus.

Her cousins, Adriana and Georgio, who were around her age, took her hand and led her on over to a nearby park, where she would meet her dad's parents. Adriana spoke in her best English, "Marta, this is Mama Oriana, though we call her Mama O."

Marta sat her backpack on the ground and handed her guitar to Georgio. Mama O stood up from the park bench she had been sitting on. She stood tall and was slim but looked strong, with a weathered, aged face, dark in color, from many years out being in the sun. She wore a summery dress to her shins with a loose belt tied around her hips, open-toed sandals, and a shawl around her neck. Her hair was long and gray, but young in texture. What stood out more to Marta as much as anything were her glistening green eyes. It was if she was looking in a mirror of what her older self would look like. Marta stepped forward and embraced her, and Mama O's eyes swelled up with tears. Then her grandfather spoke.

"Certo Mama, Certo let me meet our little Niptina from America! I am your Papa Dominico," he said, as he grabbed his wife gently from the shoulders to pull her away from Marta. He then reached out to hold each of Marta's hands in his, stepped back to stretch their arms, and looked at her with a big smile on his face. Marta saw before her an average man in height and build with strong arms and stocky legs. He was only old in the face, like Mama O, and many of the wrinkles were from his ear-to-ear smile as he looked at her over the top of his glasses, which sat on the edge of his nose.

"You know, Mama, I know why I fell in love with you so many years ago as I see your beauty in our Niptina's face. Come here child," he said to Marta, wo smiled while he pulled her into to hug and kissed her on the forehead.

"Grazie, Papa!" responded Marta.

"Oh, my child. Call me Papa Domi," he said as he stepped away from her and turned to another person. "This is your father's sister, Silvana."

Silvana stepped forward to meet her niece and reached across and hugged her as if there was no tomorrow, as did Marta. Marta had heard so much about her from her two cousins. She was her father's twin, and by all accounts they did everything together until the time he left home and Italy.

"You are of my brother," Silvana said, "but your mother must have been of much wonderful beauty!"

"Grazie, you are much too kind," responded Marta, as the two of them hugged and kissed each other on the cheek. Papa Domi noticed Mama O's face was wet with tears and put his arm around her waist to bring her close to him.

"Now, now!" he spoke as he took a handkerchief from his rear pocket and wiped the tears from her face. "Let's all get a move on. We have some driving to do up the mountain."

Marta kept her arm around Silvana and reached for Mama O to come join her as her cousins grabbed her guitar and backpack. Papa Domi led the way as they walked to the parking area. Her cousins had come in one car while her grandparents and aunt came in another.

"You ride with your cousins and get to know them, as I am sure they have plenty to share with you while I drive Mama and Papa," said Silvana. She hugged and kissed Mama and Papa as well as her aunt and then jumped in the car with her cousins. Both vehicles took off out of town and along the road that led up the mountain to the very small town of Abetone.

What a welcome, Marta thought to herself as the car wound around the snaking turns up the mountainous road. As she looked out the window at the beautiful scenery, she could see the Mediterranean in the distance and watched as the further they drove up it disappeared into the horizon. The contour of the land and vegetation changed as well. Everything was so green and again she thought just how beautiful it all was. Sure enough, her cousins filled her in on everything in their lives. Adriana spoke of her boyfriends and her brother Georgio's athletic prowess. She also found out they didn't live in Abetone; only her grandparents still lived there, having never wanted to leave—only coming off the mountain a few times a year on special occasions like today. Her cousins lived in a suburb of Pisa because of her uncle's work and their mother being a teacher. She discovered her uncle would join them later in the week. She learned a lot more on that ride up the mountain then she did in communication with them on

Facebook and FaceTime. It was different in person—much more fun and personable—yet the online times made it feel as if they had been together for years. She couldn't wait to see the area in person, for all she knew was that Abetone was a part of the Tuscany Mountains of Pistoia and the snow- skiing was supposed to be fantastic, but Marta was there in midst of summer.

Marta spent her days sharing time with her grandmother and grandfather and the nights with her cousins. She would go along with Mama O and Adriana and pick blueberries. Mama O, Adriana, and Silvana showed her how to preserve them and taught her many of the family recipes, with Papa Domi being more than happy to sample the results. They cooked and baked and ate, and she never drank so much wine before. Though she was not of age in the States, she had been to a few parties and drank mostly beer. She wasn't even that keen on alcohol, but here was different, and it was in moderation, although Papa Domi did love his wine.

Papa Domi took her on hikes and taught her the history of the family and how it came to be at the top of this mountain many years ago. She was impressed with his strength and endurance for as old as he was. Papa Domi said the secret was in the family genes and to never retire. He told Marta that retiring was giving up on life.

He said, "Marta, you can be forced to quit what you are doing or want to quit what you are doing, but then find something else to do. Never be idle. You lose your smile when you are idle."

Marta also learned a great deal about her father and was shown many pictures of him that she never saw back in California, as there were not many of him due to her parents' short time together. One evening while looking over photos of her father when he was a child, Papa Domi sat down at the piano. As he started tinkering with the keys, he spoke.

"I used to play this to your father and Silvana when they were children and again to your cousins," he said. He started playing an Old Italian children's song, "Ci Vuole Un Fiore," and began to sing the first verse in animated Italian.

Silvana walked over from the kitchen, sat down next to her father, and sang the second verse with him.

When they were done, Silvana kissed Papa on the cheek and Marta, her cousins, and Mama applauded. Marta reached into her nearby backpack and pulled out the notebook in which she had been writing down songs from the various towns she had journeyed through along the way. Papa saw this and asked, "What is that, my child?"

"It is a book where I keep all the new songs I have learned on my trip," she replied.

Papa Domi sighed, turned to face the piano, and reached above to a pile of books and papers atop it, thumbing through them. Once he found what he was searching for, he pulled it from the stack, looked at it briefly, kissed it, and turned toward Marta with a smile.

"Marta, this was your father's and now it should be yours."

He handed it over to her as she reached to receive it. Silvana rubbed her father's shoulders as he sat back onto the piano bench.

"You are most definitely your father's child," he said to her.

Marta opened the book, seeing that it contained songs her father had written down, including the dates he found them and the dates he had learned them.

"Oh my God," she said as she flipped through the pages. "This is amazing, Papa!" Marta got up and went over to Papa

Domi and gave him a big thank you hug. Silvana and Mama O wiped tears from their eyes and her cousins smiled.

"Okay, come to the table!" Mama O shouted as she clapped her hands. "I have Marta's favorite meal for her tonight." Marta walked over to the table and saw it was spaghetti and meatballs.

"But Mama, how did you know that . . ." Mama O stopped her before she could finish. "It was your father's favorite, so it must be yours!" she winked at Marta. They sat at the table and Mama O gave a toast

Marta was enjoying every minute of her time with family, but her stay was coming to an end. The timing was perfect in a sense, as it was nearing mid-August, a time when most of Italy shuts down for the celebration of Ferragsto, the end of harvest. It was one of the few times Mama and Papa came down off the mountain, as Abetone would be a ghost town; everyone would be vacationing down near the ocean beaches.

It was all set that they would stay with Aunt Silvana, her husband, Uncle Gio and the cousins near the beach of Viareggo. Here, Marta would spend one more week with the family. Her cousins surprised her in that they knew how to surf, but Georgio attempted to show her how to kite surf. For the first time, at this beach, though she saw there were surfers out on the water, there were probably twice as many kite surfers. It wasn't like that in San Diego or along the Southern California coast. She did see that more in Northern California and Oregon as she went up the west coast by train to Vancouver for a class trip, since the winds are more prevalent there.

When she first headed out on the beach of Viareggo, it was really busy. Marta had never quite seen anything so crazy other than the 4th of July back home, when the locals pretty much stayed away from the insanity. The difference here was that it was double the locals and not as many tourists, unless you counted all the locals who only participated a few times a year as tourists. She still attempted to kite surf and realized quickly she didn't have the arm strength to fully benefit from it like her cousin Georgio did, although she thought with time and less of a crowd, she could get the hang of it. Just the same, she admired her cousin and his graciousness for the time spent trying to teach her.

The week was spectacular, as she also met many other distant relatives, like grand aunts and uncles and second and third cousins who all made her seem like a big part of the family. She went on tours of Pisa and almost every night, Uncle Gio and Aunt Silvana would have a long table set up with food galore. They ate and drank, and Marta felt spoiled by her Italian family; according to her cousins, it was grander than past festivals past because of her presence—but Georgio and Adriana both said that it was still not too far from how they regularly celebrated.

"Un sacco d'amore, lots of love!" Marta said.

"Si. Grande amore!" Georgio said, and the three of them laughed and toasted, shouting "La mia famiglia!"

Papa Domi and the others heard them and there was silence. They looked down the long table and giggled, Mama and Papa smiled, and Papa shouted "La mia famiglia!"

Then everyone else along both sides of the table, whether sitting or standing—including Marta, Georgio, and Adriana—repeated it with their glasses to the air: "La mia famiglia!"

They all continued to drink, eat, and sing through the night into the early morning. Marta and others had played guitar as well. With Adriana insisting, Marta played a song she had learned while in Italy, "Regalami il Tuo Sogno" ("Give Me the Gift of Your Dream"). She surprised everyone by singing it in Italian.

Marta finished the song softly, and as she looked around the fire that had dwindled down some, she saw her Italian family, some holding one another like Mama O sitting next to Papa Domi with her head resting on his shoulder and he with his arm around her. She saw other couples hugging as well holding each other's hand and her cousins all sitting with their heads in their hands. All were smiling.

"Grazie, signorina Marta!" said Aunt Silvana with a huge smile and others chimed in as well.

"Bellissimo!"

"Fantastico!"

"Meraviglioso!"

Marta smiled graciously and sat back against the legs of the chair she was leaning against and stared into the fire, as did everyone else.

The next day was spent sleeping in, then preparing for her to leave the following morning. It was heart wrenching, but she didn't let it show until she found Mama O alone in the kitchen at the sink. Mama heard someone come into the kitchen, turned and saw Marta, and smiled. Marta ran over to her and wrapped her arms around her, and the two began to cry silently as they held each other tightly.

"Sara figlio ok" (it will be okay child), Mama assured her.

Mama walked her over to the table and sat her down in a chair.

"You sit while I make you something to eat," she said.

Soon everyone was drifting into the kitchen and they were scattered about, some sitting and some standing, as they spoke of the night before and how they were going to miss Marta. Papa Domi was the last to wander in.

"La Mia Bella Famiglia" (my beautiful family), he said with his arms spread wide open.

"Buongiorno, Papa," came from around the room.

Papa walked over to Marta, bent over, and gave her a kiss on the forehead. Marta reached up behind her and held Papa tightly around his neck, not wanting to let him go. Papa tapped her gently on her forearm.

"Ti amo! Ti amo, I love you," he said softly to her.

He straightened up, pulled out a chair and sat down next to Marta. The group began to eat, laugh, and talk about the time spent with Marta and how they were all going to miss her and she, them.

The following day, Marta collected her things and began the hard process of saying goodbye to each person in the family. She exchanged little trinkets with her cousins, then said loving yet painful goodbyes to Mama O and Papa Domi. Tears were streaming down everyone's loving faces as she pulled away and eased herself into the awaiting car with Uncle Geo and Aunt Silvana, who would take her to the airport in Pisa for her flight back to the States. The car ride didn't seem long; they soon arrived at the airport and Marta got out, gave her aunt and uncle big hugs, and they parted ways.

Marta walked through the busy airport in a different head space, already missing her Italian family. She checked in to her flight and then checked her guitar and backpack, only carrying on a small purse that was big enough to contain her phone and iPad, her father's books of music and notes, plus some money and little odds and ends. She sat for a while in the terminal, looking out onto the tarmac where they were loading up the plane she was to get on shortly. She tried to see them loading her guitar and backpack, but she wasn't able to before the clerk at the desk announced boarding to New York. Marta got up from her seat when they called her row, followed the line of people down the corridor to the entrance of the plane, and walked down to her seat.

She was seated by a window and no one was seated in her aisle, which made it easier for her to get situated. She grabbed a pillow and blanket from one of the overhead compartments before sitting down, so she could try to sleep on the long flight. She settled herself in and sat there staring out the window onto the tarmac, watching all the workers around her plane and other docked at the terminal. She was cordial to the middle-aged couple who sat down next to her and found they were Italians going to America for a vacation. After chatting for a while, the plane finally pulled away from the dock, made its journey onto the runway, and off into the sky—above the clouds into a bright blue universe.

She asked the couple if it would be all right to pull the shade down over the window and when they were fine with it, she did so and then lay her head against the pillow she had tucked against the plane wall. While relaxing, she took out the trinkets her cousins gave her. Georgio had given her a small skeleton key, saying it was a key to her Italian heart so it is always easy to open. Adriana gave her a small pin of a beautiful butterfly made of pewter with wings of some sort of green glass, telling her it represented her freedom to be who she wishes to be.

She sat forward after deciding to tie the two trinkets to strands of her hair, which was getting long from the months of travel, and then she added the keychain she got from Hugh. She tucked her head back against the pillow, and after playing a bit with the trinkets, slowly closed her eyes and fell into a sound, dream-filled sleep.

When Marta finally arrived back to San Diego, she shared all of her travels with Mama and Papa Alfaro and her great-uncle Pietro. Then it was time to go off to college at San Diego State, studying music. She continued playing her guitar around campus, in the school band, and at various functions for friends and family as well as an occasional local talent contest.

"You're damn good!" great-uncle Pietro said to her after the two of them jammed together in the backyard of her grandparents' home one night after a weekend get together with family.

She worked hard at everything for the next four years while attending SDSU. She did side jobs in the food and beverage industry from waitress to hostess. She met many new friends and lost some as well. She continued to exchange trinkets along the way, attaching them to her hair that was now weaved into manageable and very attractive dreadlocks. As always with Marta, she did her research, so when asked by her grandmother why she decided to do such a thing, Marta replied, "It's a representation of my soul, Mama! My freedom of spirit and the warrior in me that never gives up!"

From that day on, Mama Alfaro never questioned her reasoning again, embracing it instead, as she knew her granddaughter's strong will and independence were blessings from God.

Marta graduated with honors with a degree in musicology, but she didn't attend the graduation ceremony, much to her family's surprise. Her reasoning was that she didn't want to gloat, as she would have been sitting separately from her other friends and students. She didn't, however, object to the family providing a giant celebration at home with neighbors, friends, and family— and that they did.

FAMILIA DI SURF

(Family of the Surf)

Marta paddled on her board through the breaks in the waves until she got out to the others, and that's when all the name calling and teasing began. She gave it back just as good as they dished it out and it was all in fun. Marta was the only female among this group of surfers who met up every morning at this location. She was among the most consistent through the years; some would come and stay for a while and either move on in life or find they didn't fit in. Occasionally, other girls would join, but they never stayed. Maybe they felt threatened by Marta, who was a good surfer, or just like the other guys who came and went, maybe they didn't fit in. For the most part, for the last five years it was the same guys plus Marta. The companionship built in the waves extended out of the water as well. She knew all the others' strengths and weaknesses and would use them to her advantage to make a comment or to bait one against another, but they all would laugh at the end. They were tight-knit like that.

Together, they were a unit of fun and laughter, with constant ribbing every morning. Although Marta was a woman, she was like one of the guys, for she had earned their respect as a surfer long ago. In fact, she was just as good, if not better than most of them. The guys would all admit it was probably them who made her better by challenging her to some crazy tricks and stunts. She failed many times, but she had an instinct that she could do it and would keep trying until she not only did it—which was all the others expected—but keep at it until she perfected it.

There was Chucky, Danny, Larson, G—short for Gregory, Manny, and Dale Da Dude. At first, Marta added boy after each of their names—Danny boy, Chucky boy, etc.—but with time, that changed, and she just referred to them by their first names except when she would tease them, with the exception of Dale.

Chuck's older brother Dale was autistic. Marta called him Dale Da Dude to give him a sense of importance; it was a plus that all of them loved the character Jeff Bridges played in the movie the "The Big Lebowski," The Dude. When Marta first got to know Chuck and Dale, she started calling him Da Dude because Dale was a pretty damn good surfer. When Chuck noticed his brother light up when Marta called him that, he and the others started to call him Dale Da Dude as well. Chuck was his brother's keeper even though Dale got along pretty well on his own, able to live by himself and even provide for himself. The group never treated him any different from anybody else—they ribbed him and he gave it right back.

Danny was of Japanese descent. His family lived in the Kearny Mesa area of San Diego. His family had been in America for five generations, since back in WWI, when his great-great-great-grandfather came to the U.S. as an Japanese diplomat. During WWII, his great-grandparents were interred in American prison camps after the bombing of Pearl Harbor, even though they were born in America and were American citizens. His grandfather was part of the Vietnam protests in the late '60s at Cal State Berkley and ended up selling insurance. His dad became a part of the technology boom and worked for Qualcomm in San Diego as a chief engineer. Danny studied whatever came to his liking at the time at the University of California San Diego. When asked by the others what he was going to major in, he always came back with, "life and whatever direction it leads me."

Larson called himself a mutt, since he had a diverse background—a bit German, Irish, Scandinavian, and Scottish. He was at San Diego State before being kicked out for bad grades. So, he moved back home—father's orders—and would not be allowed to go back to SDSU until he made the Dean's List at Mira Costa Community College, where he was studying business management. During his short stint at SDSU, his parents had converted their garage into an extra room that they rented out for extra cash. Now, that was his bedroom, since the one he once shared with his younger brother was now his younger brother's.

Gregory, or G for short, was what you'd call the average American-looking white male. He was not attending school. He had moved to Southern California from Maine just to get away from the cold. He had learned to surf on the East Coast. Nobody knew if he still had family back there. He never spoke much of them and when he did it was always in the past tense. The group would mock his East Coast accent at times and he would always tell them they were doing it wrong, and then do his best imitation of Ben Affleck having a conversation with Matt Damon. He was also quite a jokester, although Marta could see that side of him would only come out when the others would talk about family, and he'd conveniently change the subject. He was a hell of a surfer and when asked how he learned to surf living in Maine, he told them it is a whole different kind of beast out there, cold water but high surf when the storms came through. He'd milk cows in the morning and surf in the afternoon. G was working two jobs.

He bartended at one of the restaurants off the boardwalk in Mission Beach, working one shift for brunch before going to a second shift at a tattoo parlor not far from where Marta worked on Garnett Street. The bar had a clientele of tourists and college kids, and on weekends, it was crazy with sports enthusiasts, especially during football season. He made good money there. The tattoo place was one of several on Garnett Street. He made good money there when he'd get a client, but it was more or less a time filler to keep up his own tattoos. He rented a studio above the tattoo shop, which made it nice to come back from the Mission Beach area and not have to go anywhere but to bed. He was Mr. Money Bags to the others because he was just focusing on saving for now, as he didn't know what he wanted for his future.

Then there was Manny, a childhood friend of Marta's from the Old Town days. Manny's mother was of Mexican American heritage and his father, African American descent. He looked up to Marta, as he learned surfing with her and she helped tutor him through school. She occasionally called him her Galahad, since he was her protector all through school, including college. Manny did not attend college, but went to work for his family's upholstery shop full time. They made good money doing furniture and auto upholstery. Marta always told him he could do whatever he wanted, and yet he chose the family business. He was proud of that and it wasn't all that bad. He also played guitar, learning alongside Marta, and they would occasionally play together whenever she came back to see her grandparents. Manny was her conduit to the old neighborhood. He would bring things to her from her grandparents or she would send things with him to give to them. When he didn't bring something for a while, she would smile and say, "I guess it's time for me to go make a visit," and that she would do.

"Why so slow swimming out here, Curl Gurl?" Danny said.

Curl Gurl was the nickname they had for her. They always argued over who got credit for that nickname and whether it was about her hair or her surfing.

"The usual," Marta responded.

"What's that Marta?" laughed Chuck.

"Had to take my morning pee," chuckled Marta, winking at Chuck, who returned a big smile. "Never have to go until I hit the water."

Some of the guys chuckled together while the rest went "ooooo" at the same time. Marta laughed with them and then a couple tried for a wave and caught it. As they rode it out, the others watched and patiently waited for the next one. When they caught one, Marta and whoever else would go for it and if one got in the way of the other, they would peel off and let the other ride it out. This was part of the camaraderie they had—respecting one another to be able to enjoy the time. None were competitive surfers, although most of the guys had tried at one time or another when they were younger. For now, they just competed among themselves.

FAMILIA DI SANCHEZ

(Family of Sanchez)

Marta didn't know what she wanted to do after graduation, but she knew she wasn't ready to leave the San Diego area. She did want to be out on her own and have a little less structure and discipline in her life; she wanted to explore the world of freedom before taking on the world so seriously as it seemed everyone else was doing. So, she often looked around the area to determine where she might live. Ocean Beach was nice and youthful, but the beach area was small, which made the surf often crowded. Mission Beach had good surf, but also had a lot of tourists and beginners, and the surf schools were often in the way as well. She decided on Pacific Beach; even though there were still the novice surfers there, it was not as bad near the Crystal Pier and up to Bird Rock or Tourmaline Park, as some called it, which was very popular with the locals and the occasional visiting pro.

She found a nice little second floor apartment, one street in from Garnett and across from a middle school. It backed up to an alley that was shared by many stores, small shops, restaurants, and bars, and she lucked out by getting a wait staff job at the café across the alley, kitty-corner from her apartment. The owner, Emanuel, of Costa Rican descent, liked her attitude and that she lived right there, figuring she would never be late for work—and she wasn't. She called him Boss, as she felt that sounded better than calling him Emanuel, and he didn't like being called Mr. Sanchez.

Marta started working every day around 8:00 a.m. and she worked through until 4:00 p.m. when the café would close; it only served breakfast and lunch. Emanuel tried serving dinner for a couple years, but found it too competitive, as people were bringing in more specialty chefs and he just couldn't do that right now. His was a small family business, including his two sons, Carlos and Johnny. Occasionally, Carlos's wife, Ezzie, would come in and help with the wait staff, especially when their two young children were in school. There were also a couple cousins who helped with the dishes and cleanup.

Emanuel had been a widower for several years. Marta was the only one at the cafe who was not family and Emanuel loved that, as her good work ethic made the family not be lazy as it could get at times. Marta would occasionally work with Carlos and John in the kitchen and throw in some suggestions she had learned from her grandmother. They were constantly experimenting, something that was necessary to stay on top of things in the competitive San Diego restaurant scene—to maintain a good reputation and ensure they could pay the rent for the building the restaurant occupied, which was always going up. They needed to do what they could to stay ahead of the game to survive. Marta was trusted by the family; she had worked her way into their hearts by fitting in so nicely into their routine.

IL PRESENTE

(The Present)

Out on the surf, one by one, the guys would peel off and head in to call it a day, get to school, or get to work.

"Later, Curl Gurl," Danny said.

"See ya tomorrow, Marta," Larson said.

"Yea, later, Marta," Chucky said.

"Bye, Marta," Dale Da Dude said, with a big smile as he followed his brother.

As Dale caught a wave and got up, he yelled, "Love you, Marta!" as he always did every time he and his brother left.

Marta yelled, "Love you too, Dude!"

Manny signed off with a peace sign that he pressed to his heart, and away he went. G was the only one left and he was waiting patiently for the next wave to come with Marta.

"If you have nothing to do later tonight, Curl Gurl, swing by the pub," he said. "I'd like to talk to you."

He turned as the wave got closer, winked at Marta, and started paddling; unlike the others, he rode the wave lying on his belly. Marta thought both the wink and G not surfing in were a bit odd, but then she focused on her next wave. Marta was always hanging on for one last good wave and would almost always be one of the last off the water—unless one of the guys had time and wanted to just sit and chat or had girl problems to share with her. That would often push her to the very limit of when she needed to get back to the restaurant to work, but this time she was alone and had plenty of time to try to catch another good wave.

She sat on her board waiting, turning her head back and forth, looking behind her for a wave approaching and ahead to see that her path in front would be clear, without a young boogie board rider in the way or another surfer coming in on her action. Finally, she caught one with her eye. She lay down on her board and started paddling with her hands. She could start to feel the power beneath her and the wave about to crest. In just a blink of an eye, she got the board pointed right and she was up on her feet, balancing the board on the wave. She had good balance and her feet barely moved as she maneuvered the board up and down, occasionally wiping her nose with one hand.

She caught a wave with good momentum and maneuvered it all the way into the shore. She fell off backwards into the shallow water, got to her feet, shoved her board alongside her, and began to walk out of the surf. In one motion, she released her ankle from the board's safety strap, picked up the board, and finished walking in.

Cap was standing there not far from shore, where he still had his cardboard shack in view to eye potential trespassers, but ready to meet Marta.

"Looking good out there, darlin'," he said, as he grabbed the board from her and they both headed back to his shelter.

"Yea, some good waves today," she responded. "Wish I had more time, but being Friday and all, the Boss will be counting on me."

They reached the shelter and Cap laid the board back across the supports he had made to hold it in place. He picked up the towels he used as a cover and underhand tossed one to Marta, while he started placing the others over the board. Marta began wiping herself down.

"Tell Johnny the cannoli passed the taste test. He's good to go," Cap said, as he extended his arm and fist toward Marta.

Marta exchanged the fist-bump with Cap, bent down to pick up her skateboard, and turned to run up the stairs.

"Have a good day, Cap! I'll see you around later," she yelled.

"You too, darlin'," he responded.

Cap threw the last towel back onto the board, then crawled back under it to lie down. He threw his blanket over himself and proceeded to fall right back to sleep, with his toes exposed to the morning air.

FAMILIA DI CAP

(Family of Cap)

Marta was back on her skateboard and making her way over to Garnett Street and back up to her place. Now there were more people on the street at this time of the morning—bicyclists, joggers, tourists, and shop owners. Then there were the homeless, who seemed to disappear in the shadows of the night but reappear in the morning, laying in a lot of the spaces created by a number of the buildings that were natural places for them to sleep at night and not bother anybody.

It was the same thing every morning for Marta—same people, same faces, and same observations. Some she knew by name and others she only knew by face; most of those were of the homeless. Some shop owners would treat them with some respect as a human being, but others would be very brutal toward them, going as far as kicking them, hosing them down, or even hitting them with a broom to get them out of the way. This was how Marta met Cap one morning.

It was in about her first month working at the Sanchez's cafe. She was in her routine of surfing every morning, but back then she was carrying her board down from her apartment. Instead of coming through the alley entrance, she would come around to the front of the café and say good morning to Emanuel on her way to the beach. One morning, she came around and saw

Johnny outside kicking a homeless man who had been sleeping in the cubby at the entrance of the cafe.

"Come on, you stinking bastard, move your fucking smelly ass!" yelled Johnny, as he kicked some more. Marta noticed a tattoo on the homeless man's arm, ran up to them, and stuck her board in between Johnny and the homeless man.

"Johnny, stop! Please, stop!" Johnny looked at her a bit stunned and Marta said to him, "You go inside, and I'll deal with this!" as she pushed her board toward him. "Go on, Johnny. I got it covered. Besides, you don't have time for this!" she strongly voiced. "Have your father bring out a cup of coffee and a cannoli!"

Johnny looked at her and saw the seriousness in her eyes; he knew she was right and deep down he was wrong. He knew she was good with people.

"All right! All right! You got this, Marta!" he said, then turned and went inside.

Marta leaned her board up against the café window, took the homeless man by the arm, brought him over to a bench that was just a little ways away, and sat him down.

"Are you okay?" she asked as he started to cough.

He nodded his head and after clearing his throat, said, "Yes, darlin', I'm fine."

Johnny appeared again with the coffee and cannoli.

"Here ya go, Marta" he said. The homeless man leaned away in fear. Marta put her hands on his shoulders and said to him, "It's okay!"

Then she turned to Johnny.

"Thanks, Johnny. I'll see you in a couple hours."

Johnny, who was still a bit stunned, turned and went back inside. Marta then sat down with the coffee and cannoli and said to the man.

"You know, I really don't drink coffee. Would you like this coffee?" The man couldn't help but smell its aroma and he spoke hesitantly as he slowly reached for it.

"Well, if you're not to pleasure your lips with it, I would kindly do so, darlin'," he said.

Marta handed him the coffee and then said, "I really can't eat this cannoli, either, as I don't like to eat before I go surfing. You can have it as well if you wish."

The man looked at her in wonder, and as he did, he could see her glistening green eyes—her face was lit up from the streetlamp above—and the light flickered off the many trinkets in her hair.

"Darlin', you are a sweet angel, are you not?" he said to her.

Marta chuckled and said, "Far from that sir! But hey, my name is Marta; may I ask yours?"

He took a sip of the coffee and said, "Ahhhh, Cap is my name, darlin'. Yes, darlin', that is some damn good coffee."

"Well, Cap, I have to get down to the beach and try to get in some wave action before it's too late and I have to get back here to work."

Cap got a bit anxious and said, "Darlin', you must let me carry your board for you for your kind-heartedness."

Without hesitating, Marta responded, "Well, let's get going then. I can carry my board while you finish your coffee."

They both arose from the bench. Marta looked at Cap as he got up. He didn't have a distasteful odor to himself as Johnny had stated; in fact, Marta recognized the smell. He smelled like the cologne her grandfather wore, Old Spice, she thought. She felt that was odd, as would almost anyone, since most of the homeless around San Diego had a bit of a foul odor to them—definitely dirty clothes and skin darkened by a combination of dirt and sun. She grabbed her board and they began to walk down the sidewalk.

"Do you have any other belongings, Cap?" asked Marta.

Cap took a swallow of coffee "Ahhh, that's tasty. Down under the pier."

Marta thought it was odd that he would leave his things alone, as most homeless were pretty possessive and would at times fight with one another if someone invaded their space. Marta and Cap had walked to the first intersection and were waiting for the light to change when Cap tipped his head back, finished the last swig of the coffee, and turned to walk over to the streetlamp, where there was a garbage can. He opened the flapper on the side and threw the empty cup into the opening. When he let go of the flapper, it made a banging noise that was unusually loud. Cap kind of ducked when this happened as he walked back toward Marta.

Marta took note of his behavior as she was a studier of people and knew there were different kinds of homeless. Cap was barefoot and wearing old, tattered, filthy Army fatigues with one pant leg rolled up to just below his knee and the other down to where he was walking on the hem. She could tell he had been walking on it for a while because the hem was so frayed it was basically gone. He was also wearing a dirty short-sleeved t-shirt with a print on it, but the combination of the morning darkness and the dirt over it made it hard to make out what it was. The light changed so they could walk and Cap quickly took the board from Marta.

"Thank you kindly, sir!" she said.

"My pleasure, darlin'," he replied.

Cap wrapped his long, muscular arm around the surfboard and tucked it under his armpit. He then went to scratch his nose, and Marta saw the tattoo again. It was on the underside of his left forearm. Her first instinct had been correct—he was military. She'd seen that tattoo around through the years growing up. Her uncle had one, Emanuel also had one, and she'd seen others with one while attending college; many ex-military used the GI bill to go to school. There was a large military presence around San Diego—active, inactive, and retired—and many had distinguishable tattoos for the various branches. Cap's was the emblem of the U.S. Marine Corps. It consisted of the world with an anchor pierced through it and an eagle perched on the top with its wings spread. Above the eagle's wings he had tattooed the letters USMC and under the world Semper Fi was tattooed. Its colors were red, white, and blue—but it was covered with a lot of dirt.

Together, they started walking across the street and then back on the sidewalk toward the beach. Marta continued to observe him. Cap was tall, a good six feet at a minimum, she thought. He was built, muscular, but thin. He was very much unshaven and had a beard that looked like he had been cutting it himself, along with his hair, which was down to his shoulders, all choppy looking and of course, dirty. He looked almost as though he was one of those cavemen from the auto insurance commercials she use to see on TV and the billboards around town, or even Animal of *Sesame Street*.

"Thanks, Cap for helping me down to the beach," Marta said.

"It is I who should be thanking you, darlin'," he responded. "Today, you were my angel of mercy who came to my rescue."

Marta smiled. "Well, it was very unnecessary of him to be kicking you as if you were some stubborn animal."

"He had a right, as I was asleep at his stoop and he was just waking me up."

They continued crossing the next street and walking down the sidewalk, speaking only occasionally as Cap was observing her as well.

"You're different!" he said to her. Marta turned her head in wonder and he saw the confused look on her face. "You don't ask me a lot of questions. Though I can sense you have a lot you keep to yourself. You're an observer."

Marta didn't respond right away, but smiled at his assessment.

"Ahhh, I like your communication of approval," Cap said while observing her smile.

Marta knew there were many types of homeless people around the area. There were college dropouts who had gotten hooked on drugs or alcohol and middle-aged men and women who were using a substance as well—some of whom were surprisingly "well to do" at one time, but took the partying too seriously, and bit by bit had lost everything and couldn't kick the habit.

Then there were the ones who actually had some sort of mental health issue. With them, there was really no way to deal with them sometimes, unless somehow, some way, a person of authority could get them into some sort of care; the police would not do anything with most of the homeless unless they broke a law. Most of the drug-dependent homeless Marta saw would come and go, often returning after failing some sort of treatment program or walking away from help.

Then there were the veterans, who had trouble adjusting to reality once they got back into the States. There were a lot of them around. Most were alcoholics, but some used a drug of some sort as well. Whatever "their poison," it was primarily used to escape or hide their emotional pain. She knew this to be the case with Cap after seeing his tattoo, though she did not know what his crutch may be. Her reluctance to maintain a conversation with Cap was twofold: she didn't know how she should address the subject of his military service and it was her first experience speaking with someone from the street. She had been an observer plenty of times and saw many different and mostly confrontational experiences. Most did not turn out well for one person or the other. It was why she previously intervened when she saw Johnny kicking Cap.

They crossed Mission Boulevard and headed straight toward Crystal Pier. Cap started down the stairs to the beach and Marta followed. He turned to the left, under the pier, with Marta on his heels. He walked up to a makeshift home of cardboard, more like a lean-to type structure. Marta noticed the place was quite orderly. There wasn't a bunch of worthless stuff stacked around and scattered like she had seen many homeless do—no "shopping cart madness," as she called it.

"Welcome to mi casa, darlin'," Cap said.

"Sweet," Marta said, immediately embarrassed that she had said that.

Cap, aware of it, said, "No, it's not, but it's okay. It's all I need. Where do you surf, darlin'?"

"Actually, I surf right over here, to the right of the pier." As she said that, she realized that until now, she never really noticed this part of the pier—and she had been surfing here for nearly a year. She always came down the stairs and headed right to the surf. Occasionally, she would walk to the south side and try the surf there, but she would cut across farther down toward the water line—but she had always had better luck on the north side.

"Good choice. The breaks are better on the north side then the south," Cap said. He handed the board to Marta and she handed him the cannoli, still wrapped in foil. She started walking away toward the surf, then stopped, turned, and said, "Thanks, Cap! I much appreciate it." Cap waved with his right hand, almost like a two-fingered salute, but from his chest instead of his forehead.

She started to walk away when Cap yelled, "Darlin'!" She turned and he jogged over to her through the sand. "Say, I was wondering if I could be the keeper of the board?" Marta gave him a confused look. "I mean, since I live right here, I could keep the board for you and that way you don't have to carry it all the way down here all the time and then carry it back again to your place every day."

"Oh, um," Marta said.

"You go out and surf and clear your mind and when you come back you'll have an answer for me," Cap said.

How interesting, she thought as she nodded. "Okay, okay. I'll do that."

She walked to where the sand met the surf, then started to run, and finally threw the board and herself down on it onto the surf at the same time. She began to paddle out and join the others.

When she got out there, Dale Da Dude said, "Hi, Curl Gurl."

Marta smiled and replied, "Hi, Dude."

All the others said hi and gave her high fives as well.

Larson asked, "Who's the guy, Marta, new boyfriend?"

"No, Larson boy, you know you're the only one for me," she said sarcastically.

Manny then responded, laughingly, "Ouch, you break my heart Marta."

Marta pushed him off his board. And they all laughed.

"Serves you right, Manny. You all know Marta loves me," said Dale Da Dude with a smile.

"That I do, Dude. I do love you the most," said Marta.

As she turned to look toward the beach, she saw Cap still standing there. Then he slowly sat down in the sand cross-legged and placed his hands on each knee as if he was practicing yoga, but then he leaned back into the sand with both hands, uncrossed his legs, stretched, and laid down with his arms behind his head.

Marta continued to surf with the guys and as usual, they all stripped away to the shore one by one except for Dale Da Dude and his brother, Chuckie, who left together with the same ritual as always.

Dale yelling out, "Love you, Marta."

Marta returning, "Love you, Dude."

Marta, last as usual, caught a good wave and surfed it almost all the way in, but then she collapsed to her chest and surfed the rest of the way into shore lying down. When she hit the low surf, she hopped off into the shallow water, picked up her board, unhooked her ankle from it, and started walking over to Cap, who was still lying down in the sand and looked asleep. Marta pinched her nose as to squeeze some of the saltwater out of it and then wiped her hand over her whole face. Cap hardly moved, but he opened up one eye with a squint and didn't say anything. Marta was intrigued.

She smiled and looked up into the blue sky and then said, "Okay."

Cap raised one hand from out from under his head and held it out to her in a fist. She made a fist as well and reached over and bumped his.

He then said, "One favor, if I might ask?"

"Sure," Marta said.

"You bring me a cup of coffee and one of them rolls or whatever it is every morning as well."

Marta stuck the board in the sand, so it was standing upright.

"Sure, I can do that," she said.

Cap then closed his eye, placed his hand back under his head, and said, "See you in the morning, darlin'."

Marta began to walk away slowly at first, but then she picked up pace. She wondered what she had just done. The board was expensive, and she really couldn't afford to lose it, but she felt it was in safe hands and for whatever reason she felt she was doing Cap some service in trusting him. She hustled back up the stairs to the top of Crystal Pier and on down Garnett to her little place in the morning sun.

DI SANCHEZ, PRESENTE

(The Sanchezes, Present)

Marta was about eighteen months into working with the Sanchez family at the café. She was part of the wait staff when she started, but as time went by she would end up helping out where ever she was needed. This morning when she entered through the alley door, she saw the place was busy. She walked into the kitchen area, when Carlos saw her and spoke in Spanish

"Te necesito la cocina Marta." (I need you in the kitchen, Marta). Marta came over to Carlos and responded, "Como" (what).

"I need you to be expeditor, so Johnny can help with food prep," he told her.

So, she went over to the tickets and started reading them off; Carlos and Johnny would tell her where they were with orders, so she could get up to speed. Soon, they were all in sync with the wait staff and Emanuel was much more relaxed and could mingle with customers. This particular morning rush was unusual, but they weren't complaining. As soon as things settled down, they only had about forty-five minutes of a breather and then they got another rush for lunch. That continued all the way until four in the afternoon, when it was time for them to close their doors.

Emanuel escorted out the last customers, thanking them for coming and hoping their meal was pleasant. He locked the doors, turned the sign over that said they were closed, walked into the kitchen, and sat on a stool by the edge of the prep table.

"Oh my, what a day, but a good day, yes?" he asked.

"Si Papa," said Johnny, wiping the brow of his head and smiling.

"Si Papa," followed Carlos, while the brothers, Marta, and the rest of the staff continued to work to get things cleaned up and prepped for the next day.

"We not have a day like that in a while. It feels good," Emanuel said.

They continued to work and wrap things up before Johnny excused himself. "I need to get going as the kids have football game tonight."

"Yes! Yes!" said Emanuel. Carlos then helped his father up off the stool where he always sat when not doing anything.

"Marta, can you close up tonight please?" asked Carlos.

"Sure," said Marta.

Carlos, his wife Ezzie, Johnny, and Emanuel left the cafe via the back door, which Marta locked behind them. It was just Marta and Rueben, who had finished cleaning the dishes and was putting everything in its place as Marta pulled the dirty tablecloths and replaced them with fresh ones. When Rueben finished, he came into the seating area where Marta was, grabbed the dirty linen, and put it in a bag.

"Estoy listos para dejar Senorita Marta," Rueben said.

"Si," said Marta, and she followed Rueben out of the seating area, down the hall to the back door. Marta unlocked the door and let Rueben out with the duffle of dirty linen.

"Buena noches Marta," Rueben said.

"Buena noches," Marta replied.

Marta then went back to the front of the cafe. She linked her cell phone to its sound system, set it to one of the many personal stations she had set up on her Spotify account, and pressed play. She then went back to setting the silverware and napkins for the morning service. She was busy working, enjoying the music, and getting a lot accomplished when there was a knock on the front window that kind of startled her. It was G and another guy. Marta went over and opened the front door to let them in.

"What's going on, G? I thought I was to meet you later." Marta asked as the two came in.

"I finished up my shift at the bar and then got to the tattoo parlor and it was dead, so I took off early," G responded. "Marta, this is Ron." Ron reached out to shake Marta's hand and Marta shook it.

"Nice to meet you, Marta. Gregory has told me much about you," he said.

"Well, that's nice of him," Marta said, kind of confused.

"Can we talk now, Marta?" G asked.

"Sure," Marta said. "Let's sit here."

G and Ron sat down as Marta locked the front door, took out a chair, spun it around, sat in it, and rested her arms on its back, with her chin on her forearms. She said with a smile, "What's up, G boy"?

G kind of hesitated, swallowed, and looked at Ron, who smiled. Marta observed them both, then sat back and straightened up her back, and her jaw dropped.

"No fucking way," she said. "Get the fuck out of town."

Both G and Ron were a bit surprised by her actions.

"What, Marta? What?" G said.

Marta stood up, got behind her chair and leaned on it, then straightened up and turned and paced a couple of times, and turned to G.

"You two?" she asked. "You two? Son of a bitch, G!"

Thinking Marta was upset with him, G quietly said, "Marta?"

Marta walk over to Ron, who like G did not know what to expect.

"Well stand up and give me a hug!"

Ron looked at G, slowly stood up, and gave Marta a hug. She then turned to look at G and said, "Well?"

G got up to hug her as well, and Marta gave him a kiss on the cheek as a light goes off in G's head that Marta knows what he wanted to talk about.

"How did you figure it out?" he asked.

"I could tell the minute he looked at you!" Marta replied.

She went back over to her chair and sat down, as did the other two.

"I never would have thought, G. I guess I was too stereo-typical to even think you were gay, even with good ol' Ron here. Not a bit of femininity out of him, either, but I can read eyes. I'm good at that," Marta said.

G reached over and grabbed Ron's hand, which was resting on top of the table. They all sat in brief silence. Marta looked at both of them with a grin on her face.

"Fucking eh, G!" she said to break the silence.

"Marta, you have no idea how happy I am you're okay with this," G said. "Though, somehow, I knew out of everyone, you'd have no issues with it!"

"Que sera sera, my friend. God's in control of all that shit, not me," she said. "So, I take it you have not said anything to the others?"

"No, you're the only one who has even seen us together. Nobody at either job has seen us. I wanted to come to you first so you can help me, um, us with this. Sort of break it to them all, uh, slowly," explained G.

"Of course, G, of course." G and Ron got up from the table as did Marta and they hugged each other.

Marta looked straight into G's eyes. "At your own pace, G. At your guys' own pace and when you're ready I'll be there for you!"

G smiled. Marta walked over and unlocked the door.

"Thank you, Marta. Gregory was right about you!" Ron said.

Marta smiled and replied, "Well, I'm glad one of us was right, because I was sure wrong about him, except that you're getting a good guy."

Ron looked at G and smiled and then they both looked at Marta. G reached out and squeezed Marta's hand, released it, and then turned and walked out the door. Marta closed the door behind them and locked it. She stood there and waved to them both as they walked down the sidewalk together. She watched them for a bit and then G reached over and kissed Ron. Marta opened her mouth, took in a deep breath, hesitated and released it, and smiled.

"Son of a bitch!" she whispered to herself, shaking her head in disbelief and then looking up and pointing to the ceiling. "You watch over them . . . please!" Marta went about finishing up for the night and then shut off all the lights but a couple so the local beat cops could see while patrolling. She unlocked the back door, stepped out, and locked it behind her, then walked across the alley and up the stairs to her apartment. She stopped at the top and as she was just about to enter her place, the streetlamp turned on and shined onto her porch. About 7:00 p.m., she thought, about right for early fall.

DI SURF, IL PRESENTE

(The Surf, The Present)

It was Saturday, Marta's day off, but Marta still followed the same routine she had become accustomed to every morning. She skateboarded down Garnett Street until she reached the pier, picked up her skateboard, and headed down the stairs. When she reached the bottom and headed toward the lean-to near the pier, she saw there was no Cap and no surfboard. She walked closer and found the cardboard walls still there, as were all Cap's belongings, but no board and no Cap.

Then she heard a loud shriek, turned to look, and saw Cap was down by the surf; the board was laying in the sand and he was on his hands and knees. She dropped the skateboard, slipped off her flip-flops, and headed toward Cap with coffee and cannoli in hand. As she moved closer, she saw he was waxing her board for her. He usually did that for her, but it was always ready when she got to his little cardboard home. The closer she got to Cap, she heard the pounding of a wave and looked up to see the guys all out in the water, yelling at her to get out there. She also saw Ron standing on the beach not far from Cap. She waved to Ron and he waved back.

Cap stood up as she approached and picked up the board. "Darlin', you better get your tush out there. Storm's a-coming. I'd say about six- to eight-foot surf right now. It's going to be a good day!"

Marta handed Cap his coffee and cannoli, and said, "Well okay then. Thanks, Cap!"

They fist-bumped. She then grabbed the board from Cap and ran into the surf. She threw herself up over the first wave, landed in the water on the board, and started paddling out while Manny and Danny came in surfing on a pretty good size wave. The guys were yelling and having a good time. She looked down the coastline and as far as she could see there were surfers. She continued fighting the incoming waves, paddling out toward the crew. She and G made eye contact as she approached. She smiled and gave him a look as to whether he told the others; he got it and shook his head no.

Then Dale Da Dude called out to Marta. "Marta! Hurry, you're going to miss it!" He pointed to a wave coming that he was paddling hard himself to catch. Marta and G both turned their boards and started paddling hard as well. Dale got up and yelled as did G, but Marta just missed it, so she turned around and started paddling back out to join Larson and Chuckie. She no sooner got to Chuckie, when he said, "you snooze, you lose," they started paddling past her, caught the next wave, and were gone.

As she sat there by herself for a brief moment, she saw all her friends when she looked toward shore—the ones on the beach, the ones paddling back out, and the ones surfing in. She thought to herself how lucky she was, and then she started to paddle hard as she felt the swell of the next wave coming, and she caught it. She rode it out on her stomach briefly then stood up, got her balance, and let out a big yell like the others had with her fists pumping in the air. One by one, the others yelled back at her as she rode in: "You go, Curl Gurl! You go!"

The wave was perfect for all these guys of somewhat average talent. She was sure the closer the storm got, the more it would weed out them and others until there were just a few along the coast who would continue to surf. That's how it had been in the past. Of course, she and her friends had all tried to tempt fate. There is a learning curve in all such things, but there is that moment when you can tell whether you were born and meant for this or that it was not to ever be anything but a recreational act of fun for you to participate in until your body couldn't take it anymore.

She, Manny, and Danny had gone down to Baja Mexico one time while she was in college when a storm was brewing of the coast near Rosarito. Manny and Danny came on campus searching for her, room by room, until they found her in a classroom—and told the professor it was a matter of family importance for Marta to come with them. Of course, Marta was in shock and continued to be as she ran down the hall of the building with Manny and Danny on each side of her—until they got her out to Manny's truck with their surfboards all strapped down in the back and leaning on the roof of the cab. She let out a loud whoop and the three of them got in, with Marta in the middle, and away they went.

Lots of surfers made the trip to test their skills. The surf off Calafia, near Rosarito, was six to eight feet when they arrived, and by noon it was a good ten-feet plus. Marta prided herself on being in great shape cardiovascular wise. She had always given one hundred percent in all she did, especially athletics, while growing up. She played soccer, basketball, and softball. Her uncle called her a "chica poco femnina," a tomboy.

Throughout the morning, they took breaks to save their energy, but as the storm moved off the coast, the waves got taller and seemed even more powerful. It took more effort to get out to where the swells began and as they did, the more tired they got. Marta, being stubborn as she was and as competitive, kept trying as even Manny and Danny realized they were outmatched by Mother Nature's fury. There were others still out there with her, to whom she felt she had to prove herself, and she almost did. She caught a good wave and got a good ride for a couple minutes, but it caught her quickly from behind.

Manny and Danny saw her get swallowed by the wave and its heavy thunderous pounding. They looked for her. There was nothing for a moment until her board came spitting out straight into the air. Danny ran into the water to get the board while both of them kept looking for Marta. Others were starting to get concerned as well, but then she came up, and came up fast. Manny and a couple others on the shore went running into the surf to get her as they could see she was struggling. They helped swim her in and the closer they got to shore, when they could get to their feet, Marta shooed them off her. She stood there in ankle deep surf, bent over and threw up the saltwater she had swallowed. Manny placed his hand on her back.

"You going to be okay, Marta?"

She nodded her head yes and stood up, started walking out of the water and onto the beach a few yards, and sat down facing the ocean. Manny followed her and sat next to her. Danny came running over with her board; the power of the wave had ripped the ankle cuff right off her foot. He tossed it on the sand behind them and sat down as well.

"You all right, Marta?" he asked. Marta turned her head to the side, away from the boys, and spit.

"Yes," she answered. Danny looked at Manny, who just shrugged his shoulders.

"I'm going to go get you a bottle of water," Danny said.

Off he went back to the shore road where they were parked along with many other vehicles. Marta took a big long sniff with her nose, hacked her throat, turned her head away from Manny, spit out a big bunch of snot, and said, "That's the last time I have salt with my food."

Manny paused, then looked at Marta and started to laugh after catching the reference of the saltwater mixing with the contents of her stomach. Marta smiled and giggled, then spit again. Manny helped her up and they walked off to join Danny. That was the last time she or the others tried to push themselves beyond their natural surfing capabilities, choosing to watch the pros do it instead.

Surfing was just recreational to the group. When conditions got challenging, the guys and Marta realized it was time for the pros and those who were there to test their skills to see where they fell in. One by one, Marta and the guys surfed in and sat as group on the beach, along with Cap and Ron, the latter sitting next to G, so the two could put their arms around each other. They watched the ones who continued to brave the surf and saw some remarkable moves. Skateboarding on water, Cap called it.

Again, though not on the water, the group broke off one by one. Chuckie left with his brother Dale Da Dude, and as always, Dale told Marta he loved her and Marta returned the love with the same gesture of the two-finger kiss. Then it was just her and Cap. They both got up out of the sand. Cap picked up her board and they walked back to his cardboard home under the pier. She helped Cap put the board over the makeshift structure and cover it with towels.

"What a morning, eh, Cap?" Marta said. Cap finished with the last towel.

"Yep, darlin', grand it was." He looked up over to her. "You're good, Marta."

That perked Marta's ears, as that was the first time she had ever heard him call her by her name.

"I'll catch ya in the morning, darlin'."

He put his fist out as usual and Marta slowly bumped it with hers. He smiled, and she did, too, then turned slowly, picked up her skateboard and flip-flops, and headed up the stairs to the street. When she got to the base of the stairs, she turned and looked back toward Cap. She thought about him saying her name for the first time. She felt it a big breakthrough in their relationship. She knew he had her back and he knew she trusted him. When she got to the top, it started to sprinkle. She looked up to the sky, let the water hit her face, circled her tongue around her lips, and licked the fresh rainwater on them—then opened her mouth to take in some more. She could have ducked under cover to wait for the rain to subside, but chose to walk on instead.

The rain started to fall harder, in a steady, quiet, almost peaceful spatter as it hit the pavement in front of her. She paid attention to the change in the sound of the rainfall as she walked up the sidewalk and it dropped on the cars, trees, and plants. She listened to the sounds of the cars running through it on the street and the people running through it on the sidewalk to get to their destination. The sound was mostly pleasing to everyone, as it was sound they rarely heard in Southern California, after nearly seven years of drought most of the state and the West Coast had been experiencing. It felt very soothing to Marta as she continued to take her time walking up the street to her apartment in the steady falling rain.

DI CAP

(The Cap)

Marta had been in a deep sleep when she was awakened by a loud crash. She sat up quickly in her bed and saw a flash of light through her window, and it wasn't long after that another loud crack of thunder rattled the walls and her bed.

"Wow," she said aloud.

She thought to herself that it felt as if the cloud was hanging low right over her apartment. She started to lay back down then again, and then a flash followed a few seconds later by another rattling loud clap of thunder kept her from telexing; this one caused the windows to rattle and even the glassware she had stacked in the kitchen sink after washing the dishes earlier. She threw off the sheet that was covering her naked body, crawled the length of her bed to the window, and pulled back the blinds.

"Oh, wow," she said.

She saw the wind blowing strongly and the rain pouring down in buckets. She made her way off her bed and over to the small kitchen table to grab her cell phone, which was still attached to her charger. She opened her weather app so she could check the daily surf report. The first thing she saw was a Red Alert for high tide and large waves all along the coast. Cap came to her mind almost immediately. She set down her phone, picked up a pair of jean shorts from the floor, pulled them on, zipped them up, and snapped the buttons together. She went over to the door and slipped on a pair of tennis shoes, tied them quickly, and grabbed a hooded sweatshirt hanging from a hook, putting it on over her head and shoulders and pulling it down to her waist. She swung open the door and almost immediately was hit with the wind and rain. She thought how nice it would be to have a raincoat, but she had nothing like that—most people didn't, because it seldom rains in Southern California. She did have an umbrella, but thought about how useless it would be in the wind. She carefully went down the stairs—which resembled a continuous waterfall of water—and when she hit the pavement of the alley, she started jogging quickly down it, made a turn at the next street, and then again onto Garnett toward the Crystal Pier.

She ran down the sidewalk through the puddles and water falling off the roofs of storefronts as quickly as she could. Because it so rarely rains in Southern California, a lot of places didn't have proper water drainage or gutters, so the water was pouring off the roofs. When that got to be too much of an obstacle, Marta chose to just run down the street. It was way after bar time and there was very little traffic if any out in this storm, yet she was careful. It still continued to flash lightning and crack loud, low thunder that startled her each time, even though she knew it was coming after every flash. It was such a low crash of thunder that she could feel the vibration from the ground in her feet as she ran.

The closer she got to the pier, the louder the pounding of the waves on the shore was, and she thought how she had never heard them that loud ever in her life. She got to the stairs at the top of the pier leading down to the beach and couldn't believe her eyes. The waves were not only crashing the shore with fierce strength, the tide was only a few yards from the base of the stairs instead of the typical seventy-five to one hundred yards it would be on a normal day. It was if the whole beach had disappeared. She slowly made her way down the stairs with the wind and rain still blowing strong and continuous lightning and thunder. When she reached the bottom, she darted toward what she could make out to be Cap's cardboard shack and yelled out, "Cap! Cap!"

When she got closer, she could see the shack had collapsed on one side. Her surfboard was still on top of it, but on an angle and it was popping up and down with the wind. She went to her hands and knees and crawled to what was not much of an opening.

"Cap!" she yelled out again.

She felt around through the wet towels and found one of his legs. She then began to pull the towels off him and he began to tug against her, not knowing what was happening.

"Cap, it's me, Marta," she called out.

She thought he must have heard her, as he let go of the towel. When she got closer to him, she found him cuddled up like a child, with his knees to his chest. Then the lightning flashed again and as it did she watched him close his eyes, then put his hands over his ears. When the thunder clapped, he yelled out as if he was trying to drown out the noise with his own voice. Marta grabbed his arm; he resisted at first and pulled away from her.

"Come with me, Cap. We have to get out of here quickly," she yelled. "Please, Cap!"

Cap slowly started to crawl toward her and came out into the open. Marta could tell he was frightened, like a child would be. She helped him up and grabbed his hand.

"Let's go!" she said, as she grabbed his arm and started to pull him. At first, he stopped her, let go of her hand, and went to pick up the surfboard.

"No, Cap," she yelled. "Forget about that!"

She grabbed his hand again and pulled him toward her. She headed for the stairs with Cap in tow. Between the crash of thunder and the pounding of the waves, Marta thought to herself, "Christ, it is loud." Though it was slippery, she and Cap managed to slowly get up the stairs. Cap was barefoot, and he seemed to slip more than she did with her shoes on. When they got to the top of the stairs, she put an arm around Cap, and he one around her, and they navigated each other up Garnett Street, through the wind and rain, down the alley, and up the stairs to her apartment.

LA TEMPEST

(The Storm)

Marta and Cap were soaked from the rain as they entered her apartment. They stood there for a moment and looked at each other. Marta then went to a small hall closet and pulled out a fresh towel and washcloth.

"Here, Cap," she said as she handed them to him. "Why don't you go ahead and get out of those wet clothes and take a shower? While you're doing that, I'll run down to the café and get us something to eat."

Cap took the towel and washcloth and just stood there. Marta stood still as well, waiting for a reaction, but when she didn't get one, she decided one of two things could happen if she just left. Either he'd go ahead and shower or when she got back he would be gone. She wasn't too keen on the second one, but she had to risk it.

"Well, okay then, the bathroom is right over there," she said, and she put her wet hood back over her head and out the door she went, down the stairs and through the back door of the café from the alley.

When Marta left, Cap stood briefly and then looked around the small but quaint apartment. He walked slowly over to the bathroom, laid down the towel and washcloth on the tank of the toilet, undressed himself, turned the water on in the shower, grabbed the washcloth, and stepped in over the tub and under the shower, pulling the shower curtain closed. It had been a long time since Cap had taken a real shower with warm water, soap, and shampoo. He was used to the showers down by the beach that were cold and primarily for the public to rinse off the salt and sand from the ocean and beach at the end of the day. But lately, with all the water shortages in the state, the local munic- ipalities had shut down a lot of showers as part of a state-wide effort to save water, so all Cap had to use was the sink in public beach bathrooms.

Cap reached down to the soap dish and brought the soap to his nose. It smelled of Marta. Now he knew why Marta smelled like she did every morning when she came to get her surfboard. He rubbed the bar in his hands instead of using the washcloth. He rubbed the soap until it lathered up pretty good, then rubbed the parts of his face that were not covered by beard—rubbing hard. He then began to scrub his body using the washcloth. When he was done with that, he did the same with the shampoo and washed his hair and beard. He scrubbed with his fingertips to get down deep into his long hair. He rinsed off, and as he did, he saw dirt flow off him and spin down through the drain of the tub. He then decided to start over again, washing and shampooing for a second time and rinsing.

When he was done, he shut off the shower, stepped out and grabbed the towel, and began to dry off. He wrapped the towel around his waist and then looked into the steam-covered mirror above the sink. He saw a face he only barely recognized from reflections in storefront windows or an occasional car side mirror. He wiped the mirror somewhat clear of the steam to see himself more clearly and began to feel the hair of his beard. He opened the medicine cabinet behind the mirror, found a small pair of scissors, took them out, shut the cabinet, and stared into the mirror.

By this time, Marta had come back into the apartment with some Styrofoam containers and two plastic cups full of coffee. She set them down on the small table next to her small kitchen and then went back to shut the door. As she did, she noticed the bathroom door was halfway open and Cap was standing there staring at the mirror. After she shut the apartment door, she pulled off her wet sweatshirt and hung it back on the hook, walked over to the chair by her bed, and slipped on a t-shirt that was laying over the back. When she turned around, she could see Cap more clearly, standing in front of the mirror, bare-chested with the towel wrapped around his waist—and nothing but muscle hanging from his somewhat thin body. She saw he was trying to cut the hair of his beard, but was having trouble with the small scissors, so she walked into her kitchen and pulled out a pair of larger shears from a drawer. She walked over to the bathroom, knocked a couple of times on the door, and then pushed it open the rest of the way. Cap turned and looked as she slowly pulled his hand down with the small scissors, took them from him, and placed them on the edge of the sink. Marta then turned his face toward her and looked him in the eye. She noticed for the very first time his piercing blue eyes. "Oh my God," she thought to herself and fell into a brief trance. She caught herself, shook it off, raised the shears, and began to slowly trim his beard.

At first, she cut off big chunks of hair, as his beard hung long. She dropped each handful of hair into the wastebasket next to the sink. Cap never took his eyes off her and never said a word. Marta could feel his stare upon her, but kept along with the trimming. When she got closer to his chin, she grabbed a comb off the back of the sink, then switched to using the smaller scissors Cap had tried to use before. With them and the comb, she trimmed his beard short but evenly around his face. When she was done, she lifted his chin and turned his head both ways.

"Well, Cap, I must say you have a good-looking face. What do you say we cut the hair on your head as well?"

Cap just nodded once. Marta switched back to the shears and began again with cutting big chunks of hair, which was well below his shoulders. It was very quiet as the lightning and thunder had ceased for the moment. All that could be heard were the sounds of the rain falling on the roof of the apartment and the shears each time Marta cut some of Cap's hair. She cut the hair on his head short, but a bit longer than the length she cut his beard. When she was done, she took a little of her own hair product, rubbed it in his hair, and massaged his head as well. That was the first time she felt his eyes not looking at her—and she saw his eyes were closed as he felt her soothing hands running through his hair and scalp. Marta then grabbed him by the shoulders and faced him toward the now steam-free mirror.

"There ya go, Cap," she said.

Marta looked at him in the mirror and was surprised about how good looking of a man he was. Cap opened his eyes and looked into the mirror as well. He saw Marta smiling, looking over his shoulder, and then he looked at himself. All that could be heard was the continuing sound of the rain falling on the roof above them. Cap saw a man he had not seen in a long time. He cracked a small smile and then a tear dropped from the corner of his eye, and Marta saw it. She couldn't tell if it was of pain, sorrow, or joy. She leaned over from behind him and kissed the side of his cheek. Cap watched her from the mirror as she kissed him; he then turned and cupped a hand on her cheek as she eased away from the kiss.

Though it was sudden, to Marta it was still gentle. She could feel the roughness of the calloused skin on his hand, but she turned her face into it until her lips found his palm and she kissed it. She then reached up and grabbed the same hand gently with hers, and with her other hand, she reached behind his neck and pulled his head toward her, slowly, until their lips connected, softly, and they kissed, lips closed, slowly, and briefly. He pulled back some and looked into her beautiful green eyes as she looked into his eyes of blue. She slowly released him and stepped back. Their eyes locked on each other, she began to pull her t-shirt over her head and let it drop to the floor. She then unbuttoned and unzipped her shorts and let them fall to the floor as well. Though Marta stood naked before him, Cap's eyes were still connected with hers.

She took a step closer to him, unwrapped the towel around his waist and let it fall to the floor. She placed one hand on his chest and with the other she reached down to his now erect penis. She brought her lips back to his briefly, gently touching and breaking apart, then together again with pressure. The kiss became passionate and rhythm like, and all the while she continued to stroke his penis. He placed his hands on her hips while she moved her hand from his chest to his shoulder. She could feel his body react to her stroking; his breath raced through their kissing until all at once she felt his body tense in a convulsive state and he moaned as he ejaculated. She held him tight to her as she felt his body quiver with each ejaculation while she continued to stroke him.

They stood there briefly with his head over her shoulder, his chin across the back of her neck, as she stopped stroking his penis and let it go limp in her hand. She heard him begin to cry softly. She placed her other hand on the back of his head and ran her fingers through his hair. He then eased away from her until they were released from each other's grasp. She looked at him as he bowed his head down and sat down on the side of the tub.

"I'm sorry, I'm so sorry. It's been a long . . . long time," Cap said softly.

Marta soaked a washcloth with warm water, knelt down to the floor in front of Cap, and washed the semen from his lower body and penis.

"Shhhhh, it's all good," she replied.

When she had him wiped down, she stood back up, rinsed out the cloth, and washed herself off as well. She draped the washcloth over the edge of the sink, grabbed Cap's hand, led him out of the bathroom, and over to her bed. She crawled in and pulled his hand toward her as he crawled in alongside of her with his back to her. She slid her body up tighter to him until she was spooning with him, then she pulled the covers up over them both. She stroked his head, he turned, and they kissed. He then looked into her eyes. Marta smiled, and he smiled in return. His eyes lay heavy and within a moment he fell asleep.

Marta tucked herself closer to his body by reaching around his waist, held his hand, and laid her head on the pillow against his back. All she could hear was the soothing sound of the rain on the roof and Cap's steady but soft breathing. She had never been with a man before. She had been with young men who had not yet experienced life and were immature according to her standards, thus she had a few sexual encounters that were not much to her liking. There was a boy she dated her senior year in high school and although she loved him, she knew it wasn't love. She realized it more when she went off to Europe after graduation and discovered a big part of her inner self. Somewhere along the way, she quit writing him and ended it in person when she got back to San Diego.

Then there was someone her freshman year in college, a fellow musician. It was the first time she felt in love with someone who she thought felt the same. Oh, she knew others had loved her, but she had not felt it in return. There was never all the parameters all in place, meaning everything clicked: personalities, interests, and of course, sex. Not until this classmate. It all went well for a few years until she found out he had been seeing not one, not two, but several other women the whole time. She was devastated. It was the first she had her heart broken and ever since then, it had hindered the thought of being with a man again because of their childish and selfish ways. It was why she liked being one of the guys in the surfing group; she never felt threatened or intimidated by any of them and it was the same vice versa. No one crossed the line, although she had crushed a little on G, as she thought he was her type, but any thoughts of that obviously came to an end once she met Ron. No, instead she focused on her music and work, letting life take her from one day to the next until it would tell her, "Okay, Marta, it's time to take me a little more seriously and move on into some more responsibility." Right then, the rain started to lull her to sleep, so life was telling her to go with what's gotten her this far. She kissed Cap on the shoulder and felt him gently squeeze her hand. She smiled, and soon they were both in a deep sleep.

Clap! Bang! Clap! Bang! The thunder shook the whole building, rattled the windows, and woke Marta, but more so Cap, as he had sprung from the bed over to the side of the apartment door as if he was ready to attack anyone who entered.

"Cap," said Marta.

She saw he was so focused on what was outside of the door that he did not hear her. She thought it was like he wasn't even in the present moment. Then she yelled his name. "Cap!" She yelled again, "Cap!"

Cap turned, and when he saw her, his body seemed to release a bit of the defensive tension he was showing. Marta slowly crawled from the bed, onto the floor over to him, and gently touched his hand with hers. When she did, his tension totally released, and he sat back against the door, wiping his face with both hands.

"I'm sorry, darlin'. It was a bad dream!"

"That's okay," Marta said softly. "Want to tell me about it?"

"No. No," he mumbled.

Marta wanted to find out more about Cap, so she pushed him just a little bit. She positioned herself alongside of him, resting her back against the wall as well, and crossed her feet out in front of her, clasped her hands, and placed them on her lap.

"When I was younger, and I was a waken by a bad dream, my nonna use to say it is better to speak of a dream and find meaning to it then to hold it in and be captive to it."

"Nonna?" he asked.

"It's Italian for grandmother," she replied.

"This is not a dream, Marta; this is a recurring nightmare!"

Marta noticed that he was going back and forth, calling her darlin' and Marta. She thought it was a sign of him getting used to her; trusting her. Though they had known each other now for nearly two years, he'd only recently called her Marta, and she knew enough that it was a sign of his vulnerability. He was letting down the wall that was not only between the two of them, but between all others as well. She was sure this was the closest anyone had gotten to him in a long time, and obviously she was closer to him than he had allowed her to be before. After all, the two of them were sitting on the floor, naked. Hell, she thought, she had kissed him for the first time and jacked him off in the same night. She reached over and squeezed his hand again.

"Even more so to let it out," she said.

"Marta, you don't understand. It's a recurring dream of actual events that keep . . . that just keep running through and through my head." He tried to explain. "They are not good, and you will not want to hear them. I've tried telling them before to professionals and I can't get them out."

"What do you mean professionals?" she asked.

"Military staff, medical staff, psychiatrists, psychologists and therapists!" said Cap.

Marta grabbed his arm and twisted it so the tattoo of the Marine emblem showed, then said, "Marines?"

"Yes!" he replied.

"Did you ever get the story out, Cap?" she asked. "To anyone?"

There was silence for a few minutes, as Marta didn't want to push the issue with him. Cap looked into Marta's eyes, felt her hand in his and knew he was in a safe place with her—but he was not sure he should share his horror to her. Yet, he felt her warmth and obvious compassion from the very first time they met out front of the café sidewalk, when he was on his back being kicked and she stepped in. He knew the two of them shared an intimacy that went way beyond anything he ever shared with his fellow soldiers, family, or old friends, and yet they barely knew each other. The connection was there, and he knew she knew it as well. Maybe, just maybe, this could be the beginning to the end of all of it if he shared with Marta.

"I . . . I had already served two deployments to Afghanistan. When I initially signed up for the service, it was after 9/11. I was a young buck right out of high school and I wanted to go after the assholes that did that damage on our soil, so I signed right up. My parents didn't want me to, as I was their only child. But I did anyway. When . . . when they sent us over there for the first time, I began to see how things were fucked up. It was nothing like our basic training, organized and following a set of rules. The very first words out of our squad leader were, "Out here boys, we have to make up our rules as we go along, as the enemy here doesn't follow any rules." We still had protocol for the most part, but it would change constantly in regard to the way the enemy was fighting. That first deployment I saw a lot of fucked up shit." Cap took in a deep breath; Marta put her arm around his shoulder and held him closer as he continued.

"When I came home after that first deployment, I stopped in an airport bar to have a drink while I waited for the plane to take me on the next leg home. A couple of older guys were in there and saw my uniform. They introduced themselves as ex-Marines. One asked how it felt to be fighting a war like the one they had fought in. I asked what war that was. Vietnam, they said. I said, what do you mean? We are fighting the people who attacked us on our own soil. Then they said I really needed to get caught up on the news. They explained the whole Iraq oil issue. How there were not any weapons of mass destruction and that really Bin Laden was the only one behind the whole plot of 9/11, not a country, but a group, the Taliban, which were just part of the drug business. They wanted to get their poppy plants out for world distribution of heroin, and Bin Laden was tired of America getting in the way. They explained that the Taliban was no different than the Mexican or Columbian drug cartels.

"I just shook them off and said you old guys are nuts. Then one of them said, 'Look brother, we aren't any different in blood. We fought the same war as you. Thought it was for freedom but it was for policy. We lost a lot of brothers in Nam and I don't just mean Marines, I mean all the branches of service and for what? God be with yah! Oorah,' he said as they were leaving. Then the second one did the same, so I 'Oorahed' in return.

"By the time my second deployment was over, I was beginning to wonder if what they said was right. We would come across acres and acres of poppy plants and were ordered not to destroy them. When we questioned that order, we got the same damn answer. Don't question, just do. The locals were terrified at the thought that we would destroy the crops, for the Taliban would kill them if they didn't fight back. I had already seen enough death on both sides of the war. I killed and was nearly killed several times myself, but was saved by others and I saved others as well. By the time I came home after the second deployment, my parents saw the change in me. I never talked to them or anyone about my time over there. I was seriously ready to call it quits when I was asked to be deployed one more time with a promotion. I had already been promoted a number of times throughout my service, mostly because the ones in front of me were killed in action or discharged, so the few who decided to stay advanced in rank. Now, I wasn't made captain; I couldn't be at the time. Though guys under me started calling me Cap for short, partly in fun, but also because they had a lot more trust and respect in me to lead them then others before me or at that time. I was just their squad leader. Then I got calls from others in my squad begging me to come back because they only trusted me to lead them. My mother asked me not to, but my dad said it was my choice to make, even though I knew in his heart and mind, he really didn't want me to go as well."

Cap began to shake his head and was breathing deeper. He brought his knees up to his chest, wrapped his arms around them, and rested his forehead on his knees. Marta rubbed his back and as she did, he raised his head and looked into her eyes again. He started to speak and then stopped to think for a second, then he said, "Marta, the rest of this is not going to be good."

Marta looked into his eyes and could see the pain in them. They were like, sort of, without life. She could tell he was hurting, but she could also tell he was weighed down by what he was carrying.

"Cap, all I can say is what your dad told you. You have to decide for yourself."

She rubbed the back of his neck while he closed his eyes and raised his head to the ceiling. He opened his eyes, saw the ceiling fan spinning around and around, and tried for a moment to focus on one fan blade and follow it around in its circle. As he did, his head started to move in the same circular motion and when he got to where he was able to follow it a few revolutions around, he stopped, brought his head back down, and focused his eyes on the light from the streetlamp coming through the blinds across the way in the kitchen window.

Cap continued. "I didn't want to let the guys down. I knew what could happen. We were tightknit, and they did look up to me. Some didn't think it was right of the others to expect me to come back, and yet those same young men were just as glad to see me there. By this time, more and more Afghani police and army were working together with us. It meant a lot of briefings with their squad leaders as well as our own briefings. This time, our orders were to go door to door and clear streets of IED. That is short for 'improvised explosive device.' We had dealt with this before, but more so on open roads and fields, where there were mines everywhere.

"Now we were stationed outside of a city named Kunduz. We shared barracks with the Afghani army, separated only by half walls, meaning they didn't go all the way to the ceiling. The very first night we heard screaming from the other side of the walls. I didn't know what it was until another squad leader told me it was one of the Afghani police commanders and his boy toy. I asked him to explain that to me. He begins to tell me how many of the Afghani police had boy sex slaves; it is actually a practice called 'bach bazi'—translated to 'boy play'—and all American soldiers and Marines were instructed to ignore it and not intervene. Well, I said I hadn't been instructed and started to get up from my bunk when he pushed me back. 'You have now, by me,' he said, and then he proceeds to tell me to stay put and tells me a story as to why. He says it's because we are working with them and need every one of them to be able to help back us up. He said they need to trust us and we need to be able to trust them. He then said an Army soldier tried to do something and the Afghani police officer he reported ended up shooting him in his sleep. I asked what happened to the police officer and they said nothing, as nothing could be proven. During the whole time we were in this discussion, the screaming went on.

"We had been there a few weeks, out on several missions of clearing streets and buildings, when some of the local women would come up to us and complain about their children being taken by the Afghani police and being raped and murdered; the villagers thought the Afghani police were worse than the Taliban. All we could do was report it to our superiors, and when we did, we were continually told not to interfere. One night, the screaming in the barracks from the other side of the wall wouldn't stop. The men on our side were getting furious and I did all I could to stop an uprising. The next morning, I confronted the Afghani officer and he just laughed at me and said it was none of my business. I reported the incident to my commander and it was just taken as 'Duly Noted.'"

"OMG!" said Marta. Cap reached a hand over to her and rested it on her leg, where she firmly held it.

"I reported back to not only my squad, but to other squad leaders as well. That day, we were sent out to clear more IEDs. My squad and I were following a Humvee down a narrow street, meticulously searching and finding a number of IEDs. Things were moving smoothly. We were only about 10 feet from the back of the Humvee when there was a big explosion. Its concussion threw me backward, along with several other soldiers. As I laid there, I saw the Humvee going up in the air, along with the gunner and a couple other bodies in a cloud of smoke and dirt. I continued to watch as the bodies fell to the ground and the Humvee on top of them, on its side.

"There was nothing but chaos. I saw the gunner lying on the ground with one leg trapped under the truck. I got up and ran to him; I could see he was saying something, but I couldn't hear him. That's when I realized the blast knocked out my hearing. I turned and yelled at others to come and help lift up the truck. I looked inside the wreckage and found two other soldiers, both dead. All of the sudden, as a number of Marines started to lift the truck, we came under enemy fire. I didn't know until I turned my head and saw my sergeant down on one knee, his lips moving and no words coming out of his mouth, motioning me to get down. Another squad returned the enemy fire to try and hold them off as a group of Marines lifted the Humvee up off the gunner and got him to safety. The sergeant, two other soldiers, and I went back for the two dead soldiers inside the truck. All of the sudden my ears popped, and I could hear my sergeant telling me we only had one body bag left.

"I yelled out to grab a sleeping bag and we got one soldier into a body bag. We pulled the loose debris off the other soldier, and found he was missing his right leg from the knee down. When the sergeant who was with me went to grab the dead soldier's shoulders, his right arm nearly ripped off, as it was only being held together by his flak jacket. We got him inside the sleeping bag, found his leg and laid it on top of him, zipped him in, and got the hell out of there." Marta could feel Cap starting to shake and his breathing became quicker. She didn't respond other than to squeeze his arm now and then to let him know everything was okay. Cap continued.

"We got back to the barracks with two dead soldiers and three wounded. We all started to unwind as much as possible and forget the day's events as much as we could. You try not to get close to these guys, knowing you may not see each other from one minute to the next, but in all actuality, we are brothers. Just when we were all settling down our nerves, the screaming begins from beyond the wall. We all tried to ignore it, but I couldn't handle it anymore; I jumped from my cot and headed out the door, with some of the men trying to stop me, but my sergeant pushed them back and followed me. The others then followed behind us, but when the sergeant and I entered the Afghani police officer's barracks, the others stayed outside. When we got in there, we couldn't believe what we saw. A young boy, not much older than 14 or 15, was chained to the son of bitch's bed!"

Marta felt Cap's body begin to tense up and saw a tear running down his face, but there was anger in his voice as he continued.

"The motherfucker had the boy bent over the end of the bed and he was fucking the kid. The kid was screaming and crying. I went over and pushed him off the kid, slammed him against the wall, and told him this will not be allowed! He just laughed and said I had no authority over him. Well, I lost it—probably because of the day's earlier events—and punched the son of bitch in the face. As he went back against the wall, I hit him and again and again. He fell to the floor. When I stood over him, he just looked up at me with blood coming from his nose and mouth, laughing. That's when the sergeant came over and started kicking him, and I joined him. We both were just beating the shit out of him when some of other soldiers came in, MPs, and pulled us both off him. We were brought back to the barracks and told not to move. It was a quiet night for once, but the next morning they came and got me and the sergeant and the next thing we knew we were boarding a plane, on our way back to the States."

Cap sat in silence and Marta could see he was mentally drained. She was as well, as she couldn't imagine anything like what he experienced. She thought it best to stop right there, so she stood up and extended her hands down to him. He looked up and extended his hands to her, clasping hers, so she could help him to his feet. She then saw there were still tears on his face; she gently wiped them off with her thumb. She then leaned forward, kissed him on the lips, and looked into his eyes once again.

"Are you hungry?"

Cap nodded his head yes. She grabbed his hand and led him over a stool in front of the kitchen counter. Cap sat down as Marta opened the fridge and got out the food she had picked up earlier in the morning from the café. Cap just watched in amazement as her beautiful naked figure moved around, taking care of business without a care in the world that she was butt naked. He chuckled as he realized he was butt ass naked as well. She paused to look at him with a smile.

"What?"

"Nothing, it was just a thought."

She put one dish in the microwave, then got some silverware out of a drawer and placed it in front of Cap. She then opened the fridge again.

"We have water or um bottled water," she chuckled.

He smiled at her and said, "bottled water is fine."

She grabbed two bottles and placed them on the counter. The buzzer on the microwave rang, she removed the food from it and placed it in front of him, and then she placed hers inside the microwave and waited. She saw Cap wasn't eating and realized he was waiting for her.

"I see someone was taught some manners. You go ahead and start without me, eat!"

Cap smiled and started eating. She watched him as she wait-ed for her food. She wondered about the rest of his story—how this seemly courageous man ended up living in a cardboard shack under a pier. The buzzer of the microwave rang, interrupting her thoughts. She grabbed her food and set it on the counter, where she stood there and began eating naked across from the very intriguing naked man. Cap chuckled again.

"What?" Marta asked as she smiled at him.

"I never went on a first date before where we ended up hav-ing dinner naked," he said.

Marta began to laugh, and they laughed together. Cap stopped and took another bite. He chewed the food a few times, all the while looking at Marta. She saw the look in his eyes of a man in need. He got up from the stool and walked around into the kitchen. She turned to him, expecting him and ready for him. He wrapped his arms around her waist and drew her to him as she wrapped her arms around his neck. He pushed her food aside and lifted her up on the counter. Marta raised her legs up and rested her feet on the counter's edge. He then slowly started kissing the inside of her knees working back and forth between each of her thighs. When he reached the lips of her pussy, she was already soaked with wetness. As he touched her gently with just one finger, she moaned and arched her back while lifting her legs, one each over each of Cap's shoulders. As he inserted two fingers of one hand inside her and used the other to spread her lips apart, he tongued her clit with a flicker.

Marta moaned and placed the palm of one hand in her mouth, biting down to quiet herself while balancing herself with her other hand on the counter. She then leaned forward, releas-ing her hand from her mouth. She reached down and grabbed

Cap by his hair, pulled his head up, brought his lips to hers, and passionately kissed him. She felt his erection alongside her inner knee and when she couldn't hold back any more, she reached down, grabbed his hard cock, and whispered in his ear.

"How long has it been?" she asked.

"At least four years," he replied.

"You should be good to go then," she said. He knew what she meant.

"Yes, and you?" he asked.

"I'm good to go as well," she replied as she slipped him inside of her.

He started thrusting furiously fast, but she slowed him down.

"I'm sorry," he said.

"It's perfectly fine, it's wonderful!" she replied, softly shushing him.

They stayed there in the kitchen for a while and then he lifted her up, turned, and carried her to the bed—all the while remaining locked in intercourse. They both collapsed on the bed until they had rolled over to where he was on his back and she on top. She shifted from sitting upright on him to down on his chest and then back up again to where she was squatting over him, balancing herself with her hands on his chest. That's where she was when she had her first orgasm and where she was when she felt him ready to explode. That he did, as she felt his ejaculation against her inner walls. She let her knees collapse to the bed and sat fully down onto his erection. She grabbed his hands from her hips, placed them on her breasts, and guided his hands around them as she moved her hips slowly up and down. They both moaned and grunted with ecstasy.

She could feel him deep inside her. Each of his thrusts came with an explosion that enveloped her with another orgasm. When she felt he was done, she moved her hips deliberately more slowly until she felt she had drained him of every drop, and she collapsed her chest on his with him still inside of her. There she stayed, kissing his chest tenderly, while he rubbed her back and stroked her hair until they both drifted off to sleep.

QUEL CHE SARA SARA

(What Will Be Will Be)

Marta's body clock awoke her as usual. It did not matter what time of the night or how early in the morning she would fall asleep, she always woke between 4:30 and 5:00 a.m. She awoke to the sound of the rain still falling at a steady rate, but also to the wonderful warmth of Cap's body lying next to her. She watched him as he slept like a woman watches a newborn baby to see if it's still breathing. She looked at his well-chiseled, thin body and wondered how the man she had come to know as being bright and seemingly emotionally strong ended up in the streets, homeless. She had so many thoughts and questions for him after hearing his story, but didn't know how or when she should approach him to learn more. She only knew she wanted to get to know him better, as obviously she was attracted to him sexually, but she knew there was more than that luring her closer to him.

She also knew something about the delicacy of the situation from her grandmother's stories of her great-uncle Pietro, coming back from Vietnam. The war was never to be spoken of unless it was brought up by him, and he only did on rare occasions. Cap's story was not the first she had heard of war atrocities. She and her grandfather were in the garage one summer morning; Pops was tinkering at his workbench while Marta was waxing her surfboard, when her great-uncle Pietro came into the garage, picked up an old plastic milk crate, turned it on its side, and sat down.

"Buenos dias," he said.

"Buenos dias a usted tambien mi hermano," (Good morning to you as well my brother), said her grandfather.

"Good morning, Uncle Pietro," said Marta.

He sat there a bit and seemed fidgety and agitated. Marta and her grandfather noticed but continued working on their little projects.

"You know this whole damn Middle East war has got me all pissed off at what's happening to our soldiers when they come back here to the U.S.," he said.

"Que?" (What?) replied her grandfather.

"These men and now woman, God bless them, are coming back here all fucked up and nothing is happening to help them out! The same fucking thing happened to me when I got back here except we got spit in the face like it was our fault we fought in that war!" He was angry and went on.

"We were fucking drafted and forced to go. Dios malditos putos politicos!" (God Damn fucking politicians!) We should get the same damn care they do, and they do nothing! They have no problem supporting us over there, but back here we are fucking forgotten and some of us are still fucking dying!"

He stood up slightly, bent over to look at the milk crate, and found it was on top of a piece of scrap wood, so he tilted the crate slightly and brushed the piece of wood aside with the back of his hand before sitting back down.

"I read this morning that twenty-two ex-servicemen and women commit suicide a day and some are dying a slow damn death each day through drugs and alcohol! Well no fucking shit!

That's me! That's totally me!!! What do you think is going to happen when you fucking go into a village of some foreign country and shoot all night until your gun is so hot you can cook eggs and fucking bacon on it!!!" he said angrily.

Marta and her grandfather stopped what they were doing, turned, and listen. They had heard his rants before, but never heard him say one thing about his own experiences overseas.

"We shot all night and then walk into a village and there's nothing but dead farm animals all over the place, just butchered by our gunfire. Then out of nowhere a damn old Vietnamese woman comes from a hut and starts hitting one of our men and yelling in Vietnamese for us killing her animals. Then more people come out of their huts. Come to find out they had all been hiding in tunnels under their village dug by the enemy. The enemy was why we were supposed to be in that village. Then we have to start fucking crawling in those damn tunnels to search for the fuckers.

"Then all hell breaks loose, explosions happen underground, and then we are under fire by the villagers—who are actually the enemy in disguise. They used the actual villagers as shields, so innocent men, women, and children are shot and killed by the enemy and us. It was a motherfucking clusterfuck! Sometimes we are even shooting at each other by mistake because the fire and explosions came from everywhere. We were so fucking paranoid after that, that no one trusted any Vietnamese person, not even children. You couldn't. It fucking sucked! All that bullshit over there for someone else's fucking war and we come back to protests and humiliation and crap."

They watch him become fidgety with the milk crate under him as they listened to him continue.

"There was no such thing as a goddamn debriefing or fucking detox from that shit over there. I came home off a ship down here at Naval Base San Diego and walked home. No one said or asked a damn word other than my family and even then, I didn't respond! All the while all sorts of shit was going on in my head! I found the only way to forget that shit was to work during the day and drink at night!!! Now the same fucking shit is going on today and those fucking members of Congress who cut the VA budget bitch about how the VA is underperforming!"

Great-uncle Pietro got up from the crate.

"Goddamn milk crate!" he shouted, kicking it over and storming out of the garage.

Marta and her grandfather watched him leave, waving his arms up in the air and yelling, "Putos congresistas, todos ustedes pueden ir al inferno!" (Fucking members of Congress, may you all go to hell!) Then he walked down the street and out of their sight.

"Wow," said Marta.

"That was the first time in forty years since he got back from Vietnam that he has ever said anything about what had happened over there. That's a good start, though," her grandfather said.

"What do you mean?" asked Marta.

"It is a good start to recovery. He will soon be fine," her grandfather replied.

Marta took that memory to heart in comparing it with Cap's situation. Maybe Cap also would come out of his shell, now that he had spoken his heart out to her. She crawled out of bed and covered him up with the sheet. She went to the kitchen and cleaned up from the night before, and then went into the bathroom and did the same, picking up the hair clippings from Cap's head and beard. She also picked up his camouflage pants that were almost in rags and his t-shirt. She took the shears she had cut his hair with and used them to cut the frayed legs off at the knee and threw the cut portions and his t-shirt in the waste can. She turned on the shower, stepped into it with the pants in hand, squeezed a little shampoo out of the bottle, and began to wash them. When she was done, she flipped them over the shower rod to dry. She then took off the band keeping her waist-long dreads from falling into her face, shook them free, and let the water spill over her body.

Her dreads were not the matte type, but a braided style, and not the corn row variety, but the type where you really could not tell where one dread started from the next. She had it done in college after having a deep discussion with a classmate about the many different origins and meanings of how and why some cultures wore their hair. She shampooed her dreads one by one and then washed her body while the shampoo sat in her hair. When she was done washing, she rinsed herself clean from head to foot. She turned off the shower, grabbed a towel and dried herself, and then quietly dressed for work.

She wrote a note to let Cap to let know, if he should awake, where she was and that she would be back with food in hand shortly. She opened the door out onto the back deck and the rain hit her in the face almost immediately. She shut the door behind her quietly, hustled down the stairs and across the alley, avoiding the standing water, and walked into the café. In that short period of time, she was almost soaked from the rain. She walked briskly through the kitchen and said good morning to everyone with her usual smile, grabbed a couple kitchen hand towels off the shelf, and went into the women's restroom to dry off as much as possible before putting on her hairnet.

When she thought she was more presentable, she walked out, tossed the towels in the laundry bag, headed back into the kitchen, and addressed the guys.

"What's up fellas?" she said to Carlos, Johnny, and Rueben.

"By the looks of you, it's still storming out there pretty well," Carlos said.

"Yes, it is. The wind is unreal. The rain feels like bees hitting you," she responded.

Marta joined Carlos and Johnny with the food prep for the day's crowd as Rueben took care of the miscellaneous things to be done before opening. They were a half hour into the prep when Johnny's cell phone went off.

"Hey, Pops, what's up?" Johnny answered. "Okay, no worries," he said, hung up, and put the phone back in his rear pocket. "Pops says he was on his way here, but a road is washed out, so he's going back home. He said to have Marta run the front for the day."

Marta's first thought was Cap, back at the apartment. Carlos looked over to Marta.

"Well there you have it, Marta, you finally got control of everything," he said.

She knew he was being sarcastic, but Johnny wasn't. He liked Marta, but they butted heads like a brother and sister would.

"Well, that's what she thinks," Johnny said.

Marta turned around, took the towel draped over her shoulder, and snapped Johnny in the ass.

"Son of a bitch, Marta!" he yelled, and Marta dashed out to the front of the café as Johnny made a couple steps toward her.

"Okay, brother," said Carlos, and Johnny returned to prepping for the day.

When Marta got out to the front of the café, she saw it was still raining pretty hard and the wind was whipping the rain like sheets through the air. She turned on the open sign and lights for the overhang outside and unlocked the door. She pushed open the door slightly to make sure it was totally unlocked and when she did, the wind caught it and almost ripped it out of her hands, but she caught it, shut the door, and locked it again. She thought this was definitely going to be a problem; if they had any customers at all, she would have to unlock the door when they came in and lock it behind them.

She went back into the kitchen to let the brothers know and they decided to have Rueben help her out as much as possible. Marta went back out front and sat down by the door where Boss (Emanuel) usually sat when customers came in. She looked through the front window, watching the wind still blowing the rain almost sideways, including the rainwater that was pouring off the awning that hung across the front of the café. It was very hard to see the storefronts across the street and that was without any cars parked in the street, which was definitely a rarity. Normally, on a good day, which was almost every day of the year in San Diego, there wouldn't be a parking place available. There was really no day off in an area like Pacific Beach, certainly not for any food service businesses. On a normal day, there were a lot of tourism dollars to be made in the area. But this was not normal. This was different.

Marta sat there for a good half hour and saw only a hand full of cars driving down Garnett Street in the flow of the water that was running down toward the ocean. When she first sat down, she had noticed the water along the curb was running alongside of it, and now she noticed the water had risen to just about even with the top of the curve. Rueben came out and sat down at the table next to her. When they realized there were no orders coming through to the kitchen, Johnny and Carlos came out front and joined them. Johnny sat down with Reuben and Carlos just stood there.

"Wow," said Johnny. "Guess this is El Nino settling in."

"Yea," said Carlos. "Doesn't look like much business is going to be happening today. I can't even see whether there's even any movement across the street in the other shops."

"It's been getting worse and worse since I first turned on our sign earlier," Marta said.

Just then, a flash of lightning occurred, and soon after a large sound of thunder came crashing from the heavens—and the whole place shook.

"Mary Jesus y Jose" (Mary, Jesus and Joseph), said Reuben, as he made the sign of the cross across his chest.

Marta sat up straight as she thought of Cap. After another flash of lightning and gigantic sound of thunder rattled the front window, Marta jumped straight up from her chair with a distraught look on her face. The three men saw her startled look.

"You okay, Marta? It's just some thunder," Carlos said.

Marta turned and looked at Carlos, Johnny, and Reuben.

"I'm fine, but I just remembered I left my windows and patio door open in the apartment. I'm sure there's water all over." She looked at Carlos. "I have to run really quick and take care of it, Carlos." Marta turned and started to leave when Carlos shouted out, "Marta!" She turned around but continued walking backward as she looked at Carlos. "Just stay there and I'll call you if we get anything going here."

"Really? Will do. Thanks, Carlos!" she replied.

She jogged down the hall, but stopped in the kitchen, made a couple quick plates of food, and covered them well in Styrofoam containers before heading to the back door. Once outside, she got nailed with the wind and rain, and had to make sure the door was closed behind her as she pushed it hard with her butt until it latched. She was already soaking wet before she even got to the base of the stairs of her place, and the water was falling hard off the roof and down the steps as she made her way up. It flashed lightning and thundered loudly again—so loud she thought the stairs were going to collapse from the concussion. She continued up the stairs, but slipped and fell; balancing the food with her hands, she couldn't break her fall and she hit one of the steps just below the kneecap. She let out a small yelp, but got up and continued on to the apartment. She stacked the food in one hand and opened the screen door, which the wind took and slammed it against the porch railing. She then opened the door and stepped into the apartment. She quickly placed the food containers on the floor and reached around to close the screen and entry doors, again making sure the latter was shut behind her with her butt.

She turned to shake the water off her and remove her wet shoes, and when she looked up, saw Cap was not in the bed and the covers were gone. She picked up the food containers and walked by the bathroom; Cap wasn't in there, either. As she got closer to the kitchen, she did not see him, and the thought went through her mind that he had run off in this storm. As she got to the kitchen, she saw that indeed she had left the door open to the front balcony. She set down the food on the counter and went to close it, finding Cap sitting in a chair with the bedcovers draped around him and over his head. The balcony was sort of protected by the elements, as it had a wall on both sides and a roof over it;

since the storm was coming up from the south, and this was the north side of the building, the rain and the wind were not blowing as hard. Right now, it felt like an occasional mist hitting the balcony, even though not more than six feet away, it was coming down in sheets.

She approached Cap slowly, not knowing what to expect, then the lightning flashed again, and the thunder was just as intense. Cap barely budged and just flinched a bit, which surprised her.

"Cap!" she cautiously called out as she approached him.

He seemed to shrug more from hearing her voice than he did from the sound of the thunder. As he pulled off the covers and turned his head to look at her, she moved toward him and knelt on one knee, while at the same time squinting in slight pain by bending the knee she just banged on the steps. She put an arm around his back.

"Are you okay?" she asked.

Cap noticed her knee and saw a trickle of blood coming from it. He looked up at Marta.

"Yes, but are you okay?" he asked, as he stood up grabbing a hand of hers helping her up to her feet.

"What do you mean?" she asked.

"Marta, your knee?" He pointed to her knee and she saw the blood.

"Yes, I slipped on the steps, but I guess I hadn't realized I had cut myself."

He directed her inside and sat her down on a kitchen stool. He threw off the covers and let them fall to the floor. Marta watched his naked ass as he walked around the kitchen. He took a dish towel and ran it under warm water in the sink. Another flash of lightning and clap of thunder made him flinch just a bit. He looked up and saw Marta smiling. He smiled back.

"What?" he asked.

"Oh, nothing," she chuckled.

They looked at each other for a little longer.

"Under the sink there is a first aid kit," she said.

Cap handed her the dish towel. She started to dab the area of the wound on her knee and realized it wasn't as big a deal as they thought.

"No stitches needed. Just a couple Band-Aids will suffice," she said.

He retrieved the first aid kit, set it on the counter in front of her, opened it, reached in, and grabbed the size he thought would work. He tore off the covering, and knelt down in front of Marta's knee, and as soon as she had dabbed the area dry, he placed the bandage over her cut. He then leaned forward and kissed her knee.

"There, there, darlin'. Baby all better," he said in a baby type voice.

Marta, who loved how he always addressed her as darlin', smiled and playfully slapped him on his shoulder, and they both laughed it off. Cap then noticed the guitar leaning against the wall behind Marta.

"Do you play that or is it just a piece of wall art?" he said, smiling.

Marta turned around and picked up the guitar, gave it a quick tune-up, and without saying a thing, started playing a Spanish love song. Cap sat back on the floor, still naked, crossing his legs and leaning back, propping himself up with his hands and arms, and watched as her picking started out slow then quickened.

He was mesmerized by her playing and focus. She looked at the guitar and watched her own fingers as she meticulously moved around the instrument as if they were a part of it. Then she started to sing, in Spanish, the song, "Mi Vida Sin tu Amor."

It seemed the further into the song she got, the more focused she was. This went on for about five minutes, and then she slowed it down and finished. She looked up at Cap with a grin.

"Does that answer your question?" Cap looked at her in amazement.

"Why the fuck are you working in a café?" he said. "Did you write that?"

Marta laughed as she set the guitar back up against the wall and turned back around in the stool.

"Because I have been playing this and other instruments my whole life and I want to see what else is out there for me before I get serious about life," she said, "and no, I did not write that. It's called 'Mi Vida Sin Tu Amor' and that's the short version."

Cap slowly nodded his head, appreciating her honesty.

"It was beautiful! What does it mean? What was it about?" he asked.

"It's about two lovers and one expressing to the other how life would be without their love."

"Ah, I get it, I get it!" he said. "I wish I had done that as well." Marta looked a little confused and he saw it on her face. "I mean take a break from all the seriousness of life."

She thought to herself that this was a man, since returning from war in the Middle East, who really had no responsibilities. Surely, his living under a pier in a cardboard hut brought none to her mind a person could have.

"Why can't you do it now, Cap? What's stopping you?" she asked him.

The lightning flashed again, and the thunder clapped soon after. Cap flinched and sat there in silenced, looking into Marta's eyes. She decided it would be better to let the subject go until another time and broke the ice.

"Well, we need to get you into some clothes, as I will never get anything accomplished with a naked man around the place," she said with a smile.

Cap returned the smile with a seemingly reluctant grin of his own—that Marta noticed.

"What's wrong?" she asked.

Cap now looked more like a whipped puppy dog.

"Marta, I haven't any money."

Marta got up, walked briskly over to the bathroom, grabbed his pants off the shower curtain rod, and tossed them over to him. Cap caught them and stood up. He noticed they were cut into shorts and washed, and then began putting them on. She turned to rummage through a few oversized sweatshirts she had hung up on hooks by the door.

"I have a question for you, Cap," she said as she found what she was looking for and tossed that over to Cap as well. "That should fit you."

"What's the question?" asked Cap.

As Cap was slipping on Marta's hooded sweatshirt, she walked over to him, reached down, and grabbed one of his hands.

"Cap, do you like me?" she asked.

"Well of course, darlin', I have always liked you, ever since the day you stopped Johnny from kicking me. You put a lot of trust into me that day, something I hadn't felt from anyone since I was in the service."

"I understand that, and I do trust you, but do you like all of me?" she asked.

Cap knew what she was asking and that to him meant getting close to somebody—something he always had trouble with.

"Darlin', I like all of you, but you don't really know me."

Marta noticed he went back to calling her darlin' instead of Marta.

"I know, and you really don't know me, but that's the point. We like each other and I want to get to know you and want you to get to know me. If you're in agreement with that, I really don't care about you having any money, Cap. All I care about is your happiness; that's worth more to me than anything at this time."

Cap stood there thinking and kind of biting his lower lip. Marta saw that and knew he was in thought. She gave him his space, knowing what little she did about the homeless and more so about homeless veterans, so she didn't push. That was hard for her to do, for Marta was always a focused person who fought hard to get her way and was often competitive—as she always felt she had something to prove. It ruined many relationships and friendships as she grew into a young adult. She didn't want to get her heart broken again, but with Cap, she felt something different inside of her. She tugged at his hand and pulled him along with her toward the door.

"Come on, it'll be okay," she said.

When they got to the door, she turned around and planted a kiss on his lips. Cap didn't resist it; in fact, he enjoyed it. There was something about Marta he just couldn't put a finger on, but he felt more at ease with her then he did with his own family and even more than he did with his service buddies.

Marta opened the door and out they went. The rain and wind had subsided some as if they were in the eye of the storm. They headed down the stairs through the alley and turned left on the side street and then right onto Garnett. It was just sprinkling lightly as they headed down the sidewalk. Cap was still barefoot, and Marta still had her hair net on from the café.

Garnett Street is full of every kind of bar, restaurant, and shop you can think of. On one of her many trips down and back on Garnett from her morning surf, she counted sixteen different places that served pizza alone. She found eight tattoo parlors and about the same amount of Hookah joints and hair salons. You are guaranteed to find a restaurant on the street that will specialize in food from anywhere around the world and a bar that will serve beer and alcohol from around the world or even brewed locally. There were probably just as many liquor stores as there were tattoo parlors. Then there were shops selling everything from insurance and bicycles to phones and tires. There were auto, motorcycle/scooter shops and a bunch of individually owned yoga clubs and gyms. Then of course there were several places selling beachwear, many of which were designs created by the owners. Clothing shops abounded, along with many tourist trap stores selling souvenirs. And, there were used furniture and secondhand shops, thrift shops, Goodwill, and the Salvation Army.

Marta and Cap walked through the light rain and occasional downpour of water coming from shop roofs without awnings. They reached a thrift store she would often visit to find items from recent estates, donated after someone had passed away. Some items would be out of style, but Marta might get them anyway, making them into her own style and setting her own trends. She was always complimented on her appearance when she met up with her surf family or just went out on her own at local clubs to dance. When asked by other women where she found an outfit, she always responded, "Oh it's just something I whipped together myself."

Marta and Cap walked in from the deserted wet streets. They stood at the entrance and wiped the rain off them as best they could, so as not to track a lot of water. The owner was behind the counter, leaning on it and staring out the window.

"Hi, Marta," she said.

"Hi, Angie," Marta said. "We're going to look around for some things for this guy."

"Help yourself, dear; the store is all yours. You're my only customers," Angie responded depressingly.

Marta grabbed Cap's hand and led him over to the area of thrift clothing for men. When they got there, she stopped Cap in his tracks and went down the aisle, looking for items of clothing she thought might look good on him. She would pull some off the rack and come back down the aisle to see if it would be okay.

"That shirt looks good with your eyes, but I don't know about the length," she said, then removed it and held another one up to his chin. "That one's long enough but I just don't know about the color. What do you think, Angie?"

Soon the two women were dressing and judging Cap. Cap didn't know how to respond, as he had never had this much attention while shopping, even as a kid when his mother bought his clothes. She would usually shop while he was in school, and when he got home and walked into his room, there would be new clothes on the bed for him and to try on. When he'd come down for dinner, she'd ask him what he thought and if everything fit. If he didn't like something or it didn't fit, she would return it. As he got older, he learned that if he didn't like something, he would just tell his mother it didn't fit, and she would return it and get something else. She soon caught on and said to him one day, "My boy, here's one hundred dollars. Go out and get yourself some new clothes you like. I'm at a loss for what you young kids like today."

Now he was a grown man and although he dated through high school and occasionally on his leaves from service, he never really had a woman into him enough to want to dress him and actually enjoy doing so—and now he had not only one woman, but two. Besides, he already knew what Marta wants, Marta gets. Her tenacity could come off as annoying at times and pushy to others. But he liked that about her. In the short time he had known her, he saw that attitude of hers got things done and it was a character he liked in the men in his squad in Afghanistan. Cap knew how to deal with it.

They settled on a couple pairs of shorts; some jeans, t-shirts, and dress shirts; a pair of old, beat-up Chuck Taylors; and a pair of flip flops, which Cap put on his feet immediately and instantly felt some relief. They met Angie at the counter, where she totaled the bill on a receipt pad.

"That's forty-three dollars and seventy-six cents, Marta dear," she said as she tore off the copy underneath the original and handed it over to her.

While Marta was digging in her purse, Cap was waiting by the door and saw a help wanted sign in the window. When he thought neither woman was watching, he grabbed it and tucked it under his shirt. Marta settled up with Angie.

"Thank you, dear," she said to Marta. "Nice to have met you," she shouted to Cap, who raised up his chin in acknowledgement.

"Love," responded Marta, with her signature two-finger blow kiss.

Marta and Cap walked out to see the rain had subsided to a small mist, but it was still a very dark and gloomy day—and it looked like the storm could pick up again at any moment. There was a humid breeze shooting down the street that would become stronger every time they walked past gaps between buildings or crossed one of the east-west streets. As they made their way back toward the apartment, Marta noticed the traffic picking up and more people on the sidewalks, so she thought she should go by the café to see if she was needed. As they arrived at the entrance, she saw her surfboard leaning up against the wall.

"Oh my God!" she said. Cap saw what she was looking at.

"It's your surfboard!" he said.

Then there was a knock on the glass window from inside, and they both looked to see it was Dale Da Dude. He was waving, and they could see him mouthing Marta's name. They entered the café and to their left were four of the guys: Dale, his brother Chuckie, Manny, and Danny.

"We found your board!" Dale said.

"I can see that, Dale; thank you so much!" she said.

She walked toward Dale, sat the bag of clothes on a table next to one where the guys were sitting, and gave Dale a hug. Cap just stood by the entrance, smiling but not moving. He didn't know how the guys would react to him being with Marta.

"When the weather eased up, Manny and I decided to go down and check out the beach, and that's when we saw Chuck and Dale," Danny said.

"Yea, we checked out what was left of the beach," Chuckie said. "That's when Dale mentioned Cap, so we all ran up toward the pier and there was nothing left of his shack or the board."

Dale started staring at Cap and the other guys kind of glanced over at him as well and Cap stood with a bit of uneasiness. Dale walked a little closer to him.

"But Dale saw a surfboard up in the cross members of the underside of pier, along with a ton of kelp," Danny said. "He yelled that it was yours. That's a good twenty feet up, so you can imagine the height of the surf."

"I climbed up, got it down, and found it wasn't in too bad of shape," Manny said.

"Thank you! Thank you so much, you guys!" she said to them all.

"Marta, we also looked up and down the beach and around and saw no sign of Cap," Chuckie exclaimed.

The guys all sat in silence as Marta looked over to Cap with a devilish smile. Marta and Cap each realized no one had recognized him. Dale walked closer to Cap, paused, and then quickly went back over to his brother to whisper in his ear. Chuckie stood up.

"No fucking way!" he said.

Manny and Danny looked at Chuckie and simultaneously said, "What?"

"I found Cap! I found Cap!" Dale sounded in excitement.

Danny and Manny looked at Cap, a cleaned up guy they didn't recognize.

"What the fuck?" Manny said.

All the guys got up, went over to Cap, looked at him, and then gave him palm shakes and hugs.

"We thought for sure you were a goner dude!" Danny said.

They sat back down at the table.

"I was sound asleep last night and was awakened by the thunder and wind. The first thing on my mind was Cap, so I ran down and got him just in time, brought him back to my place, got him cleaned up, and voila!" Marta said.

"Damn Marta, good job," Manny said.

"So, wait a minute, he's been with you in that tiny little apartment of yours since the storm started?" asked Danny.

Cap and Marta knew what Danny was getting at and Cap saw that Marta was going to respond, but he beat her to it.

"Marta made up a nice little place on the floor for me to sleep on," Cap answered.

Marta looked at Cap as if saying why not tell them the truth, but she elected not to say anything. Then her eyes caught the front entrance of the café and she happened to see G and Ron holding each other and beginning to kiss. She knew the guys didn't know anything about G's relationship and G obviously didn't know they were inside the café. G and Ron kissed.

"Oh, dios mio!" Manny said.

Marta didn't have to turn to see who responded to what they had just seen, as she knew Manny was the only other one who spoke Spanish.

"It's G boy!" Dale Da Dude said excitedly.

Danny stopped his questioning to turn his head to see what Manny was talking about.

"Oh boy," Chuckie said.

"What in the fuck?" said Danny, as he got up and went out the door. Marta got up and followed. When the others got up, she turned her head toward them and shouted while pointing her finger at them, "Don't one of you fuckers leave that table!" She looked them all in the eyes and they all stood there halfway out of their seats except Dale.

"Don't worry, Marta. We won't," he said.

Marta turned toward the door and could hear Danny going off on G. She slowly pushed open the door, went outside, and moved slowly toward them. Before she got to the boys or even said a word, Danny screamed at her, "Shut the fuck up, Marta! I don't want to hear your preaching right now!"

Marta moved over by Ron and held his hand, as they both waited to see what was going to happen or be said next. Danny then pushed G with both hands in his chest and Ron tried to step in, but Marta squeezed his hand and held him back.

"But Marta?" Ron said, and Marta held his hand even tighter.

"What the fuck, Danny?" said G after Danny shoved him a couple times.

"What the fuck? What the fuck? What the fuck are you doing kissing that guy? Huh, what the fuck is wrong with you?" Danny said again and again, continuing to shove G

The guys inside were watching and by this time so were Carlos, Johnny, and Rueben. Carlos asked what was going on.

"Danny doesn't like it that G was kissing Ron," Dale Da Dude replied.

"No fucking shit!" Johnny was astonished.

The argument was going on right in front of the café's window. Everyone except maybe Danny and G could hear the thunder rumbling in the distance, but Danny kept yelling at G.

"I've worked out with you in the gym and partied with you with women, dude! What the fuck is this?" Danny said as he looked at Ron and then back at G.

G just kept letting Danny be verbally abusive and pissed off at him. All of a sudden, the sky turned dark.

"Gonna be a boomer, Chuckie," Dale Da Dude said.

There was a flash of lightning and big sound of thunder that not only rattled the windows and the building, but everyone in the café as well. Marta looked through the window and locked eyes with Cap, who gave her a thumbs up that he was okay. Marta then released Ron's hand and tried stepping in between Danny and G as the rain started slowly coming down.

"God damn it, Marta!" Danny said. Marta responded by stepping aside again, seeing G nod to her and Ron that he was all right.

"Danny, I understand you're upset, but your behavior is inappropriate, brother. You're pissed off! I get it and yet I don't!" G said.

Danny stopped shoving G, turned away from him, walked away back toward the café entrance, and went inside. The guys sat back down, while Carlos, Johnny, and Rueben just stood there.

"Danny, you okay?" asked Chuckie.

Danny nodded his head yes and sat down. Back outside, the rain began to fall harder and the lightning and thunder began to pick up, though not as intense as they were earlier. Marta and Ron went over to G, grabbed him, and brought him under the awning of the entrance.

"You do know what that was about, don't you, G?" asked Ron.

G looked at Ron with a blank stare, and Ron and Marta waited for him to answer. When G just stood there and didn't respond, Ron answered his own question.

"Well, think about how hard it has been for you to come out. Until just recently, with all the news, it's been hard for a lot of us to come out and that tends to isolate us. All of this frustration and anger builds up inside some of us because we don't know who to share it with in fear of receiving a negative response or consequences," Ron said.

"Son of a bitch, first you, G, and now Danny!" was Marta's response.

G looked at Marta and back at Ron, and then turned and looked through the window inside toward the guys—seeing Danny with his head in his hands, resting his elbows on the table. G turned back to Ron, squeezed his hand, leaned over, and kissed him on the lips. He then let go of Ron's hand and turned toward Marta, who had just opened the door to the café. As he started to walk, Marta grabbed his hand, leaned into him, kissed him on the cheek, and smiled. G walked in with Ron and Marta behind him. He walked toward the guys' table and they all looked toward him, except Danny. Carlos, Johnny, and Rueben moved to the side; Manny got up from next to Danny and stepped away. The others still didn't know what was going on. G walked over to Danny and sat down in the chair Manny had vacated. Then Marta broke from Ron, walked over to Cap, stood behind him, and rubbed her hand through his hair before placing it on his shoulder. When she did this, the Manny sort of put two and two together. He just smiled, shook his head and said, "Ay caramba!"

Marta stuck out her tongue at Manny and smiled at him.

"Danny," said G. "Hey, buddy. I'm sorry . . . I . . . had no idea."

G didn't know if he should put his arm around him, and after a first attempt, he pulled it back without touching him. Danny still had his head in his hands and was staring down at the table.

"Dan, I don't know what to say or how I should say it other than I'm sorry," G said.

There was silence for a bit and everybody was looking to each other as to what to say or do—and then the silence was broken by Johnny.

"Hell, it's a surprise to us as well that G is gay, but what the fuck, as long as he doesn't hit on me for Christ sake, I'm fine with it."

Danny raised his head and slapped his hands on the table, both palms cupping enough to make a pop instead of a slap, looked around at everyone and caught each one in the eyes as he spoke calmly. "I am gay as well!"

"Oh cogerme, voy a volver a la cocina!" (Oh, fuck me, I'm going back into the kitchen), Johnny said, turning and walking away.

The others were silent.

"Hey, Dude! So, what? Why should it change the way any of your friends feel about you? I lost many a friend. Dude, you're lucky. All your friends are still here. Not one of them has gotten up and left you," Cap said.

Dale Da Dude got up, walked over to Danny and G, and put his arms around both of them.

"I love both of you guys," he said.

Then out of the blue, Larson walked into the café.

"Hey, guys, what's new?" he said.

They all looked at each other and started laughing hysterically, while Larson stood there with a blank smile on his face—not having a clue what had been going on.

CASA MIA E CASA TUE

(My Home is Your Home)

Marta stepped back and took it all in. Cap saw her and stood at her side. She knew what Cap had said was as important to her friends as it was to her.

"Thank you!" she said to him, reaching down and grabbing his hand as well the bag of clothes, and they sneaked away from the group. They went past the kitchen where Johnny was too busy on the phone to notice them and through the back door. They ran through the rain, again, up the stairs and into her apartment.

"Well, that was a most exciting and interesting trip," she said.

Cap smiled, went over to the bed and sort of made it by throwing the sheet and blanket back on it and smoothing it out. He kicked off his flip-flops, stacked the pillows against the wall, and then laid down, staring at the ceiling. Marta set the bag down, removed the hair net from her head, and let her dreads fall, fluffing them some. She walked into the kitchen, grabbed a water bottle out of the fridge, and walked on over to the bed. She stood there looking at Cap, smiling, while she removed her shoes one at a time, using her feet to do so. She opened the bottle of water, took a swig, and offered it to Cap, who shook his head no. She placed the cap back on the bottle and smiled at him. He returned the smile as she crawled in alongside him, gave him a quick kiss, and laid her head on his chest.

Cap went to run his hand through Marta's hair, but then realized he couldn't with her dreads. His hand hung awkwardly in the air and he chuckled a little, then just placed it on her head and kind of patted it.

"What?" she said, after hearing his little laugh.

"Oh nothing," he responded.

This was all new to him. It had been so long since he'd been with a woman—three years in the service and there was a woman or two he could remember, then almost year back in the States before he ended up in the streets, which was at least two or maybe three years ago. He really couldn't remember how long he'd been away from things. He needed to adjust to all this interaction since he had been absent from it for a long while. He loved the group of people Marta was surrounded by; they made him feel like he was in a squad again. They were all like family and he felt that, especially today. They all had each other's back. They even had their own squad leader in the lone wolf, the only woman, Marta. There was a reason for that as well, he thought. He related it to his service days when there were women who served as well. Not many were leaders, and those who were, weren't strong like Marta. He thought about how she would have been good in the service. He thought of her as stronger than even himself. It was obvious to him, with her having taken so much control over him since the storm, control over what little affairs he had. After all, it was she who rescued him from the beach.

He rubbed her shoulder as she laid there, still on his chest, and she rubbed his stomach gently in response and spoke.

"Cap, my place is yours. I mean, you can stay here and come and go as you please. I don't want you to feel you have to or I need you to. I just don't want you to think about or worry about having to go back to living under the pier or someplace else for that matter. No strings attached either, Cap. My place is yours. Okay?"

Cap squeezed her shoulder, gently signaling he heard her, and Marta smiled and closed her eyes. Before long, Cap could feel the rhythm of her breathing and knew she had fallen asleep. The rain kept falling on the roof, his eyes became heavy, and it wasn't long before he had fallen asleep as well.

E SOLO UN ALTRO GIORNO

(It's Just Another Day)

El Nino is a Spanish word associated with a band of ocean water that develops in the central and east-central equatorial region of the Pacific Ocean. It creates a much wetter winter all along the West Coast of the U.S. California had been in a seven-year drought, the severity of which was reflected by a record number of fires and a statewide mandatory water rationing system. Even though San Diego and its citizens were doing a great job of conserving water, the El Nino gave a much-needed reprieve to the rationing, but also meant flooding and other issues around the city. It had been raining on and off for nearly a month and most of that time it was a hard rain. Every day, the number of lightning strikes was breaking records. The cloud cover was lower than normal, which amplified the thunder and made the walls and windows shake in any building. Many times, the vibrations could be felt through your feet while standing still. The rain was so intense that almost daily, the streets, gutters, and waterways could not handle the overflow, so there was flooding everywhere. Garnett Street was no exception.

There wasn't much surfing going on with the group. Not so much because of the weather, but with the beaches being closed from accidental sewer spills or overflows. When they could surf, the waves were big, but the riptides were treacherous. It was definitely not for the average surfer, although many did try to test their skills. People came from all over the world to surf up and down the California coast during this El Nino. The good news was the group was together and supportive of each other more than ever. Danny and G were never judged by the others or questioned. Dale Da Dude was becoming more independent of his brother. The group was a good part of that success, with Chuckie insisting nobody treat his brother any different than anybody else.

Cap had begun to settle in with Marta by now and they were getting to know each other's habits. Marta still wasn't pushing Cap much. He liked that about her, but he knew she was struggling with it. He knew it was against her nature not to know something about everything, and he was still a mystery to her and the others as well. Cap took the job at the thrift store even though Marta wasn't demanding it. He wanted to pay his way in the relationship, plus he wanted to try to get back into society again and he thought it would be a good start. Marta continued at the café, and because there wasn't much surfing going on, she switched to working out at the gym before work. She sometimes skipped that to experiment in the kitchen with Carlos and Johnny on new dishes to present their customers. All the businesses were struggling some, as tourism dropped off with the rain. No sunny beach weather meant fewer customers to eat or shop nearby, so everyone was looking for an advantage to bring in new customers.

Marta started work earlier than Cap, thus she finished before him as well. He would often come back to the apartment and hear her playing on her guitar, perhaps trying something new she had written. He would just sit at the top of the steps and listen until she was done. He didn't want to interrupt her. She caught on to this after a few times, when she felt it odd that he walked in right after she had finished playing. She wanted him there. She said he was inspiration for her. He gave her new energy and drive.

"Why, Marta?" Cap asked her one day.

"I want to share my experience with you. Before I always felt alone, wondering why or who I was doing it for, besides family," she said.

"Well, what about other people out there who haven't heard your music, your words?" he asked.

"I don't have a problem sharing the finished product with others, but I want to feel that each time I perform I am performing for that one person who inspires me. That each and every time that moment is special and unique," Marta responded.

Cap got it. He understood probably better than Marta understood herself. It was because he felt that way as well. Everything he had done before today was for his country and for himself. He felt betrayed by his country, by its hypocrisy when dealing with policy in fighting fights he felt were never meant to be won. And, he and others returned to be given nothing more than a handshake or pat on the back for risking their lives. He thought only about himself when he chose to go to the streets to live life without a care for others or even for himself at times. He didn't think of how his parents would feel about losing their son. He made it back from the Middle East in one piece only to disappear into the invisibility of the shadows of the nearly one point six million homeless in America. His own experience on the streets was a testament to the fact that volunteers were trying, but the politicians who put most of them in the streets to begin with were not. Cap now wanted out. He knew he needed help. But not from Marta. This was bigger than Marta. He realized that a few days earlier while working at the thrift shop.

He was hanging clothing on the racks when a man of color came into the store with a young boy of not more than ten or eleven. He spoke to the boy in a language Cap understood all too well, Pashto. That is one of the languages used in Afghanistan and Pakistan. Cap was not fluent in it, but he knew enough of it to know that's what the man spoke. The man told the boy to stay near him. They walked through the shop and the man was checking things out throughout the store. He went back to the furniture items, then to the household goods like plates, glassware, and utensils. Often the boy would lag behind. When he did, the man would scold him and the boy would bow his head and run closer to his father.

The incident was triggering memories in Cap's head of the war. The man then turned down the aisle where Cap was and the two briefly locked eyes. The man turned his head away and back to the clothing. He noticed his son was not near him again and he yelled the boy's name. Cap started getting agitated. The man left the aisle and Cap followed him as the man continued to yell for the boy. The man found the boy in an area full of used toys for sale. The boy was sitting on the floor, playing with a toy he had found. The man was angry; he went over to the boy, grabbed his arm, yanked him up in the air, and yelled at him some more.

Cap snapped, ran up behind the man, and put a choke hold on him. He demanded he let go of the boy and he did, but Cap didn't let go of the man. Almost immediately, the boy started kicking and hitting Cap and yelling at him to let go of his father. Cap could not hear the boy, as he only saw his lips moving. Angie heard the commotion and came from out of the back room. She ran up to Cap, asked what was going on, and grabbed a hold of his arm to try and release it from around the man's neck. Cap looked at her but could only see her lips moving as well. All of a sudden, he could hear the boy and Angie, and he realized where he was and what he was doing.

He released the man, who immediately gasped for air and then grabbed his son and hurried to leave the store. Angie followed them, trying to comfort the man and apologize to him. The man said nothing, as the fright on his face, as well as on the boy's, said it all, and they left the store. Angie watched them head down the sidewalk, then went over to Cap, who had sat down on one of the chairs that were for sale.

She asked Cap if he was okay and what had happened. He told her, apologized, and asked that she not tell Marta about it. She was understanding and wrote down a name of a person she spoke to when she had issues she couldn't share with others. He put the piece of paper in his pocket, thanked her, and asked if he could leave early to get his thoughts together. She agreed, gave him a hug, and said everything would be okay. The man never came back, nor did he call the police, something Cap feared.

The incident scared him more than he had realized. The first thing that came across his mind was Marta. It brought a feeling through his body, mainly his heart, that he had never felt before. He walked down Garnett Street to the pier, then down the stairs and over to where his cardboard shack use to be. There weren't any remnants of it, except some pieces hanging high up in the upper cross members. This showed him how lucky he was that Marta came along, as he was very much frozen in a state of confusion at the time. He was sure the beach crew had cleaned up anything that was left, as they combed most of the beach after the main storm had come through.

He sat down in the sand in the approximate area of where the shack had been. The waves were still pounding the shoreline and the beach was much smaller than it had been before the storms hit. He watched as the waves hit against the pier's pylons. He looked above at all the piping and plumbing of the water supply and sewer returns of the cottages above the pier. He squeezed the sand with both hands, lifted his arms out in front of him, and slowly released the sand from his hands, letting every last grain fall. After sitting there for a few minutes, he got up onto his feet, slapped his hands, and said, shaking his head, "Nope, never again."

It was then and there that he decided he needed to make a change—a change for the better.

Cap walked up the stairs to a much busier Garnett Street. The weather this day was not bad, even though rain was still in the forecast. He took his time making his way back to the apartment. He thought about getting the help he needed from the VA, but their incompetence the first two times around was what brought him to the streets. The first time, they assigned him a young psychologist right out of college who had no firsthand experience with Post Traumatic Stress Disorder—PTSD as it was called for short—in soldiers. He never asked what Cap thought were pertinent questions; he just prescribed pills and told him to try and forget about it.

The second time, he was asked questions, but still ordered to take pills. Cap just felt totally down more than up while on the pills. That's when he threw them away and started living under the pier. It was more therapeutic than anything else, but it certainly was not unconventional. He stuck his hands in his pockets, and when he did he found the piece of paper Angie had given him with the name of a person who might be able to help. He decided to give someone from outside the military a shot. He felt it was his best way of becoming somewhat of a man again.

He came to the thrift shop and walked in. Angie was sitting behind the counter texting someone on her cell phone when she saw him enter. She watched him as he walked up, set the piece of paper on the counter, and asked if he could borrow her phone. He had left the one Marta had gotten him in the apartment; he feared she would be home and he wanted to keep this from her. Angie said sure, in fact she made the call for him and was able to set up a time for Cap later the following day. He thanked Angie again for her help and understanding.

He took off for the apartment, thinking Marta would be there playing the guitar when he arrived, but she wasn't. He did, however, hear her singing. He opened the door and walked in to find the song was coming from the bathroom and the shower was running. He slipped off his flip-flops by the door, quietly closed it behind him, walked over to the bed, and sat down on its edge. The bathroom was directly across and the door was open, so he could see the silhouette of Marta's naked body behind the shower curtain. The way she had one foot propped up on the edge of the tub looked as though she was shaving her legs. She stopped singing and started humming whatever song she had been singing.

Cap stood up, pulled his shirt up over his shoulders and threw it on the bed, then un-snapped his jeans and let them fall to the floor before walking into the bathroom. He pulled the shower curtain open, startling Marta a bit, then he stepped into the shower with her.

"Oh, my sir, I shall scream for help if you don't, if you . . ." she said when Cap interrupted her.

"If I don't what?" he said with a smile.

"If you don't quickly ravish me right here and now!" she said with a big grin.

Cap grabbed her with both hands on her ass cheeks and pulled her to him. Their lips passionately locked. Cap then spun her around, so her back was to him, while she slightly bent over with one hand bracing herself against the shower wall. She reached between her legs with the other hand, grabbed his erect cock, and slipped it inside of her as she pushed her ass against his thighs. He let her thrust her ass against him instead of him thrusting into her. He liked it when she was in control of the sex and she did as well. He seemed to last longer when she was and the sensation for both of them was more intense—not that Marta didn't like the "wham bam thank you ma'am" routine once in a while, as she had surprised him a few times.

One of those times was at her grandparent's house in her old bedroom, the very day he met them for the first time. He tried holding onto her hips, but the water from the shower made it difficult, so he reached one hand around her waist and placed the other in hers as they massaged her breasts together. They were united in ecstatic pleasure. He kissed her around her neck, nibbled at her ear, and then rested his head on the back of hers until they both climaxed in one of the most intense sex sessions they had had together.

"Wow!" said Marta. "My body is shuddering!"

Cap was silent, still holding on to her tightly, not yet wanting to let go. Marta could feel his heart pounding through his chest onto her back; she reached her arm up and behind until she felt the back of his head and held it gently. He slowly released her, and she slowly turned around and faced him. He passionately kissed Marta as if there was no tomorrow. She returned it without question. He slowly released from her lips and brushed some of her water-soaked dreads from her face, all the while using his body to keep the spray of the shower from her eyes.

He looked into her mesmerizing green eyes and knew right then and there, in his heart, that he couldn't continue to hurt her anymore. All of this with Marta, from her saving him from being kicked in the street and being keeper of her board to everything that had happened since, was all part of a plan—a plan he had no control over, as it was preordained for him by a higher power than he had ever experienced or been involved with before in his life. "Everything happens for a reason" was what one of his squad members use to say every day, but Cap refused to accept that, for what kind of God would allow the carnage he experienced and saw for those years he served to happen? But he now felt an awakening in his soul brought on by Marta; it was good and he wanted to be able to give back, but he knew he had a lot of work to do on himself. He and Marta finished washing each other and had playful fun doing so. When they were done, they toweled off, got dressed, and headed off down Garnett Street to one of the pizza joints.

It was a playful evening as they sat and ate. They talked and joked and even danced between the tables of other customers when a song played that they both liked. The whole evening was wonderful. Marta was feeling the best she had ever felt around a man in her life. But Cap was truly at a crossroads. He wanted to be there with her, but he knew it was going to take some doing. He hoped tomorrow's counseling session would get him some place closer to Marta. They started back to the apartment when it began sprinkling, and the closer they got to home, the harder the rain started to fall. They dashed down the alley, up the stairs, and into the apartment. They kissed, undressed each other, and fell to the bed, bodies entangled—making passionate love until they were exhausted but feeling complete. After kissing Cap, Marta fell asleep on his chest, as she always did, with his arm around her, as he always did. Cap's eyes stared at the ceiling as he listened to Marta's breathing and the rain hitting the roof, and soon, from the rhythm of both, his eyes closed as well.

IL MIGLIOR USO DELLA VITA E` L'AMORE

(The Best Use of Life Is Love)

Marta woke up as usual, by her body clock. When she didn't feel Cap next to her, she looked over to the bathroom, lit up only by the little nightlight, and saw it was empty. She got up and walked over toward the front balcony, opening the sliding door and poking her head out, but still no Cap, just the emptiness of the early morning with the steady rhythm of rain still falling. She figured he must have gone for a walk. With the rain, there would be no surfing for her, even though there would still be some of the guys out there, so she got ready to go work out at the gym. She figured she would more than likely run into Cap somewhere on the street.

She donned her workout gear, threw on a hooded sweatshirt, and headed out the door, down the steps, through the alley, a left and right turn, and then down Garnett Street at a light jog through the rain. It wasn't a raining hard, but it was a steady rain. She stopped for a moment and continued to jog in place, realizing she had forgotten her headphones for listening to music while she worked out; she thought for a moment of going back to the apartment, but decided against it. Instead, she continued with her jog. She could hear the sound of her feet splashing with every step she took on the wet concrete of the sidewalk. She saw the usual establishments getting ready to open at this time of morning, the owners dealing again and again with shooing away one homeless person after another at the usual places they would hole up at night out of the rain.

She continued to the front door of the gym, entered, walked to the women's locker room, grabbed a towel, and went immediately to one of the stalls, as she all of the sudden had to pee. When finished, she went to wash her hands, removed her wet sweatshirt, wiped her hands and face clean, stood in front of the mirror, and stared at herself for a moment. Then, another women turned on a blow dryer to wake her from her trance. She left the bathroom and went on out into the gym area to begin her normal workout for the day. About halfway through, her stomach started to feel odd. At first, she ignored it and continued to work out, but then it kicked up again and she thought she was going to be sick. She quit her workout, put her sweatshirt back on, and flipped the hood over her head. She got to the door of the club, stopped, and turned around to jog back into the women's bathroom. She bent over one of the toilets and hurled, but it was a dry heave, as nothing came out. She did this three times, just spitting saliva out into the bowl. She wiped her mouth with her sweatshirt sleeve when she felt she was okay. She just shook it off as some sort of food poisoning from the previous night out with Cap and then thought maybe that was what happened to Cap—he was not feeling well and chose to leave the apartment rather than get sick there, as he was always thinking about her and not wanting to disturb her.

She headed back out of the bathroom, out of the club, and onto Garnett, heading back to the apartment. She started walking at first, then when she felt she would be okay, she jogged again.

She went through the rain up the street, two turns off Garnett, through the alley, up the stairs, and into the apartment.

"Cap!" she called out for him.

She looked around the small place and there was still no sign of him. She thought it odd, but not enough to worry. She removed her clothes, jumped in the shower, and proceeded to get ready for work at the café. She left a note for him to swing by the café on his way to work and signed it, "Love, Curl Gurl." She headed down the stairs, across the alley, and through the rear door of the café. She walked right to the front of the café to see if by chance Cap might be sitting there drinking a coffee and having a cannoli, but he wasn't. She walked into the kitchen, said her good mornings to Carlos, Johnny, and Reuben, and began what had become her daily ritual of going over the day's menu with the guys and starting prep. When she was done, she went out front and assisted Emanuel with setting tables. Halfway through that she felt sick again, and she excused herself to go to the bathroom, but she didn't throw up as the feeling went away. She got herself together and got back out in the café as customers started coming in. They had a pretty good crowd and soon, like the others, she was busy. Cap wasn't on her mind, and although she felt woozy a couple more times, she fought through it and continued.

After the morning shift, when they all got a little bit of breather before the lunch crowd would descend upon them, she made a little lunch for Cap as she always did and ran the three blocks to the thrift shop to give it to him. When she got there, she walked in and saw Angie at the counter.

"Hey, Angie!" Angie looked up and had a blank look on her face. "Is Cap in the back? I brought him his lunch." She continued to walk toward the back of the shop.

"Marta!" called Angie. "Cap isn't back there. He's not here, Marta."

Angie saw the stunned look on Marta's face, picked up an envelope from the side of the cash register, walked out from behind the counter over to Marta, and handed the envelope to her.

"I found this on the counter this morning when I walked in."

Marta took the envelope from her, her hand shaking as she did. Marta saw Darlin' written across it. She opened it, pulled out a note, and began to read it. As she did, she began to get ill and felt like throwing up, this time for a different reason.

"Marta, are you all right?" Angie asked.

Marta ran for the door and made it outside to the street between two parked cars. She had dropped the letter and envelope on the sidewalk, but Angie picked them both up, as she had followed Marta out the door. Marta steadied herself on the front bumper of one car and the rear of the other, and when she did, the car alarm on the second vehicle went off and startled her and Angie briefly as Marta proceeded to throw up on the street. Angie rubbed her back.

"Marta, are you okay?" she asked again.

After the third time, Marta figured that was all she was going to hurl, so she stood up straight, with Angie helping her. The owner of the car with the alarm came out of one of the other shops to shut it off, and saw the two women behind his vehicle. When he saw the mess on the street behind his car, he backed away and asked, "Are you okay, miss?"

Marta nodded her head and walked backward over the curb and onto the sidewalk. She stood there for a moment, then looked at Angie with a look of fear on her face before turning and running down the sidewalk through the light crowd in the light rain toward the pier.

"Marta!" yelled Angie, waving the letter that was still in her hand.

Marta was not turning around and even if she heard Angie, she ignored her shouts. Angie took the letter and envelope and placed it in her back pocket. A couple people entered her shop; she followed them and asked if they could come back later, as she needed to close the shop temporarily. They obliged, Angie closed up, and headed toward the pier in pursuit of Marta.

Marta ran down Garnett and cut across the traffic, dodging a few cars to get up to the pier, down the steps, onto the beach, and under the pier—where she had hoped to find Cap. She stood near where his shack used to be, breathing hard from the run, trying to catch her breath with her hands on her hips, and then clasping them together on the top of her head. She walked around the area.

"Cap! Cap! Oh, Cap!" she cried softly.

She fell to the sand on her butt and then put her hands behind her to prop herself up with her knees bent and her feet still in the sand. Still catching her breath, she spoke softly.

"I'm here Cap! I'll be here Cap! I'll be here waiting for you Cap!"

Angie came to a stop at the bottom of the stairs when she saw Marta and sat down on the last step, letting her have her space. The waves pounded the shore. The mist from the waves and the light rain hit Angie's face as well as Marta's as she stared off into the horizon.

SUSURROS DEL CORAZON

(Whispers of the Heart)

The ocean wind was blowing steadily across the beach. On dryer occasions, this would mean being pelted with sand while lying on the beach, however, with all the recent rain and the earlier high tide, the sand was still wet. Marta had laid out a beach towel over the wet sand and sat there with her legs stretched out, one arm back bracing herself and the other resting on her pregnant belly. She sat there under Crystal Pier, most of the time focusing her eyes on the main cross timber about 20 yards in front of her. It was if she was looking for a sign of some sort, a sign of the past to suddenly become present. She let her eyes wander—looking up to all the piping running under the pier from the housing above it, then to the left side of the pier and the scarcely populated beach to the south. She turned to the right and to the same vision to the north, with the exception of all the surfers who made a trail from the pier up to the Birdrock cliffs. From time to time, a seagull would fly through, and occasionally one would rest on one of the many cross members under the pier or on the pipes. Oddly, they would only stay briefly before flying off. It was as if they knew Marta was wanting time and space from everyone and everything.

After picking up the note the day Cap had left, Angie read it and eventually returned it to Marta. Marta had gathered parts of her community together at different times—Angie and the boys, her grandparents, and the Sanchez family—reading the note aloud each time. "Darlin', I have to leave, for how long, I do not know. I need to become a man others won't fear; a man you won't fear; and most importantly, a man I won't fear. Darlin', if you can wait for me, I promise to return mended from the broken man I am now with a heart that is whole—a heart that is for you."

Marta also shared that Cap didn't know of her pregnancy and she requested everyone not judge a man who never once had judged any of them. All of them understood and respected her wishes, and as most good friends and family do, they gave her all their support in more ways than she could have imagined.

It had been about three months since Cap disappeared and about six months since the beginning of El Nino—the time their relationship had turned—making the pregnancy about that far along as well. Marta was getting all the help she needed between her grandparents; her café family; and of course, the boys, who were all involved. Each of them took turns going with her to birthing classes so everyone would be prepared in case the call came. Even Dale Da Dude participated, and she actually felt the most comfortable with him, as he always seemed to take things in stride. Whether it was his autism or just his nature, she could see how the others named him Dale Da Dude. Danny, however, was becoming her most consistent and noble knight.

It is funny how events can change the direction of people's lives. This El Nino was having an impact on everyone, not just in Marta's community, but all over San Diego and up and down the coast of California. Danny had gotten a job as a legal assistant for the San Diego Charger's team of attorneys. They were in the middle of a team location process that could put them anywhere in Southern California, so they needed a lot of extra hands to file and push paperwork. It was a perfect fit for Danny. It provided good pay, benefits, and excellent direction for him. He was able to squeeze Marta in on his insurance through the group, claiming her as a dependent. Was it legal? Not really, but it was a risk he took for his beloved friend.

G, Ron, and Danny all went in on a rental home on the corner of Windemere Street and the boardwalk, between Belmont Park in Mission Beach and the Crystal Pier in Pacific Beach. It was a big three-story home and expensive, but Ron was in real estate and got a great deal, and he was making good money. Danny, still attending law school part time, was making a good buck with the Chargers. In the short period of time he had been with them, he was given a raise, and the remainder of his education would be paid for if he passed the bar and stayed with them. G quit bartending and focused solely on the tattoo business. With the weather being very wet, it drove people indoors to do other things, and tattoos seemed to be a big thing, especially with the Millennial set—college students and young surfers. Danny, G, and Ron offered a room to Marta to help her out, and although she hated giving up her little place, which offered privacy and convenience, she took them up on their offer.

Marta shook her long, brown dreadlocks out of her face and reached to her side, where her backpack was laying, opened it up, and pulled out a writing tablet and pen. She flipped open the tablet, used her pregnant stomach as a table, and began to write. This was her late afternoon ritual, every day after work at the café when the weather was at least halfway decent. She would walk down to the pier, find a spot somewhat near where Cap's cardboard shack use to be, sit, think, and write.

Most days she would stay there for at least an hour. On days when she had a doctor's appointment or birthing class, she would stay longer. She would write and wait for one of the guys to walk down the stairs to the beach and whistle. He would walk her up the stairs and off to the appointment or class. She wrote down her thoughts and ideas, with most being lyrics for songs. She would hum and sing softly, writing down the words and notes. This was her way of creating for now and she actually found it quite soothing.

She would hardly ever hear the waves; it was as though her thought process blocked everything out and she was in a zone. In addition to writing, she would also hum sounds and sing words into her iPhone, replaying and editing her work on her own mini recording studio. When she was done, she would sit in meditation and prayer. Her meditation would empty her mind and her prayer would be for the many things on her mind to be placed in God's hands to show her direction. Her faith never wandered; although it was brief at times, it often left her teary eyed. She never ended with an "amen," but with a softly spoken, "Thank you for loving me."

Mind cleared, she sat back on both hands, took a deep breath of the ocean air, and looked to see what was happening around her. It was more of a look to see who might be watching her. In her mind, it was a hope that Cap would appear from the shadows to say she was no longer alone. She thought, why could it not be like in the old movies her grandmother always watched, where the man left the girl for some reason and then came back, and they lived happily ever after? "Why not?" she always said to herself. "Why not?"

Marta grabbed her backpack and placed the notepad and pen back inside. She then placed one arm through one of its straps and hoisted it over her shoulder. Marta took another deep breath, let it out, and pushed her pregnant body up onto her bare feet. She reached down to pick up her sandals and towel, walked over to the stairs and up to the pier, heading down the Pacific Beach part of the boardwalk toward Windemere Street.

People were taking advantage of the beaches as much as possible before the next wave of storms would come, so the walk was crowded. The strip in front of Baja Beach Café down to the Pacific Surf School was the narrowest part of the walk before it widened up. It was already difficult at times to walk with the joggers and cyclists who lived there, and even more so with tourists. That stretch was worse than the rest of the boardwalk, but everyone managed well.

A month earlier when Marta hit that section, she was anxious to get around a really slow crowd ahead of her and decided to slide past them. When she did, she got cut down by a man in a wheelchair coming the other way. She hadn't seen him. She was looking ahead, not down, and had assumed she could make it around. She landed in his lap, causing him to veer off to the side and hit the foot-tall block wall in the front of The Beach Cottages. At first, the young man was upset and started to go off on Marta about watching where she was going, but then he saw she was pregnant, reversed course, and asked her if she was okay. Marta said she was—and she apologized for the unscheduled "lap dance." This was how she met Ricky, an African American ex-serviceman. This first meeting ended with them apologizing to each other, and then going their own way. There are many regulars on the boardwalk, so the chance of meeting someone again is very high, as it was for Marta and Ricky. Each time they ran into each other, not literally, they apologized to each other until Ricky decided to stop her.

"Hey!" he shouted, pulling over in front of her to stop here. She pulled out her earbuds.

"Hi! I'm still really sorry about colliding with you the other day," she said. He reached out and gently grabbed her hand.

"My name is Ricky." Marta squeezed his hand.

"Mine is Marta."

"Well, Marta, it's nice to meet you. Now that we have actually met, let's stop apologizing to each other, okay?" he replied while shaking her hand.

With this, Marta and Ricky began to learn each other's story. Marta found that Ricky had lost both legs from stepping on a land mine while walking through the Iraqi desert in the first Gulf War. She learned he had stood nearly six foot six before the incident and had all sorts of scholarship offers to play college basketball. Instead, he chose to enlist in the Army, as his father and grandfather had done before him, even though they both wanted him to go to college instead. She discovered he had a wife and two kids. She heard him tell the story of how they were high school sweethearts and he found out his girlfriend was pregnant with their first child while stationed in Iraq. That they got married over the phone because he didn't want a child born out of wedlock, and that meant his new wife and soon-to-be child would be taken care of by the military.

She then learned about the toll it took on his wife when she found out he had been wounded. That he fought for his survival and existence while he laid in a coma for ten days. When he awoke, he found he had lost both his legs from below the knee, but had gained a new son back in the States. She learned how strong his wife's love was for him, even though he felt he was only half the man now. His wife made it clear that "the whole of a man is judged by one's heart and soul and not by one's appearance." Months after he had come back to the U.S. and had started rehabilitation, his wife became pregnant with their second child. This time, he decided they needed to have a real wedding and he worked on being able to walk on prosthetics so he could look her in the eye and say not only, "I do!" but, "I will forever love you!"

Marta's eyes teared up as she listened to his story. Then Marta told Ricky hers. He spoke his mind about Cap, understanding where he might be coming from. Ricky told her honestly that she had a 50/50 chance of ever seeing him again, and even then, his stability would still be in question. He said he had been in that position, but war has changed. Very few soldiers had witnessed death or even had to be a part of the first Gulf War because it was over in a few days. The current war was different. Ricky said when he does his weekly rehab, he sees soldiers who struggle physically, as well as many who are not physically hurt, but struggle mentally. She heard the same thing Cap has said, that the broken system of government had no problem sending men and women into harm's way, but failed to provide the care they needed when they returned. He felt he was lucky, as he had a well-grounded family and a strong wife who fought just as hard for him at home as he did for his country. He told her if she really loved Cap, she should never give up hope—not because she's having his baby, but because, like his wife, she loved the man she knew wasn't broken on the inside. If she knew she could love the inside, all the troubles they would have would be on the outside. There would be many. But Marta and Cap would survive. Marta was blown away with this man's courage, fortitude, and life view. She was respectful of his wisdom and advice. As the days went by, their friendship grew. He and his family were eventually introduced to Marta's: her grandparents, the Sanchez family, and of course her family of surfers.

Every day she either walked to the Crystal Pier or was dropped off by one of her family of surfers. In addition to writing, she would occasionally paddle out, surf for a while or just sit out beyond the waves thinking, and then come back into shore, sit on her board, and write some more. Later, she would be accompanied back to the house by Ricky or other family members. Even her grandfather and grandmother would show up on good weather days, sometimes with her great-uncle Pietro. During these walks, there would be many discussions. She found herself being more open as the others were to her as well. She learned much more about her families. She never felt as close to them all as she did now, and they felt the same about her. During the times she walked alone, she also felt closer to her own self, her own spirituality. She built confidence in herself daily and felt she was ready for this child to come into this world and to be a mother. That had been her biggest fear. Being a mother was never in her plans. She loved children and as a child she had dreamed of having them sometime in her life. That changed years ago, after being involved in a freak surfing accident. Another surfer had plowed into her back after she had just completed a wave. It was so bad that Marta had lost feeling from her waist down and thought she was going to drown; if it hadn't been for her friend Manny being right there to help, she probably would have.

Marta was in a panic as Manny got her on his board. With the help of others, he got her to shore. The lifeguards got her on a spine board and into an emergency vehicle. Manny rode alongside her in the back. By the time they got to the hospital, she had regained all her feeling. However, after x-rays and further tests over the following months, doctors told her the nerves to her reproductive system had suffered irreversible damage. The chances of her having a child were nearly two hundred million to one. Thus, Marta never planned on children and had made music her child. She and her family knew this child was a miracle. Marta felt even more than that. She felt everything leading up to where she was right now was all planned.

She felt her spirituality deeply and knew she and God were in sync. Sayings like, "things happen for a reason" and, "taking the good with the bad" had a lot of truth in them. Her talks with Ricky gave even more substance to it all. When she had sexual relationships with other men, she always practiced safe sex. But she had been also reckless at times because she felt she was naturally protected. She felt that way with Cap, but she also had a different feeling with him—one she had never felt before. Many times, in their short time together while they were making love, she had hoped and prayed that she could have his child. Many times, the feeling she experienced in their sexual relations were an "out of body experience" where she felt as though she was being born again. As they lay in each other's arms, many times Cap had said he felt the same way.

Marta felt her pregnancy was a response to her prayers and God brought the right man to her, just as he did with Joseph to Mary. Though her grandparents had raised her Catholic, Marta formed her own opinion about faith through her great-uncle and then later in college. She learned while studying music how it had a big part in developing many nations' religions. Marta had heard the story of Jesus many times as a youth and obviously through the Catholic religion when children venture into adulthood via Confirmation. She questioned whether it was Joseph or Mary who couldn't bear children, but because of their strong and obedient belief—or even if they hadn't been obedient—God blessed them with child as He had done now with Marta. The Immaculate Conception argument was based on them never having sex. But there were so many versions of the situation that Marta accepted her great-uncle's once she heard it again in college. It made sense to her because if Jesus had been an Immaculate Conception, he would not have died such an inhumanely tragic death.

She truly believed Jesus was a special human being who taught compassion and love no matter where you were from, who you were born of, or to whom. Such people have existed before and after him. They had done the same as him and had died like him, if not worse, but his teachings were the base of our faith today. This is how she grew to feel. Today, there was no organization to the faith of spirit, nor should there ever be. No roof, no walls, no rules, no commandments—just pure common sense of knowing what is right and what is wrong. Bottom line, she felt Jesus's intent was that there be no religion that is organized. Man and woman should be able to live together no matter what, as we are all in God's image. Her great-uncle pointed out that even Jesus would not approve of Christianity created and organized in his name, nor of any of its spinoffs or other religions, for that matter. He said that most wars in the world are over religion first, then over greed. He explained that was the essence of the '60s movement; love and peace were what Jesus was about, and what should be paramount now. This was Marta's practice and her belief today. It was why she felt her pregnancy—a lesson or blessing—was a miracle, a gift given to her and Cap.

Marta got through the narrow section of the boardwalk when she saw Ricky ahead, wheeling his chair toward her. As he approached, as he had done since they met, he did a wheelie and spun around a couple times. Then he landed on all four wheels right alongside her, going the same direction.

"Hello, little lady!" he said to her with a big grin. Marta smiled, grabbed his shoulder, and said, "Hello, my friend, how was your day?"

"Marvelous! Just marvelous my dear!" he responded, as he gave his wheelchair a couple strokes forward and adjusted the speed with his hands to stay with Marta's stride. "Had a great work out at the Box."

"Box?" she asked.

"Yea, you know, cross fit. Their gyms are called Boxes," he explained.

"Ah, that's right," Marta said.

"What's up Marta? You seem preoccupied," Ricky said, as Marta looked ahead and saw an opening in the seawall that led to the beach.

"Come with me," she said.

She walked into the opening and Ricky followed her. She sat on one of the upper steps leading down to the beach and he wheeled up next to her.

"Give me your hand, Ricky."

Ricky did, and she gently placed it on her belly. She looked at him and he smiled at her.

"She's moving," Ricky said. "Great feeling, isn't it?"

Marta was grinning from ear to ear, but then her face reflected confusion.

"She just started kicking today. Wait a minute. How do you know it's a she?"

"Ha ha!" he laughed "Well, I wasn't around when my son was born, but I was for my daughter. My wife had me touch her stomach then and this felt like my daughter's kick. Plus, you just referred to it as she."

"That's interesting. I did, didn't I?"

Ricky nodded his head yes and as he removed his hand from her stomach, Marta placed her own hand there and thought about it for a second. She then placed her hand in his as he helped balance to stand up. They began their walk again on down to Windemere Street. "A girl, you say?" she looked at Ricky with a smile.

"That's just my guess, Marta, a non-educated one at that," he said, laughing, as they continued down the boardwalk.

Marta hadn't thought about the baby's sex. During her check-ups, when they asked her if she wanted to know, she had said no, hoping Cap would return and they would find out together. But now things seemed to be moving faster. Time seemed to travel much quicker—who knew why—and she now thought maybe she would like to find out the sex and start thinking of names. But think was all she did for now, thinking of her child's future.

SUSURROS DE LOS SUEÑOS

(Whispers of Dreams)

Mission Boulevard runs from Belmont Park to the surfing park of Tourmaline. It stretches along Mission and Pacific beaches, separating them from the inner waters of Mission Bay. The Ocean Boardwalk follows along the shoreline of the two beaches and consists of the amusement rides and tourist shopping of Belmont Park. It includes a variety of restaurants along with various residential living from Airbnbs for tourists to expansive homes of the wealthy year-rounders. The bay side is pretty much the same, with the addition of more shops; various surf, boat, and yacht service stores; and Sea World San Diego.

In a state where every point given for an earthquake is ten times more destructive than the previous point, it seemed to be the same with El Nino of 2015-2016. The damage done to date from the flooding, mudslides, and wind was ten times that of its predecessor in 2004 and the one before that in 1998. At high tide, which is twice in a twenty-four-hour period, Mission Boulevard became flooded, along with most of the homes that sit on both sides of Mission Boulevard. Because of this, it was hard for owners who rent to tourists to get their homes occupied. Thus, tourism decreased and when tourism is affected, so is everything else in the area.

While there are those who may suffer, some others do benefit. Those who are willing to put up with a little chaos once in a while could live the life of luxury for a time. Such was the case when Danny, G, and Ron went in together on the beach rental on Windemere Street.

It was a three-story contemporary cottage that sat one house in from the boardwalk. The front door faced a walkway shared by nine other houses, which all had little patio areas. The rear of the house faced a street that was more like a small alley. Each house had one parking place plus a two-car garage and a single dumpster was provided for the ten homes that shared the alley. The bedroom in the rear of the second story, behind the kitchen, which would be the maid's quarters or guest room, was Marta's room. The other three bedrooms, including the master, were on the third story. The master, which G and Ron shared, faced the ocean. The other two in the rear each had their own bathrooms. The first floor was built to be a recreation room or hangout. If you didn't know it, you would mistake it for one of the many small bars anywhere in the San Diego area. The guys had the outside patio area around the front surrounded by sandbags to keep the surging sea water from creeping into the lower level. Almost all the homes did the same thing. The garage off the alley was another story. Although the alley was built with a slope in the middle of the road to allow the water to drain back into the main street, the storm surge was much too great for the street to handle. Many times, the guys would go to their cars, whether parked inside the garage or out in the alley, and have to wade through water. Because of this issue, they were able to get a good deal on the lease.

It was an early January, a Friday evening, and G and Ron were out on the rooftop, sitting on lawn chairs, holding hands, looking out over the ocean. They waited for the sun to set, while slowly sipping on a couple beers. They had a pretty good unobstructed view of the ocean and part of the boardwalk, even though they were the second house back. The house in front of them was a story shorter. The parts of the boardwalk they could see were the width of the alley to the south and the width of the shared walkway to the north. The high tide showed its ugly head twice a day, twelve and a half hours apart, so it was pretty predictable when the waves would increase in size and flooding would occur. When it did, the boardwalk would disappear in water and the streets would flood; Mission Boulevard would be a river twice a day. There were warning signs posted up and down the boardwalk and the boulevard, but they did not stop a lot of the locals, who knew how to navigate around them. When it was raining, things became difficult, as there really wasn't anywhere the water could go other than up. The main issue was parking and that was a problem even on dry streets. One guy went as far as attaching a boat anchor to his vehicle bumper and tying it around a telephone pole. Some thought it was a good gag at the time. But when water got so high that some smaller cars began to float down the street, others began to do the same.

This Friday night the weather was quiet. It was still partly cloudy out, but not enough to hide the sun and being able to see it set. While Ron and G were enjoying the view, Danny appeared with a beer in hand.

"Listen . . . here he comes," Danny said. G let go of Ron's hand and stood up.

"It's Vince!" G exclaimed.

They all walked to the edge of the rooftop and looked patiently toward the opening of the boardwalk facing the walkway. The music got louder, and then an elderly man on rollerblades appeared with a box radio attached to his upper chest by makeshift straps. Blaring from the radio was the Rolling Stones song, "Get off my Cloud."

"Vince!" The three of them yelled.

Vince looked up and saw the guys, gave them his trademark big grin, and waved as he disappeared behind the house in front. The guys ran to the other corner of the roof and watched as Vince reappeared. Rollerblading backward, he smiled and waved to the guys, music still blaring, and then disappeared again behind the next row of homes. The guys raised their beer bottles to the sky for him. Vince was one of the many regulars who used the boardwalk every day—part of its character. He was nearly seventy, but in good shape from all the regular rollerblading he did up and down the boardwalk. It was known that he used to be a bodybuilder in his heyday. He was very, very tan, with long gray hair; at times when he rollerblades without a shirt, his gray chest hairs stand out from his dark tan. He usually rollerbladed in cutoff shorts to his knees and a tank top, with an iPhone hooked up to his boom box blaring good old rock and roll. He usually sings along with the song or is wearing a big grin. Tourists and locals are always clamoring to get a photo with him, as if he was a big celebrity, and he is always accommodating.

While Vince's music faded away, the sound of a Coast Guard helicopter began to emerge in the distance. It sounded like it was very close, when in fact it was miles down the coast. When it did finally come into view, it was extremely loud. In normal weather conditions—with temperatures averaging seventy-five degrees year-round—the Coast Guard and lifeguards are kept extremely busy, especially with tourists, saving anywhere from thirty to forty people on the busiest weekends on just the two beaches along the boulevard. This year was different. The focus of the Coast Guard and lifeguards included not only swimmers, but surfers drawn to the big waves to test their skills. In addition, the number of fishing boats increased off the coast. The warmer waters brought a lot of record marlin fishing, as well as many other types of fishing that normally doesn't occur in the waters off the coast of Southern California. The increased fishing brought the predatory great white sharks closer to the shore, keeping everyone on their toes.

As the sun began to set, as it did earlier due to Daylight Saving Time, the buzz of helicopters, jet skis, and other water craft quieted down, replaced with the sounds of people picking up their beach chairs, umbrellas, and other things while slowly moving off the beach. The closer the sun got to the horizon, the more the sounds changed to reflect people walking the boardwalk and enjoying the various bars and restaurants along it and Mission Boulevard.

As the sound of the helicopter faded away, Ricky coasted into the guys' view.

"Ricky!" yelled Danny.

Ricky pulled up his wheelchair in a wheelie and balanced there as if it was not a problem to do so at all.

"What up?" Ricky yelled back.

"Are you staying for a while after you walk Marta back?" Danny asked.

"If the wife says it's good to go!" Ricky answered.

Danny gave him a thumbs up, Ricky spun around in a three-sixty, and he headed onto the boardwalk to meet up with Marta. Danny walked back and sat on a deck chair, G and Ron turned around and leaned against the deck railing, and they all continued to drink their beers.

"That Ricky sure is amazing with that wheelchair," G said.

"Yes, he is!" Ron responded.

"Well, he's obviously had to adapt to it, with all that's happened to him, otherwise he wouldn't have much of a life to live," Danny said.

"Truth," responded G, and Ron nodded his head in agreement.

"Danny, how's all the legal mumble jumbo going with the Chargers and stadium deals?" Ron asked.

"Well, I'm not at liberty to really say. Even if I was, all I could tell you right now is that it seems like a clusterfuck between the Charger's family and the mayor," Danny responded.

"That's what I felt after listening to the radio this morning. Sounds more like the mayor than the rest of the city council. I have come to the conclusion that this mayor has an overblown ego. Thinks about himself than others," Ron said.

G looked perplexed. Ron saw this and asked, "What?"

"Well, when did you get all political?" G asked.

"I always have been, but I usually don't express it because of the business I'm in. I cater to all kinds of people from all aspects of life and political views, but lately I have been getting pretty fed up with what I have been reading and observing, locally and nationally," Ron said.

There was silence for a second and Ron continued. "Come on you guys! You two of all people should understand what I'm talking about."

Danny started to laugh and Ron and G looked at him.

"What's so funny?" G asked.

"Just that you two have been dating and living together for a while now and you don't really know each other yet," Danny said.

G and Ron looked at each other and Ron started to laugh. "I guess when we met we didn't really have many responsibilities," Ron said. "Now that we do, everything else tends to come in play and when we see how it affects us, either good, bad, or both, we get more involved in what's happening."

"That was really a quite profound statement you just made, Ron," Danny said, holding up his beer bottle toward him and saying, "Cheers!"

G just shook his head.

"Things like that are why I fell in love with you. I guess we have a lot more to learn from each other," G said, as he leaned over and kissed Ron.

"Maybe if you two would communicate to one another in other ways besides fucking you would!" Danny said, laughing.

"You're just jealous Danny!" G said, laughing back.

Danny tilted his head to the side and shrugged his shoulder as if to say, so what if I am, and said, "Oh well."

Chuck then stepped out onto the roof deck.

"Chuckie boy!" shouted the other three.

"Where's Dale Da Dude?" G asked.

"He's down in the kitchen waiting for Marta to get home. You know how he is about that baby of hers," Chuckie said.

The guys agreed about Dale, and then heard a whistle from below. G and Ron turned to see Ricky wheeling up to the side entrance with Marta in tow. As Marta got to the door, she leaned down and gave Ricky a kiss on the forehead.

"Thank you again, my dear prince, as always," she said.

"A pleasure as always, Marta." Ricky smiled. He turned to leave, then stopped and looked up as G shouted down at him.

"You're not staying?" G questioned.

"Nah, Ronelle says Marcus has been giving her a fuss all day, so I have to get home," Ricky responded.

"Next time, later!" shouted G.

"Give my love to Ronelle," Marta said, as Ricky sped off.

"Will do," Ricky said, as he waved at Marta and to the guys above.

Marta opened the door and took the stairs up to the second floor. When she got to the top, she saw Dale Da Dude. He was at the kitchen counter, waiting anxiously for her as always. She smiled when he turned and saw her walking in. She went over to Dale and gave him a hug.

"How's my sweet Dale today?" she asked.

"Oh Marta, I am fine! How's the baby, Marta?" Dale asked excitedly.

"The baby's doing just fine, Dale boy. Just fine," Marta said. She walked over to the fridge, opened it, and reached for a bottle of coconut water. "Dale, do you want anything to drink?"

"Just a water, Marta. May I have a water?" he asked.

"That we can do," Marta said.

She grabbed a bottle of water, rolled it across the counter to Dale, and shut the door to the fridge. She went to the other end of the counter and grabbed her mail, which Danny had already separated for her. As she picked it up, she saw Dale still sitting anxiously at the counter, watching her every move. She smiled, knowing he looked forward to these times with her.

"What are you waiting for Dale? Let's go," she said.

Dale hopped off the stool, walked briskly over to Marta, and followed her. They walked into the hall behind the kitchen and into her bedroom. Dale stood at the bedroom doorway as Marta stood at her dresser briefly and laid the mail on the top of it. She then set down her backpack, walked over to her bed, and sat on the edge of it.

"Okay. Come sit, Dale," she said, motioning to him.

Dale walked over to the bed and sat down beside her. She removed the earbuds she had wrapped around her neck and hooked them up to her iPhone. She then took one earpiece and reached over to Dale to place it in his ear. Dale leaned his head toward her as she got it snuggly in his ear. She then placed the other one in her ear and fiddled with the phone until she got the Pandora station she wanted, and then adjusted the volume.

"What do you think Dale? Is the volume okay?" she asked.

Dale nodded his head yes, smiled, and said, "Yes, Marta, it's perfect for her!"

Marta looked at him and said, "That's twice now!"

"Twice, Marta?" Dale questioned.

"Yes. Ricky called the baby a 'she' as well."

"I know it's going to be a girl, Marta. The baby can't be anything but a girl because she has to be as beautiful as you," Dale said.

Marta was overwhelmed by Dale's words and left speechless. She put her arm on his back and rubbed his shoulders.

"Thank you, Dale." She kissed him on his forehead and leaned her head next to his, and they sat there listening to the music.

When she saw Dale was focused on listening, she removed the earpiece from her ear and handed it to him. He took it from her hand, like always, and placed it on Marta's belly to let the baby hear the music. He then laid his head down on Marta's belly as well, as she leaned back on the bed. She patted Dale's head and watched as he laid there listening to the music, assuming her baby was as well.

This had become the daily practice between Dale and Marta. Every day, Marta knew Dale looked forward to this and Marta actually did as well. Out of all the guys, Dale was the only one who was not needy and demanding of attention. She thought it odd that she felt that way. With his autism, Dale needed more attention and care than any of the others. However, with all of the attention put into Dale, he wasn't needy. In fact, she thought he was more of gentleman then the others. His parents, even his brother, did well in the time spent with him. In fact, she thought if the others paid more attention as he did, they would be more gentlemanly as well. But at the same time, she knew they all expressed themselves in their own way and none of them would be allowed in her world if she had not seen good qualities in them. Especially now, as all their good qualities were exposing themselves more so than before the pregnancy; at times, she thought it may be just another contest between them to see who could be the best man for her.

She smiled and laughed it off, taking the bull by the horns and scheduling time with each of them on a dry eraser board in the kitchen. It worked for the most part, and if it did not, the guys would argue and get it fixed so she did not have to worry. She never knew who was going to be there to pick her up to take her to doctor appointments or birthing classes until she would get a text from one of them at the last minute, so she knew who to expect. All she knew was that she just needed to be ready at the house, at work, or even at the pier—and one of them would be there. Dale didn't have to worry about any schedule unless the weather was really bad and Chuckie could not get them over to the house. Dale hated those days, as did Marta. It seemed on those days that Danny, G, and Ron were very bothersome. When Dale was over, nobody bothered her. Dale was an extension of her peace, and she loved that.

SUSURROS DEL CAIDO

(Whispers of the Fallen)

The car pulled up into the parking lot of the Elfin Forrest Recreational Reserve. The driver parked in one of the available parking spaces. Cap stepped out of the passenger side, stood to look at the beautiful surroundings, and took in the view of the mountain before him. It was a small mountain, but yet still a mountain in terms of what distinguishes mountains from hills. Out of the driver's side exited Suzanne, a woman in her fifties who was in pretty good physical shape. She was short in stature but large in personality and bright, very bright. Since the day Angie had given him Suzanne's phone number, Cap never questioned her motives or her seemingly unending expertise in anything she brought before him, tasks or responsibilities.

As far as Cap was concerned, Suzanne was a Godsend, an angel from heaven. The past few months had been very therapeutic, a better representation of the treatment he felt all soldiers coming back from service should be going through. He was slowly getting his peace of mind back, although he knew he wasn't quite there yet and may never be one hundred percent, but he was progressing. He still had to deal with some deep-seated issues, as Suzanne would call them, that had not yet been brought to the surface. She had an idea of what they were, but Cap was at a loss. He was still finding ways to deal with resolving the issues they had discussed. He understood what was still hidden was holding him back from being whole again. It tortured him, as he was sure it was what his fellow soldiers in arms were going through as well. It was a silent killer, a murderer of souls that was taking up to two soldiers' lives a day, by suicide.

Cap had seen it in the men he had led into battle and in others when he first landed back on American soil. He had seen it take root in heavy drinking, heavy drug use, and everything from violent behavior to total withdrawal from society. After all the other experiences of what he called, "piss poor management of a human life" by the government—which he thought had the power to do what was right but didn't—Cap ignored their services, as he saw what was going on with others. Soldiers were being prescribed one drug to help them sleep, another to keep them awake, and yet another to take away the pain. There was scheduled counseling with inexperienced therapists, psychologists, and analytical theorists who had no idea about the repercussions of war.

He was tired of it all. Tired of attending one funeral after another of Marines from his own company who had made it back, mostly in one piece, but had fallen to the demons they all had inside them—PTSD, Chronic Traumatic Encephalopathy (CTE), or something else. In his experience, no one knew how to beat or cure these demons, or even help resolve them, either. Thus, he chose to hide, and hide he did.

When he came back, he didn't even let his Mom and Dad know he was back. They found out from the hospital while he was going through therapy on base. When he found out they had been notified, he got out of bed, grabbed his fatigues, and left the hospital dressed only in his gown. He just walked out the front doors. He did not want to return to his parents a broken man.

He did not want them to see him in a condition he knew they would not see. He knew they would be able to feel it and know he was not the same son he was before he left. That pain would be more than he could bear; he felt it would have pushed him into committing suicide.

Of all the things he had to hold onto to survive, it was what he saw in his own mother while he was younger; she had battled breast cancer. She always had faith. She never wavered from her it even though they never attended a church; his mother prayed every day of her life. While growing up, he would see her stop in the middle of doing something that was frustrating her and say a prayer. If his dad was driving and slammed on the brakes suddenly or swerved to avoid an object, he would be cussing and swearing up a storm, while she would say a prayer. If she happened to be the one behind the wheel and experienced the same thing, she would pull to side of the road, say a prayer, and then get back to her journey when she was done. She would always say, "Trust in your faith, as that is what your heart and soul is made of" and his dad would always respond, "Amen to that."

Thus, Cap had chosen to disappear. He didn't want drugs or alcohol to alter his state of mind and he wanted no part of an addiction. He always felt his withdrawal from society would not be everlasting—that at some point when he felt it was safe for him to come out, he would know it. He always believed his faith would show him the way, as it did with his mother when she refused chemotherapy and would not have her breasts removed. One day she woke up and said to him and his dad, "No more worries, today is the day." She dumped all the pills she was taking down the kitchen sink, turned on the water, and switched on the garbage disposal. He remembered wondering what the hell she was doing and talking about—and his dad was as well—but she just smiled after turning off the garbage disposal and continued to make breakfast. A few weeks later, when she went to the doctor for more tests, they could not find a thing wrong with her.

Cap's faith, he felt, had begun to show him a way, and it's why he felt Marta came into his life. Everything from then on started to have some meaning to him. His dad always encouraged him to keep his eyes and ears open to everything around him, saying the answers to a lot of life's questions are there for the taking. Marta was an understanding soul who didn't judge. As he watched her interact with the people around her, he saw she never left any of those she met, and she never really came into their lives. They always came into hers and left of their own choosing. The whole time they were together, she never forced him to talk or do anything; she never even suggested. That's how it was with the rest of the group, as she allowed them to be themselves. There were no judgments on her part whatsoever. He loved that about her the most, but he didn't want her to be hurt by him. That's how he knew it was time to come out of hiding. Everything that had happened between Marta and him was a sign to that it was time for him to come back to the rest of the world. Even getting the job in the thrift store with Angie and the many talks he and Angie had were a sign. When Angie gave him Suzanne's contact information, he knew his faith was telling him it was time.

As Suzanne exited the driver's side, a woman approached her and gave her a big hug, and they kissed each other on the side of each other's cheek.

"Come on over here, James," Suzanne said to Cap, using his given name.

He shut the car door and walked around to its rear, where Suzanne stood.

"James, this is a very good friend of mine and soon a friend of yours I'm sure, Kathleen."

Kathleen reached out to shake Cap's hand. "Pleasure to meet you, James," Kathleen said with a smile.

"Likewise," Cap said.

Kathleen stood about five foot six or seven, according to his observation. She was a dark brunette—with almost black hair—and brown eyes. Like Cap, she had on a pair of hiking shoes, pants, and a long-sleeved shirt. It was early morning and the air was still cool and crisp, as the sun had not risen above the mountain that stood before them. She also had a backpack, and she held two walking sticks in one hand. As they briefly stood there, a few more cars drove into the parking lot. More hikers got out and disappeared into the forest, following the different paths that went every which way, depending on how hard or easy a hike they might want to take.

"James," Suzanne said. "Here is the plan for the day. You and Kathleen are to partake in a hike to the top of the mountain. It's only something like twelve-hundred feet. Not far. But it's the journey I want you to focus on."

Cap was always good at taking orders; other than the one time in Afghanistan that got him sent back to the States, he had always followed them, no questions asked. He had faith in Suzanne, as all her methods to fight his demons had been working thus far. They were different from the rest, even odd at times, but he felt what was odd to some may not be to others and that is why he felt the "standard" methods did not work for him. So, he had not questioned her methods before, and he knew he was not going to question them now.

"You and Kathleen are not to speak to each other on the way up. I want you to focus on keeping your eyes and ears open," Suzanne said. Wow, he said to himself as he looked over to Kathleen and she smiled.

"You may, however, choose to greet others you meet on the way up as they are coming on down or those who may pass you on the way up," Suzanne continued.

She then popped open the trunk of the car and pulled out a big straw hat. Cap removed a backpack and handed it to Suzanne, grabbed the other one and placed it on his back, and then shut the trunk's lid.

"While you two are on your way up the mountain, I'll be going on my own hike along the base. Okay, now as of this moment, no talking. Shoo! Shoo you two! Get along now!" Suzanne said as she waved them on.

Cap and Kathleen headed across the parking lot and into the tree line, following the path they were told to take. Meanwhile, Suzanne headed over to the park info center and sat down on a bench just outside the entrance. She laid the backpack down next to her, leaned back, crossed her arms, closed her eyes, and let the sun slowly move upon her face as it rose above the top of the mountain. She started to smile as she felt the warmth. Then all of the sudden, the warmth disappeared as she felt the sun go away. She opened her eyes to see Hank, the park ranger.

"Same time for a wakeup call, Suzanne?" Hank said with a smile.

"Yes sir!" she replied. "Now get out of the way, my friend! You're disrupting my tanning bed time."

Hank chuckled as he walked on into the building and Suzanne closed her eyes and soaked in the sun's rays.

Cap and Kathleen began the hike up the trail. She was ahead of him, using her walking sticks proficiently through the rough terrain of the mountain path. Cap was also managing well, as he had been in rougher spots than this while in Afghanistan, though some stretches of loose rock were a bit troublesome. On the way up, as the trail began to weave back and forth, they met other people coming down—hikers, mountain bikers, and to Cap's surprise, joggers—who he felt were crazier than those riding bikes down the treacherous path, as the trails were hell bent on creating a broken limb of some kind for those who were not careful and sure-footed. Kathleen and Cap greeted everyone who passed them going the other direction. Some responded with a quick smile, remaining focused on every step they took, and others did not respond at all, not even with a smile or nod. A few never even raised their heads or eyes in acknowledgement. Cap took a mental note and did all he could to keep pace with Kathleen, who had the advantage of using the walking sticks to assist her every step.

Onward toward the top they kept going, until they were about an hour into their hike and came upon a covered bench standing in a small clearing and veered off the main trail a few yards to look over the valley behind them. Kathleen walked up to the far side of the bench, leaned her walking sticks up over the back of it, and removed her backpack. She motioned to Cap to do the same. She then pulled a bottle of water from her pack, twisted off the cap, and took a couple swallows as she looked out over the view. Cap did the same and when Kathleen sat down, he did as well.

Cap was sweating a lot, and Kathleen noticed. She reached over to one of Cap's pant legs and tugged at the zipper that was just above the knee. Cap realized he could unzip the legs from just above the knee, removing them to have instant shorts. He wondered why he never knew that when he bought the pants. He unzipped both pant legs and removed them by easing them down past his calves and over each foot. He then rolled them up and tucked them inside his backpack.

They sat there in silence, and just when Cap was wondering when they were going to proceed the rest of the way, Kathleen spoke.

"So solider, I understand you have an interesting story to tell."

Cap was a bit stunned at first, knowing they were not supposed to be speaking to each other. Kathleen, seeing the bewildered look on his face, set him at ease.

"It's okay if we talk; we are just a few yards from the top. This is where Suzanne wanted us to stop and talk anyway."

Cap hesitated, and then asked, "Wanted us to talk?"

"Yes, Suzanne wanted us to talk soldier to soldier," Kathleen replied.

"Soldier? You served?" Cap asked.

"Yes, I was naval aviator."

"You're a commissioned officer?" Cap asked.

"Was on my way to be one, but today is about you. Suzanne told me your story, but I want to hear it myself."

Cap was taken aback by her bluntness. Suzanne was more relaxed, easygoing with her questions, and always seemed to get what she wanted from him by going slowly around things. He liked that. If Kathleen was a part of the program, he was not getting it. He was exhausted with the military's way of dealing with shit—shit he wanted to get rid of and out of his life.

"Look, like I told Suzanne, I'm done telling the story. It was hard enough telling her, and I just want to bury it forever," he explained.

Kathleen sat there and just stared into his eyes. Then she leaned into the bench, rested both her elbows over its back, and stared out over the valley. Cap sat back as well and started to feel a little more at ease. Kathleen sensed this, and then she took a deep breath, let it out, and stood up, still looking over the valley below.

"Man, I use to love flying. I grew up with it in my blood. My dad was a pilot, served in Korea. Then he came home and flew commercially. He was always gone, but when he was home he'd take me and my brother up in the sky in a little Piper Cub he owned. He'd fly us around the area where we lived, and we'd look down on the forests, lakes, rivers, and farmland, seeing how the world was from above. He'd do little maneuvers that would make our stomachs tickle. It was like being on a rollercoaster for me, but twice as fun. As we got older, my brother got interested in sports, but I wanted to learn to fly. My dad loved teaching his son to play ball, but he also enjoyed teaching his daughter how to fly."

Cap's tension began to ease and he listened intently as Kathleen continued.

"By the time I was a senior in high school, I was flying solo. Dad said I was as good as he was, but I wanted to be better. Not just better at flying aircraft, I set my goals even higher. My dad's hero was John Glenn, as he flew with him in Korea. I remember when he first heard about Glenn going into space. Dad would smile and say, 'Well what do you know, ole ass magnet is an astronaut, good for him.' Seeing dad smile like made me decide

I wanted to be an astronaut myself, and I went the same route as Glenn. I grew up in Iowa, and thus went to the University of Iowa, got a degree in engineering while in the Naval Reserve Officer Training Corp, and finished my pre-flight training there as well. I spent the next two years as a naval aviator in training. I just kept working my way up the ladder. It wasn't fucking easy!"

"I should say not!" Cap blurted out. Kathleen turned and looked at him with a questionable look on her face, as she didn't know at first how he meant what he said. Cap noticed this and tried to explain, saying, "I mean that is a tough road to hoe. Studying in all the classes and then learning to fly the big planes. I don't know how you all stay focused like you do. It takes a certain kind of person, I guess."

Kathleen eased up with her look at Cap, understanding he wasn't expressing anything less than a compliment, or even more than that. She turned back to look over the valley and continued.

"It wasn't long before I was flying T-45s over areas like this. I felt like I was literary in heaven then. My dad and mom were very proud, and my brother thought it was so cool. Life was good, very good for a while anyway. Then it all came to an end."

Cap sat up when he heard her say this and turned his eyes from the valley to her. Kathleen then turned around and looked at Cap, taking a deep breath in and letting it out.

"Look, James!" she said firmly. "I've heard your story, but you haven't told *your* story! I'm going to tell you *my* story, then I'm going to hope you get why we are here!"

Cap wasn't stupid. He felt he knew what she was getting at, but he sat there, listened, and watched, as Suzanne had instructed. He saw Kathleen's body begin to shiver, even though the sun was shining directly on her from behind, casting her shadow along the ground and up to his feet. However, she didn't waver in her eyes, looking at Cap. He knew as one soldier to another, she wanted to make sure he understood.

"We graduated from flight school, me and fourteen other women in a class of about 250. There had been women before us and we had heard stories, so I had an idea what I was getting into. Before I even started, my dad had told me stories of women in the military when he served. I always told him not to worry; I said I was tougher than they were, because he has raised me. He smiled every time I said that, even though it still didn't make him feel any better.

Anyway, a few of us went out and celebrated. A lot of the women graduates didn't go, but I did, along with one other woman. We hit up a number of the establishments throughout the night and I know I had been drinking a few, but I always was able to watch my count and be responsible. Then all of the sudden I had no idea what was going on. I mean, so much so, I do not remember how I got from a bar to someone's apartment. I can't remember if I was waking up slowly or if everything I was seeing and feeling was in slow motion, from the shock my body was going through, not wanting to believe what was happening to me. All I know is that my body wouldn't respond to what I wanted, to have it stop, and it wouldn't."

Kathleen looked at him the whole time, only stopping to blink occasionally, but she was intent on him hearing what she had to say.

"I awoke slowly to having a cock in my mouth and another inside my vagina! While I couldn't yet make out who the men were in the room, as my vision was blurry, I could see who the woman was as when her head popped off of sucking on my breast; she looked eye to eye at me. Then her voice was even more recognizable when she spoke, 'Looky, looky who's waking up!" said my fellow classmate. I tried to react, but again my body wouldn't allow it. Whatever they gave me, made me numb throughout. Slowly I began to recover and slowly they all began to take turns with me and then her, although she was more of a willing participant than I was.

"I counted about five men who had been inside of me one way or another and how many times they came inside of me or on me I have no idea. All I remember is that I blacked out again. When I came to on the floor of some bedroom, I was the only one in a strange apartment. I kept my composure, as that is how I was trained. I gathered my things—those I could find—as well as all the info on the place and who was involved. I went to the naval hospital and had a rape kit performed, all the pictures taken. I followed protocol to a 'T.' The Military Police took all the info I gathered and drilled me and drilled me as if I was the suspect instead. 'Are you sure you were not a willing participant?' was a question I got over and over and over again. They knew who the guilty were, but instead of doing anything about it they decided to bury it! You know how they fucking buried it?" she asked Cap, as she leaned over him and rested one hand on his knee and the other on the six by six-foot post that supported the roof of the bench. As she yelled the last question to Cap. a couple mountain bikers were riding by on their way down. They looked her way and while they passed, a female jogger came running up the path panting, stopped alongside them, and pulled out a bottle of water.

"Good morning," she said to Cap and Kathleen.

Kathleen stood up, smiled at the woman and said, "Good morning, miss!"

Cap got up and said good morning as well.

"Beautiful day, isn't it?" the woman said.

Cap said, "Yes, it is!"

"Indeed, it is!" Kathleen responded.

The jogger put her bottle of water back in her side pouch and said, "Well, have a great day!"

Kathleen and Cap replied, "You as well."

Cap bent over and picked up a rock about the size of a golf ball and started playing with it, walking away from Kathleen a few steps with his back to her.

"They discharged you!" he said.

Kathleen didn't hear what he had said. "What?" she asked.

Cap went and hurled the rock as far as he could, making sure he was throwing in a direction that wouldn't hit someone below. Then he turned around and looked at Kathleen. This time he was looking straight into her eyes.

"They gave you a fucking honorable discharge!" he said firmly and direct to her. "They did the same fucking thing to me!" he shouted. "After I reported the rape of the boy, the brass buried it and told me to stay focused. But I couldn't deal with it and I beat the shit out of the rapist. The problem was that the one who raped all these young boys and girls was an Afghanistan Army commander, thus my discharge and nothing happening to him."

Kathleen got back into his face, pointed all her fingers on her right hand in the middle of his chest, and yelled.

"You weren't raped, and to top it off, you didn't lose your virginity. Yes, that's right, I had never had sex with a man before that! I also lost my dream of going into space. I lost my self-respect and dignity!" She eased off of Cap and backed away from him. "Most of all, I lost my family. I was depressed as hell. I couldn't face my parents, especially my father, who adored me. When I left, I didn't go home. I lied to my parents as if everything was still all right and I was still in the service. I started drinking to kill the pain; the hurt and suicide were in my mind all the time. I was twenty-four years old and had everything taken away from me and felt like I had nowhere to go."

Cap stood there with his hands on his hips and took in a deep breath of the fresh air and looked up into the deep blue sky. Then the sound of rocks rolling down the path brought him back as a jogger came around the curve.

"Good morning," the jogger said.

Cap and Kathleen responded in kind as the jogger went on by, down the hill.

Cap picked up his backpack and started walking, resuming the hike back up the mountain path, slipping his arms through the straps to hoist the pack over his shoulders. Kathleen stood briefly, somewhat in disbelief that Cap took off before they finished their conversation. She felt he sort of left her hanging after she confessed her story. She was hoping he would come clean with his. She grabbed her backpack and hiking sticks and jogged a little bit to catch up with Cap, who had surprisingly walked a good distance away from her in a short time.

"Hey!" she said as she caught up with him.

Cap hesitated a bit, but kept walking straight forward, turning briefly only to look at Kathleen as she slipped her backpack over her shoulders. Then, he refocused on the path.

"How do you know Suzanne?" he asked Kathleen.

Kathleen was silent for a bit as they continued to hike, and she glanced at Cap, who happened to turn his head to look at her at the same time. He turned back to focus on the path, as did Kathleen.

"She's my mother," Kathleen responded.

Cap hesitated very briefly, then looked at her again, but continued hiking forward. The climb was starting to level off the closer to the top they got, and thus their pace seemed to pick up some.

"Can I ask you a question, James?"

Cap walked on in silence. Kathleen did not say anything more, just followed along, keeping up to his pace even though his stride was longer than hers. About five minutes went on since Kathleen had posed her question.

"Go ahead, ask," Cap responded. "What's your question?"

Kathleen stopped, put her hands to her hips, and took in a deep breath. "What determines the transformation of a caterpillar into a butterfly?"

Cap sensed by the sound of her voice that she was not as close to him as he thought, thus he turned to look and saw she had stopped, but he continued forward a few more steps before stopping himself. He turned and looked at her. The look in his eyes told her he was a bit irritated. Cap shook his head in frustration, shrugged his shoulders, and raised his hands up in the air. A jogger then came up from behind Kathleen and passed her. Cap and the jogger locked eyes.

"Good morning!" Cap said.

The jogger responded accordingly and continued on by.

"I swear even with all the training I had, I still do not know how people make it up this mountain running like that. He makes it look so easy," Kathleen said.

Cap looked at her in silence for a minute. She saw he was thinking.

"Doesn't the caterpillar just turn into a butterfly when it's time to turn into a butterfly? It's a nature thing," he said.

"Don't you think it's a little deeper than that?" Kathleen asked.

Cap shrugged his shoulders again. Kathleen responded to his shrug as she moved closer to him.

"From what my mom says, you are not a man of religious faith, but of spirituality. With that said, tell me what you feel is the significance of the caterpillar turning into butterfly? What determines its transformation, say, comparatively to a human?" she asked.

She began to walk past him and took over the lead up the path. As he thought, he slowly followed. He wondered if this was a test of knowledge or a test of faith of some sort, as she referred to his spirituality. He continued to follow her as the path widened and flattened out some. They came upon an intersection of paths and a signpost with several boards attached stating the name of the trails and the distance of each, and pointing the direction of each one. Just beyond the sign was a picnic area and a few porta-potties, along with a working water spigot. Kathleen walked over to the picnic area, unstrapped her backpack, and laid it on top of one the picnic tables. She then placed one foot up on the bench, untied a loose shoe string, and began to retie it.

"Can you watch my stuff for a bit while I take a bathroom break?" she asked Cap.

Cap nodded yes as she continued over to a porta-potty. He removed his backpack, set it on the picnic table, and removed a water bottle. He stepped up on the bench, and then on up on top of the table, and took in the view of the surrounding area. The sky was bluer than blue. There was a small lake off in the distance that they were higher than. He could see it was manmade, as there was a dam at one end. He caught glimpses of people spread out here and there on various trials that seemed to surround the lake. He even saw a couple people on horseback. He took in a deep breath of air through his nose; it was fresh air with not much of a scent, not even of all the sage trees, pines, and evergreen bushes that covered most of the mountain.

He started to think about the significance of the butterfly puzzle Kathleen posed to him. When Kathleen exited the porta-potty, she saw Cap standing on the table. She tucked in her shirt, walked over to the water spigot, and proceeded to wash her hands. When she was done, she shook them in the air to get off what water remained on her skin. She then wiped them each on her pant legs and walked on back over toward Cap. She stood before him and looked up at him.

"You see, a caterpillar determines when it's time based on the climate it lives in," she explained. "The warmer it is, the sooner it wills itself to metamorphize into a butterfly. The colder it is, the longer it will take to change. Sometimes, it can be a few seasons before change will come. Either way, once it does, the transformation is wonderful."

Cap looked down at Kathleen.

"The caterpillar knows its time is coming and thus doesn't give up, no matter what the circumstances," she continued. "It has faith that no matter what, everything is going to work out and it will be in essence 'born again.'"

Cap hopped down from the tabletop to the bench and then again from the bench to the ground.

Kathleen went on.

"When I realized nobody could take my soul away but my-self, I was able to express my true feelings about the whole thing that went down against me. I accepted the fact that it happened, but I didn't accept the fact that it had to continue to happen by me being silent. It's about right and wrong, James. Burying something that is wrong just eats you up. I thank God every day for my mother giving me counseling, as most mothers do, but for her having a degree in it.

"Now, I can't imagine what it's like to kill another person when you must in order to survive yourself. Especially in the situation that you and many others have experienced. But in the same breath, you have to use the experience to survive here by doing everything you can to right the wrongs. In my case, the wrongs made onto me or in your case, the ones you witnessed and are still holding onto."

She reached over to pick up her backpack and strapped it back over her shoulders.

"I'm leaving you here and going back down. I want you to head up this paved service road here for about a mile or so. You will see a sign that says the equine loop trail. Take that to the top of the ridge, then follow it on back to the main trail, which will lead you back down the mountain. There's no hurry. The rest of this trip is about you now."

Cap reached over to grab his backpack and strapped it on. They both hiked up to the paved service road. He looked down the road and then turned and looked at Kathleen. She put out her fist toward Cap and he slowly put his toward hers and bumped it. She smiled, turned, and headed in the opposite direction.

"The temperature is just perfect today! Love it! I just love it!" she shouted as she walked away from him.

He watched her until she hiked out of view behind some the tall sage trees. He turned and began to hike up the service road. He came upon the equine trial as Kathleen said he would, turned and followed it. It was a bit treacherous and he could see why it would be easier for a sure-footed horse to travel it then a human. But he was making his way up. Occasionally, he would stop and look behind him to see the view of the dam, along with the whole shoreline of the lake it created.

He started to think about Kathleen's words in reference to his situation. He didn't want to bring himself back to his tour in Afghanistan, but he was beginning to understand the reference of the caterpillar becoming a butterfly. As he hiked the trail, he started to go back in his mind to the point in the village when he and his outfit were going door to door in search of the Taliban soldiers who occupied parts of Afghanistan. Each step he took on the trail had to be meticulously taken, just as he had to overseas. Walking down the streets of the village meant taking each step with caution—of an IED being planted along the way, of a sniper being anywhere within a thousand yards or so, of women and children being used as human explosives, much against their will, or of any kind of combative situation occurring out of the blue.

As Cap took a step in the present, at this point and time, his mind was also taking one in the past. He and a few others were following the Humvee slowly up the street. Each door they would come to, his men would enter, search, and come back "clear" or in some cases coming across families and questioning them with the help of Afghani soldiers as translators to clear them. Every structure had to be cleared—rooms, tunnels, and what was found behind hidden doorways. Dogs were often used, and on many occasions, sadly sacrificed to save soldiers' lives. This was heartbreaking to a lot of the men, as some enjoyed the loyal companionship of those canines more than some of their own troops.

As Cap followed the trail, his mind started to wander. He began to hear his men in the headset he was wearing. One by one, they were reporting in to him "clear," but then a commotion caused Cap to stop in his tracks. He covered his earpiece with his hand to ensure he could make out what they were saying and understand it. One of the village residents was in an argument with an Afghani solider, but nothing was being interpreted back to him. As he stood there trying to get a response from one of his men, the Humvee kept moving forward. Cap had turned his back to the Humvee to look at the building where the commotion was taking place and just as he did there was an explosion, the force of which knocked him face first to the ground.

Cap was replaying the events he had spoken to Marta about the night of the thunderstorm. This time, he was replaying it to himself and in real time—he had gone to his hands and knees on the equine trail. In his mind, the force of the blast had flown him forward, with rocks and sand falling on and around him, knocking off his helmet, but his rifle remained in his hand. The concussion of the blast had caused a loud ringing in his ears, knocking out his hearing. When he looked up, he could barely see with all the dust and sand blowing around, but his helmet was within reach. He grabbed it; quickly put it back on; and turned onto his back, where he could just barely make out the Humvee on its side, leaning against a building about 15 yards ahead of him. He quickly got to his feet with his gun in ready position and ran to the rear of the Humvee; as he did, he could start to make out the muffled sounds of his men yelling. His earpiece was hanging down around his chin. He placed it back into his ear. His hearing started to come back faintly, but he was getting nothing but commotion on the line.

In real time, Cap had crawled up behind a boulder along the trail, pressed his back up against it, and braced his knees to help keep him from slipping. He yelled into the headset for everyone to shut up and report one by one and they did; all but the men in the Humvee were "clear." The men who were alongside of him were accounted for and barricaded in doorways on each side of the street. As the dust began to settle, he and his men gained eye contact and he also began to see the carnage, as a severed leg and arm lay out in the middle of the street. He yelled out to the Humvee and only got one response. It was the gunner, and he was pinned under the vehicle. Cap's hearing was still muffled, but he could make out what his men were saying. The dust had settled, and the commotion had been reduced to controlled alertness.

Cap yelled at his men to come and help lift the Humvee off the gunner and grab the other men inside the vehicle. Six men broke away from the protection of the buildings, ran to the side of the Humvee and started to try and lift it off the gunner's leg, with Cap grabbing the man by his armpits. Just when they thought they had it up, a shot rang out and struck one of his men's hands, ripping off several fingers, and he went down.

"Cover!" yelled Cap. Another shot ran out and a solider dropped to the ground in front of him as he went back around to the rear of the Humvee.

Cap braced his back against the Humvee's bumper. As he did, he saw a fallen soldier face down and reaching out toward him. Cap dropped his gun to his side and went to grab for the soldier's hand. They locked wrists and he began to drag him toward cover when another shot ran out. Cap got the soldier back alongside him and was still holding onto his wrist, but he felt his grip loosen. Cap realized he had literally felt the life of one of his men leave his body. He grabbed the soldier's shoulders, flipped him on his back, placed his hand on his neck, and felt for a pulse. When he turned the soldier to look at his face, part of it was gone from the exit wound of the bullet that hit him.

Cap spread his fingers wide on one hand and closed the soldier's remaining eyelid shut. Another shot ran out and then a yell was heard from the gunner still trapped under the Humvee. Cap looked to the sky as if expecting an answer from above, then slowly rolled his fallen teammate away from any more harm. The enemy was known to keep shooting at the dead to make them almost unrecognizable and to irritate the fuck out of the Allied troops, who were warned to ignore it, but had difficulty doing so.

Cap then saw another one of his men in a doorway across the street, out of line of fire, helping wrap the hand of the other soldier who was shot. He tried to get a glimpse of the gunner and peered carefully around the rear of the Humvee. He saw the gunner was still alive, lying on his back, still pinned, and unable to move. Beyond him he saw three more soldiers, two kneeling and one standing, all three in protective positions out of site of the sniper. Cap repositioned himself back against the rear bumper. He looked back down the street they had come up and saw four more of his men approaching carefully toward him, taking positions. He went to speak through his mike, only to find it was split in two, obviously by a bullet. It began to sink in a bit—how close he had just come to being killed—yet he remained focused. Then a shot ran out and he heard the gunner yell out.

"Son of a bitch!"

Cap turned to look without thinking and exposed himself, and then another shot ran out, hitting the rear of the Humvee's hood. Cap spun back into safety.

"Are you hit?" Cap yelled out to the gunner.

"Yes!!!" yelled out the gunner. "In my left fucking knee!"

Cap carefully peered around the corner and now he could see the gunner moving in pain. He looked at the others behind him and one yelled to Cap that more help was on the way. Another shot ran out and the gunner yelled again.

"Oh Christ! Oh, Jesus Christ! Oh God!"

Cap and the others turned and looked.

"He shot me again! In my hip! Oh God it hurts!"

"Goddamn!" yelled Cap.

He looked beyond the gunner and saw the others all in a state of shock and loss at being helpless. They couldn't do a thing, as that Humvee was not being moved for one man without jeopardizing several other. If he could, Cap knew he would be the first one out there to get the gunner. Cap looked back at the men who had just approached up the street for an answer of where help was, and they had none. All they knew was that they were on their way. Another vehicle would be able to block the line of fire. Another shot rang out.

"Goddam it! Gunner!" yelled Cap.

"He's fucking playing with me, Cap! My shoulder!"

"Fuck! Fuck! Fuck!" yelled almost all the others nearby.

Then one of the others yelled out to the gunner by his real name. "No, Carson!"

Cap peered around the Humvee and saw the gunner pulling his side pistol out of his holster. He was having difficulty, with his shoulder having just been shot, but he still managed to do it.

"Stand down, soldier!" Cap yelled out to the gunner.

Then another shot ran out and they all had thought the gunner had shot himself, but it was the sniper again. There wasn't a sound.

"Gunner! Are you still with us?" yelled Cap.

There was silence.

"Carson!" yelled one of the others.

There was more silence for about a minute and then the gunner responded.

"I'm here, fellas!" he softly yelled. "I'm done with this bastard though! I'm through! I'll be damned if I'm going to be his fucking mouse! Fuck him! Fuck all of this shit!" His voice got higher and louder.

Cap and the others saw he was moving his sidearm up to his chin.

"No!" they yelled.

Cap could see the gunner mouthing something just before placing the gun under his chin and pulling the trigger. Cap and the others watched as the back of gunner's head exploded from the self-inflicted gunshot. Cap looked at the others on the other side of the Humvee; they all sat backward on their legs with their jaws hanging low in disbelief. He looked at the two in the doorway, who were also in shock, and at the remaining group of his men, most who had their heads hanging low. Behind them, he could see the help coming up the street.

Cap's sadness quickly turned to anger. He picked up his gun, stood up, ran out from behind the Humvee into the street toward where the sniper was, and started shooting in that direction—out in the open.

"Come and get me you fucking coward! Come and get me!" he yelled.

He fired until he emptied a clip. The others yelled at him to get back, but he slipped another clip in and fired until that was gone. He then threw down his gun.

"Come and get me!" he yelled again, standing there alone over the deceased gunner.

When the others saw he wasn't being shot at, they came out and walked toward him. The other platoon arrived and drove its Humvee to the open side of the street to cover the men next to their fallen comrades. As Cap stood there looking over the gunner, the men rocked the Humvee off his leg and pulled him out. They then got the remaining deceased crew out of the vehicle. Because they were out of body bags, they had to put them in sleeping bags. Cap watched everything going around him like it was in slow motion. He saw the men pick up body parts here and there. He watched as they swept through the whole scene and cleaned it up. If it wasn't for the fact that there was a blown-up vehicle and blood-soaked sand and dirt, nobody would have known they were even there.

"Cap, you all right?" asked one of his men.

Though he felt like he'd been punched in the gut, he replied, "Yes."

He got up, walked over to one of the vehicles, and hopped in with the others. As they pulled away, he felt numb and all he saw was dust. One of the soldiers put a hand on his shoulder and he turned to look. That's when Cap came back to reality and saw a mule deer kicking up dust behind it, as he must have been startled by his presence. He noticed he was soaked in sweat, as he had been sitting in the direct sunlight. He realized he had not been in the present while he was reliving the events overseas for the very first time since they happened.

Cap stood up, noticed a clearing ahead of the trail before him, and continued up it until reaching a large open space with a couple picnic tables and a bench covered with a big wooden canopy. As he got closer, he also saw a tall post with a bunch of dog collars tacked to it, each with a name tag. At the top of the post was a plaque that said this was a memorial to the dogs who had explored this path many times and now were deceased. There were also a couple horse halters tacked to the post, which Cap assumed honored deceased equines. He took some time to look at each one, along with the little notes the owners had written in marker on the collars.

He then turned around to walk toward the bench and that's when he saw the view. He almost stumbled at first, as he had never seen anything so majestic. He walked over to the shaded bench, pulled off his backpack, unzipped it, and pulled out a bottle of water. It felt twenty degrees cooler in the shade. He took off his hat, poured about half the water over his head, and then drank the rest of the bottle. He set the empty bottle on the bench, then walked slowly forward out from the shade toward what appeared to be a boulder that everybody who reached the top must have climbed onto, as there was a worn path leading up to it.

Cap reached into his pants pocket, pulled out a handkerchief, and wiped his head and face dry. He then bunched the handkerchief into a ball in one hand, climbed the boulder, and stood up on it. He looked out over the horizon to the west and he could see the coastline as far south and north as his eyes would take him. He thought how the sky was so beautifully blue and clear, not a cloud anywhere to be seen. The ocean glistened like diamonds. The land before the ocean looked barren, even though he knew there was a lot of development between him and the ocean. It must have been a combination of the distance and the glare from the ocean that made it look that way—as if he was the first one to discover this beautiful view.

He turned and followed the horizon inland, slowly coming around from the north where he began to see structures in the distance that said, yes, man indeed was present. As he brought his gaze to the east, the view became magnificent. The mountains rose to their gigantic splendor and what was most impressive was that they were covered in a purple hue. He had never seen that before. He thought to himself that this is what they must have meant by the words, "purple mountain's majesties" in the song "America the Beautiful." Now he was seeing it with his own eyes.

He continued to turn and to the south he could make out the skyline of San Diego and the land beyond it, that he knew was Mexico. He followed the coast as he turned back to his original position and then he looked to the sky. He closed his eyes, opened his arms out wide, and breathed in deeply the fresh air. This time he could smell the sage and small pines. He stood like that thinking of nothing at all as a smile came across his face. He stood silently for a few minutes and then out of somewhere deep inside of him, his emotions poured out of him; he slowly went to his knees on the boulder and wept and wept and wept.

Cap came down off the mountain and stood before Kathleen and Suzanne. He was soaked in sweat. They both looked up to him. He looked down upon them and smiled. He joined them at the bench where Susanne had been sitting the whole time, and this time he told his true story, for the first time, to them. It was a real relief for him. There were several reasons he had blocked it out of his mind. First, that the gunner's family would not have received any benefits from the military had it become clear how he died, even though his death was imminent. Second, he didn't want to relive any of the horrors of war and it took all he had just to tell Marta what he did, though it wasn't complete. Cap got up from the bench, as did Kathleen with her mom.

"Soldier, you're in good hands now!" said Kathleen, as she hugged him and started on her way.

"Yes, Susanne is amazing!" responded Cap.

Kathleen turned and yelled, "No! I meant your own hands soldier!"

Cap and Suzanne sat back down, with Suzanne putting one arm around him and taking her free hand to reach over, grab his hand, and squeeze it tightly.

"I feel like I got a giant load off my back," he said to her.

"In a way you did, in a medical sense," Suzanne explained. "All your nerves loosened up, endorphins were released, and neurons started firing like they should. A lot of people don't understand what you and many others who have experienced war have is an illness. It actually could be compared to a disease and should be. Anything that creates disease of the mind is not good and eventually is no different than cancer or the common cold and in fact can be just as hard to cure. It's an addiction that can lead to other addictions. But as in any addiction, there's the misconception of what will work for one individual will work for all individuals. That's what is wrong with the military and other institutions; they take that approach when in fact every individual is different, thus why they are individuals."

Suzanne rose from the bench, stretched out, and reached her hand out to Cap. He grabbed it and eased himself off the bench. She squeezed his hand to confirm her happiness at this breakthrough. They walked toward the car and Suzanne continued.

"Our program is just one of many for our vets and others. There's Pets for Vets, which teams up veterans with animal shelters, as the animals seem to help with some and it actually benefits both of them. There are various motorcycle and car clubs for veterans as well where they get together, discuss their experiences, and how they cope. They combine group therapy with group interests. There's a lot out there and it's a matter of finding the right thing for the individual. I have this and other gimmicks up my sleeve."

As they reached the car, Suzanne opened the trunk so she and Cap could throw in their backpacks and she closed the lid. Cap walked over, opened the door for Suzanne, and she got in.

"Thank you," she said

He shut the door and walked around, opened the passenger side, slid himself in, shut the door, reached behind to grab his seatbelt and hooked it up, took a deep breath, exhaled, and leaned back into the seat as Suzanne started the car.

"This is just the beginning, my friend," she said to Cap. "It's a major big step to a number of little steps to keeping this all under control for the rest of your life."

Cap looked straight ahead out the windshield and nodded his head up and down a few times in agreement. Suzanne put the car in reverse and pulled out of the parking spot, then shifted into drive and they drove away from the mountain—the mountain Cap had climbed in more ways than one and would climb several more times in the next months, not only by himself, but with others like him, as he continued to help himself and other veterans as well. Little by little, he desensitized himself from his time overseas so he could talk about it, share experiences with others, and work on how to use it to their benefit to "pay it forward." Little did he know how far back this would end up taking him, more so than he could have imagined.

SUSURROS DE IDENTIDAD

(Whispers of Identity)

Danny's grandparents were naturally born U.S. citizens of Japanese ancestry. When the U.S. entered World War II, Franklin Delano Roosevelt ordered that all Japanese people currently residing in the States be put into internment camps. Danny's grandfather always said that was the worst thing FDR ever did as president, but that it was also the best thing he ever did, as that is where he met his wife, Danny's grandmother.

He told the story many times of how they had been living in the Pasadena area of California when one day some men in uniform came and literary told them to grab what they could, as they were being detained. In March 1942, they were sent to Santa Anita Park, where they were temporarily placed inside a horse stall until the track was set up with tents and facilities—not nearly enough for all the detainees. It was a struggle at first, but nearly 19,000 Japanese Americans were able to create a community that was pretty well organized and operated fairly efficiently under the circumstance.

Danny's grandfather spoke of how he had started working in the kitchen, helping with cleanup after every meal was served. Then this beauty overtook him when he first laid eyes on his future wife, as she was helping with the cooking. In October 1942, all the detainees would be sent elsewhere, more inland away from the coast, and both their families ended up on an Indian reservation in Wyoming. These camps had worse conditions than the race track, but both families, as well as many others, were quickly able to make things much more bearable then might be expected.

As the days progressed, his grandfather learned of a program through which some Japanese would be able to attend college on campuses in the Midwest: the National Japanese American Student Relocation Council. Both his grandparents were accepted, but they ended up not attending the same college. Although they were sent in different directions, they stayed in touch through letters, and as the war came to an end, so did the families' incarceration. Their years of study ended nearly at the same time and both graduated, he in economics and she in education. They married and moved to San Diego, where they started a family. He enlisted to serve in the Navy Air Corps, became a pilot, and served in Korea flying combat missions, while his wife taught English at a high school in Kearny Mesa. They eventually had three children, two boys and a daughter who would eventually become Danny's mother.

Danny's mom and dad met at the University of San Diego, where for some reason most of the Asian community in Southern California ends up attending college. His father studied engineering and his mother followed in her father's footsteps in economics. Upon completing his undergraduate degree, his dad was commissioned in the Army and was immediately deployed during the first Gulf War. He was stationed in a makeshift base in Iraq and for a while was staying out of any combat situations. Unfortunately, that would not last long, as three months into his tour, his unit would come under fire, and most of them, including his father, were killed. It was later to be found that they were killed by friendly fire, meaning by fellow Americans, who were given the wrong coordinates to fire upon.

Danny's dad never knew he was going to be a father, as his mother found out she was pregnant only days after she learned her husband was killed. Danny's mother finished her education and ended up working in the banking system while raising her son on her own with Danny's grandparents. She dated occasionally while raising him, but focused so much attention on him that he was very spoiled. His grandparents insisted that she be more disciplined with the boy, and she would try, but he was a pretty persuasive young man.

For a while, Danny's grandfather was really the only male influence he had while growing up besides teachers and some male friends. Then one day his mother met someone and soon they were married. Danny's new stepfather was a brilliant man, an engineer like his father, who worked for Qualcomm and was a big part of a new technology boom. He and Danny got along fine, and although he did not have children of his own, he treated Danny with respect. He also disciplined him as if he was his own, and Danny respected him for that. In the not too distant future, he would be in Danny's corner when Danny's sexuality was in question.

Danny realized at a very young age that he was not only interested in girls, but he was attracted to boys as well. He found himself sexually drawn to both sexes, although he did not have any feminine qualities. He did the typical homecoming and prom thing and dated many girls, but he always felt awkward on dates and most soon thought him strange. He found himself having more fun going out with his soccer teammates. Even though he felt close to some of his friends, he was still confused about his situation. He was very mindful about it as well and he didn't want to lose any of the close friendships he treasured.

Danny graduated the top of his class and though he was offered many academic scholarships, he was also offered several scholarships to play soccer. He chose to stay near home to be close to his mother and grandparents, following in his parents' footsteps to attend the University of San Diego. His studies would be guided toward law, while he also played and started for the men's soccer team. It was during his second year at school that he had his first sexual encounter with another player on the team. They first became close as teammates and then as friends, as he offered to teach Danny to surf. Even though he grew up in San Diego, Danny had never learned to surf, and actually had never been to the beach that much, other than on holidays such as the Fourth of July. But he began spending a lot of time at the beach after practices with his teammate and during downtime from when the season was over.

It was at the beach after a day of surfing that Danny's teammate unexpectedly kissed him after they came out of the water and onto the beach with their boards in hand. Danny was caught off guard, but he didn't back off and returned the kiss. Their relationship became deeper and sexual, developing into a close but secret one. They both knew it could never be let out to the rest of the team or they would be kicked off it for sure, and many other issues would most definitely arise from it. Thus, they treated each other in public as good friends and that's all anybody ever saw of it, including Danny's own family.

The relationship only ended after graduation, when Danny moved onto law school and his companion moved back east to accept a job closer to his family. Though they stayed in touch,

Danny found himself alone until while surfing one day he met Marta and the other surfer dudes.

Greg's kin were fifth-generation dairy farmers and one of the oldest families in Maine. G, as his sisters came to call him, was the only boy of five children and the youngest. Growing up with four older sisters was never an easy task. As a toddler, he was used as a living doll by them, dressed up in girls' clothing and having lipstick and perfume applied to him many times. His father would come in from the barn to find this and get really upset, demanding that his sisters clean him up and make him look like a respectable boy.

As he got older, G became more and more involved with the farm, as it was expected by his dad that he would ultimately take it over. His dad often ran roughshod over G, so much so at times that he realized he had to find something else to do that would give him an excuse to get away. In the often harsh, cold winters of Maine, he joined a youth wrestling club. When his father found out, he got an unexpected reaction from him, as he encouraged it and pushed him to be the best. At first, G was happy with his father's support, but as he got better, his father got tougher on him to train harder and he did.

When spring came one year, G was out mending fences on the far edge of the farm that was just across the main coastal highway, about two football fields from the coastline. When he wanted some peace to think, he would always volunteer to go out to the far pasture to do any kind of work his father wanted; sometimes would make up something to do like cut up a tree that had fallen during a storm—anything so he could get away and his father would think he was doing something constructive.

Once out there, he would hop the fence, cross the highway, hike to the edge of the sand dunes, and sit and listen to the waves as they beat against the shore. One day, he was walking down a dune and was surprised to see a surfer out in the water. He sat there and watched the man for what must have been an hour or so and realized he better get back to the farm. He came back the next day and found the man out there again; when he came in from the water, he came over to G and struck up a conversation. He found out the man and his family had just moved to the area for business from the west coast. It was not too long before G struck a deal with him to teach him how to surf.

From then on, when he wasn't at school, working on the farm, or wrestling, G was out surfing. A couple of his sisters knew something was up; they followed him one day and watched. When he saw them, he made them promise not to tell their father, and they were more than happy to agree if G would teach them how to surf. Though their father eventually found out and disapproved of the surfing, he let it be, as it seemed to make G stronger and more balanced for his wrestling. As long as chores were getting done, it ended up being fine with him. Soon, all five siblings were surfing the waves of the upper East Coast.

G's senior year included victory and tragedy. G came in second in the state wrestling tournament for his weight class. The match could have gone either way—it was that close—and as a result he earned several scholarships from various colleges. His dad kept pushing him to pick a certain school, but G had other interests that school didn't have. He also excelled at art while growing up, and his art teacher encouraged him to go to another school.

During the late spring, the North Atlantic had some tremendous waves. G and his sisters were intrigued; they were used to waves of three to six feet, but these were closer to eight to ten feet. When they arrived at their usual spot, they not only found the larger waves, but also a bigger crowd than usual. G suggested to his sisters that they may want to pass on the surf. G ran out toward the water as his sisters stood by and watched. It took forever for him to get out far enough where he could catch a wave and catch one he did. His sisters were elated and the youngest took her board and ran out to the water—with the others yelling at her, trying to convince her otherwise—but she felt if her brother could do it, so could she.

G saw her go into the water and decided to wait for her to reach him. He watched her and at the same time watched as other surfers caught a wave. His gaze went from watching his sisters on the beach and watching the one sister paddle out to watching the surfers around him. The waves would occasionally hide his sister from view, but he could see everyone on the beach, and all of the sudden, he saw them running and yelling. He couldn't see the sister who was in the water, but then other surfers near the shore were bringing in a body and board, and G hurriedly swam in on his board, body surfing instead of riding it.

When he got to the shore, there was a small crowd around his sister. One of the surfers said he didn't see her, and struck her. He was terribly sorry; G calmed him down and the others said it was okay. Another surfer said he was a med student. As he tended to their sister, someone had already called 911. Their sister was transported to the hospital, where their parents were already waiting. She had severe head trauma and underwent surgery. She remained in a coma for almost three days before she finally came to. During that time, G sensed his father's angst and he was right. His sister was going to be okay, although she would have a long recovery and need therapy. Though his father never said anything, G knew he blamed him.

A lot of the cost for his sister's care wasn't covered by insurance, which put a strain on the family to the extent that his parents had to borrow against the farm. The tension grew between father and son, and came to a head when G chose a college that was exceptional in art but didn't offer wrestling. He hadn't said anything to his family when he applied, but when the letter of acceptance came, it got into his father's hands first. G was out in the barn that day, prepping for the evening milking, when his father came in waving the letter.

"What the hell is this?" he asked, catching G by surprised as he was coming out of the milking parlor.

G had his hands full carrying buckets of warm water for washing. He set one down and grabbed the letter, began to read, and then set down the other bucket.

"It's a letter of acceptance to the college of Arts and Science at Cornell University," he replied, with a slight smile on his face that he hid it from his father as much as possible when he looked back up at him.

"There isn't a wrestling program at Cornell!" his father pointed out.

"I'm not going to college to study wrestling!" G quickly snapped back.

His father snatched the letter out of G's hand. G stood there for a brief second and then bent down to pick up the buckets of water. He stood back up, looked at his father straight in the eye as to ask if he could go past him, and continued with his work. His father crumbled the letter into a ball; placed both his hands, now fists, on his hips; and stepped aside. As G began to walk by, his father kicked one the buckets as hard as he could with his boot and the water went flying in the air and then onto G. His sister Marlene had walked into the barn just as it had happened.

"Dad!" she shouted.

He turned around and looked at her, and then walked into the milking parlor without saying a word. She walked over to G and saw he had tears running down his face.

"Are you okay, Greg?" she asked.

He just nodded yes. She went to speak, and he hushed her.

"It's okay, Marlene. Let's get to work."

The two of them finished the evening milking together and headed up to the house for dinner. They got cleaned up and sat down at the table, but their father wasn't there. Neither his mother nor his sisters spoke about the incident, even though they all knew what had happened. They tried talking about other topics, but G just sat and ate, not really listening, and was silent. He excused himself from the table, brought his empty dishes to the sink, laid them carefully in the basin, and headed to his room. As he walked by his mother, she gently grabbed his arm. He turned toward her, she brushed the hair away from his eyes, kissed him lightly on his forehead, and let him go on by.

G showered and then packed a suitcase and duffle bag with everything he really cared about having with him on a trip. When the lights were off in the house, he sneaked down the stairs and out the back quietly, somehow not disturbing anyone, even the dogs. He placed the bags in the back of his pickup, put the truck in neutral, and let it coast down the driveway before popping the clutch, starting it up, and driving away from the family farm for what he felt would be for good.

G drove, but his destination was not Cornell University. Instead, he decided to go west. When he crossed the Mississippi, he decided to go to San Diego and realized he had not taken his surfboard with him. He had lived with that surfboard in his truck, but when his sister had been hurt, he took it out so as his father wouldn't see it and be reminded of the accident. When he arrived in San Diego, he went straight to the beach. He threw all his belongings inside the cab of the truck, locked it up, and then went out to watch the few surfers who were out in the water. The sun was high, and the sky was pure blue. He then saw a seal catch a wave and ride it into shore, then scoot on over to a group of others laying on the rocks as if they were people catching the sun's rays. He laid back in the sand and was immediately overtaken by emotion, as tears poured from his eyes. He was sad and yet angry about how things were left with his father. While sad about how he left his family without saying anything, he also was overcome with joy. With all the hurt he was feeling, he was also feeling a peacefulness inside him that he had made the right decision to not go to school and come to San Diego instead.

G explored the area and found himself walking up Garnett Street looking for a job. There were plenty of opportunities for bartending, but at the time he wasn't of age. He stopped at street vendor to get something to eat. While he was waiting for his order, he saw a sign for a tattoo artist. He looked through the window and saw all the different drawings of artwork up on one wall and on another, photographs of the tattoos done by the shop's artist. He thought this would be a great way to work on his own art. Just when he thought about walking in, his food order was up. He picked it up and went back to the tattoo parlor, leaned against an empty bicycle rack in front of it, sat his soda on the sidewalk, and began eating his sandwich and fries. He watched people go into the shop. Then out came a big guy with tattoos all over his forearms that ran up inside the sleeves on his short-sleeved shirt and continued onto his neck. He walked over toward G and raised his head up as if to say, "hey."

"Mind if I smoke?" he asked.

Even though he did mind, he didn't say so and responded, "No."

"Cool," the big guy said. "Some people don't like it while they are eating."

G kind of responded in agreement, nodding his head sideways.

"There's no smoking inside," the big guy said.

"You waiting to get a tattoo?" G asked.

"No, I'm waiting to give one, but he can't make up his mind about what he wants, so while he is looking over the artwork, I'm taking a break."

"How long have you been doing this?" G asked.

The big guy took a puff on his cigarette and said, "Oh, on and off for about eight years now. I get in a groove and then I get bored and go off and do something else or cruise around to some other part of the country, but I always end up back here. Marie is a pretty cool owner."

"Cool!" G said. "I was thinking about applying for the job."

'Really?"

"Yea!" G said. "Except I really haven't done it before, but I am pretty good at art. I had a scholarship to college for art."

"Really, well let's go inside and see what you have."

"Really?" G responded.

"Hell yeah! Why not? If you have the art, the procedure isn't that difficult."

The big guy tossed his cigarette down to the sidewalk and rubbed it out with his foot. G took the last bite of his sandwich, picked up his drink and washed it down, tossed the cup and bag into the trash bin, and followed the big guy into the shop. Once inside, the big guy sat G down at one of the tables, gave him a blank pad of drawing paper and told him to draw a picture of anything, something unique to him. G thought for a moment and then he remembered the seal. He began drawing a wave with a seal, but he drew the seal on top of a surfboard on its belly. The seal had its head tilted back, eyes closed, and mouth open as to express its happiness at being on top of the water. G looked up at big guy and saw him talking to Marie, the owner.

"Here ya go," G said.

The big guy came over to pick up the sketch and brought it over Marie. While Marie and the big buy were talking, a customer was nearby, looking at all the artwork on the wall; he happened to glance at the piece G had drawn that Marie had in her hands. G could only observe what was going on; he could not hear the conversation. Soon they were done, and Marie walked over to G. She handed the drawing pad to him.

"So, you have never worked in a tattoo parlor before?" she asked G.

"No, ma'am," he responded.

"Please do not call me ma'am. I'm not that much older than you. Call me Marie or as most call me, Boss Lady," she said.

"Yes." G hesitated "Does this mean I'm hired?"

"You see that customer over there with the big guy? He's a Navy SEAL and one of our regulars," she said. "He wants that drawing you made put on him with a few little changes. Big guy is going to bring him over to you and you guys are to work out the particulars. We'll see how it goes. If you can sell him, then we'll have you draw up the art while the big guy teaches you the craft."

G stood up and went to shake her hand.

She shook it and said, "Don't think this handshake is a contract or anything. All it means is I'm giving you a shot. That was a pretty good piece you drew up."

"Um, what is the big guy's name?" G asked.

She turned and winked, "Big Guy."

He smiled as she walked away and went over to Big Guy, who along with the customer sat with him at a table to discuss the drawing. While they were talking, he noticed Marie go over to the front window and remove the help wanted sign. When she turned around, she saw he had seen her; she winked at him again, went over to the counter, pulled open a drawer, and stuffed the sign inside. G returned to the conversation and smiled.

This was not only the beginning of a new life for G, but also an adventure of self-discovery. He caught on fast and he had been there for only about two weeks when Big Guy and Marie found out he had been sleeping in the back of his pickup since arriving in San Diego. He had a tarp covering the top of the bed that made it like a makeshift tent, and he'd rotate parking along alleys or side streets so as to not disturb stores and homeowners or be harassed by the police. Marie loved his talent so much that she didn't want to lose this young man to the streets, something that happened to many who came to California. They didn't have a job and goal in mind to make it with the cost of living being as high as it was. So, Marie and Big Guy helped make a second-floor storage room into a small apartment, turning a utility room into a small kitchen with a mini-fridge, stove, and sink.

G studied hard under the guidance of Big Guy and before long he was tattooing customers without assistance. Although Marie did keep an eye on him for a while, eventually she felt at ease. The three of them worked together so much so that Marie and Big Guy would almost always use him for the pre-art sketches for especially intricate requests. They would share their cut of the money made with G or in Marie's case, give him free rent. This allowed G to save some of his money to send back home to his sister Marlene, who he was communicating with to stay in touch with the family. The money was to help with expenses for her and any of his sisters who wanted to come join him in Southern California sometime soon.

G became responsible for opening the shop every day, since he was living there. So, he started a routine of getting up and going down to the beach to jog along the shore to stay in shape; he had always been athletic and was really getting bored without having wrestling to discipline him. As soon as he saved enough, he got himself a new surfboard and began the ritual of jogging and surfing every day. If he hadn't already had a rock-solid physique from wrestling, he was now chiseled like the Greek god Adonis, as Marie would occasionally call him. He started to grow a beard, and a long one at that. It seemed a lot of the surfers and millennials were doing so. Even Big Guy, with his big balding head, grew one. At one time, he and G had a contest to see whose grew the longest in a week.

One day, as G finished up his regular routine at the beach, he came back to open the shop and there was already a customer waiting outside the door. He opened it and allowed him in. The young guy walked in and started looking at all the artwork posted on the walls; G also showed him the picture books they had of various past procedures and also told the guy they could create just about anything his wildest imagination could dream up.

"Really?" responded the customer.

"Yep, pretty much!" G said with confidence.

So, the guy pulled out a piece of paper from his back pocket, unfolded it, and laid it out on the counter for G to see. G looked it over.

"No problem! However, for this to be done properly, it should be done in stages and may require a few trips back in here, say four or five. It is an intricate piece, but it can be done and I'm your guy," G said, and noted the cost.

The customer agreed, and a relationship began that would catch both young men off guard. G was particular about his several-step art. He preferred to have customers be as patient as possible, coming back as necessary to continue the work. The skin could heal and relax properly before the next phase began, otherwise he thought the colors would not blend correctly. Marie liked this about G. He was in love with his work, not with just a paycheck, plus word about his talent was spreading and business was booming.

This was not the first time G did a multi-stage project. But it was the first time he really got to know a customer beyond the regular questions he, Marie, and Big Guy would ask to get a feel for their personalities. Even though most customers would come in with a pretty good idea of what they wanted, the three of them would put a subtle spin on the artwork to make it the customer's very own. But this customer was different for G; as the project went on, it seemed the questions got more personal, about family and friends, and likes and dislikes, and for the first time he shared a lot of his past with someone other than his sisters.

The two became close and soon they were hanging out together later in the day after G was done, heading to the local hangouts. A lot of times they would end up at G's room above the shop and pass out from the night's partying. Then one night they got back and were talking up a storm as usual while sitting on the floor drunk as skunks. They got to shouting stupid stuff to each other and laughing when G tried to get up to go to the bathroom. He tripped and fell in the other guy's lap. They laughed at first, then the guy planted a kiss on G. When he released, G stared at him briefly, but then returned the kiss—but this time it was very passionate for both of them. G broke it off and went to the bathroom as he had initially planned.

While in there, all sorts of things were spinning through his head, but he also knew he was still pretty drunk. When he came out, the guy was standing there naked. G stood there in a bit of a daze, but then he began to remove his own clothes, walked over to him, and the two embraced. The night went on with their sexual encounter lasting until they both fell asleep. In the morning, they started talking and learned it had been a first experience for both of them. The relationship went on for a few months after the tattoo was finished and then the young man disappeared. G asked around, but nobody had heard of him or knew where he lived. G didn't even know, as most of their encounters were in his room. He hadn't kept the friendship from Marie or the Big Guy, but he had kept the relationship from them. It really kind of messed with his head; he lost touch with his jogging and surfing and it was beginning to affect his job until one day he walked into the café and the world became better when he met Marta.

Manny grew up with Marta, since they were born. They attended grade school, high school, all the functions of the Catholic church required of them, and of course surfing. It was Marta who got Manny to surf. Her grandfather demanded she not ever go alone, and since Manny was already her friend, it was the perfect fit. Manny's family and hers lived on the same block and a lot them worked in the same business, down at the shipyards doing one job or another. Manny's father was an upholsterer, but his grandfather and Marta's uncle were long- time union iron workers who had worked together ever since they both made it back from Vietnam.

Manny's family had deep Mexican American roots, with a sprinkling of German as well. The German came from his grandmother's side, as her father was an escaped German prisoner of war from Fort Bliss in El Paso, Texas during the Second World War. As Manny tells it, the story was that his great-grandfather was captured by the Allied troops in Africa and he and other captured German soldiers were sent to prison camps in the U.S. When the war was coming to an end, pretty much no one really cared whether the prisoners escaped, as the only place they could go was Mexico. That is what his great-grandfather and other escapees did, and where he met his future bride.

He had gotten a job working the pecan fields of Chihuahua. She was a daughter of a wealthy farmer who was against their relationship, thus they eloped to Punta Chueca, off the coast of the Gulf of California, then crossed the border to San Diego, where they easily blended into the community; both were able to speak English and understand it fairly well. He eventually built war ships for America, and she taught English to other Mexicans.

They only had two children; one was Manny's mother and the other his aunt. Both of them married brothers who were also descendants of the Spaniards who occupied the area of California. One brother also worked in the shipyards, while Manny's father worked in the upholstery business. Manny learned both trades, but after high school he chose to follow his uncle and work in the shipyards. When he wasn't working, he was surfing with the others and was still single, although he dated.

Manny was what Marta called her "hermano guapo" or handsome brother—or when he would go out with her and her girlfriends to local clubs while she was attending college, an "hombre de las senoras" or ladies' man. Anytime he would go clubbing with her and her college girlfriends, he would always end up separating one of them from the crowd and disappearing for the rest of the night. Marta knew he was a safe bet for the girls, as even though he was a lover, he was also a gentleman.

Manny loved having a "big sister" like Marta, as he was the oldest of six children and had grown up helping his family when his father worked sometimes fifty to sixty hours a week, to help with the family income. Marta's grandfather said the family comes from "good blood," and her grandmother would always follow with, "And what makes up good blood, Papa?" "I don't know Mama," he would answer. "But I believe Marta knows." She did. "Mama, good blood is a good work ethic," Marta would say. Manny's family had that indeed.

Chuckie was born four years after Dale. According to him, he was an accident, as his parents were not planning on having more children once they realized Dale had some issues. Dale will tell you himself that he was a problem child even before he was born. "I kicked mom like a motherfucker!" he would say, much to others' amazement, and when asked why by Chuckie, he would say, "because it was too fucking dark and crowded in there!" He and Chuckie were like Abbott and Costello, or maybe Martin and Lewis, with their conversations in front of other people. Chuckie saw it as a way to keep people from laughing at Dale, and instead laugh with him. This started in grade school as their parents did everything they could to help Dale along, but seemed to get bad advice from one doctor after another.

They and Chuckie saw there really wasn't anything wrong with Dale other than he was different. Chuckie saw this one night while doing homework with Dale. Chuckie was having a hard time with a science project while the two were working at the kitchen table. Chuckie got upset with his assignment, tossed down his pencil, got up, and left the table. When he came back, he found his assignment was all completed. He asked Dale who finished his work and Dale told him he did it. Chuckie's first thought was to get upset, but when he looked into Dale's eyes, he reversed course and said thanks—and then explained why he shouldn't do that.

Chuckie and his parents realized Dale was brilliant and should be in school; his mother had been homeschooling him. Chuckie and Dale ended up being in the same class. From then on, the two were in separable. If Chuckie went out for a sport, Dale would end up being a team manager. In high school, Dale would end up going to the homecoming dance and prom with his brother and girls had no problem with this. Though very shy at times, Dale could also be very outgoing and sometimes over the top. Chuckie found a way to soothe that part of Dale—at the beach.

The water always calmed Dale, whether it was taking a bath or shower. It was hard to get him out before there would be no more hot water for anyone else. Chuckie got tired of it one day during their senior year and told Dale from now on he couldn't use the tub or shower until Chuckie had used it first. That is the way was from then on. But Chuckie also knew he couldn't have Dale use the shower every morning for hours on end to get him to be calm and focused through the rest of the day, so he started taking him to the beach before they went to school.

He got the idea remembering that when they were younger, Dale would always be more "normal" when their parents took them to the beach. Several trips down to the beach ended up becoming several trips learning how to surf, and when Dale got up on the board for the first time, Chuckie described it with the old adage, "it was like seeing a kid in a candy store!" Dale's whole body reacted jubilantly, so much so that he fell off while trying to jump up and down on the board while surfing in. Chuckie laughed, and Dale just got back on his board and went out by himself, without Chuckie. When Chuckie would get tired, Dale was still going. Dale was a master of study; he watched others and would tell Chuckie not to do this and not to do that because he saw another person do it and they wiped out really bad. Sure enough, Chuckie found Dale to be right about eighty percent of the time.

Chuckie and Dale graduated from high school in the top third of their class, with Dale getting a standing ovation from his fellow students. Chuckie went on to college, without Dale. Dale couldn't pass the college exam requirements to get in, as he had a hard time being in a large facility with thousands taking the exam at the same time, and the board would not make an exception. Chuckie stayed close by and attended San Diego State. It was there, while taking basic studies his freshman year, that he met Marta.

SUSURROS DE ESPERANZA

(Whispers of Hope)

Marta had dosed off while Dale Da Dude had his head resting on her stomach, playing music for the baby. She was awakened by a knock on her door. She and Dale sat up as Chuckie entered the doorway.

"Sorry to bother you two, but we are grilling up on the roof and Danny wants to know if you want fish or chicken?" he asked.

"Chicken, please, Chuck," Marta replied.

"Chicken or fish, Dale?"

"Chicken, but only the legs, Chuckie," Dale responded.

"Got it, bro, but why don't you come on up and make sure Danny gets it right." Chuckie winked at Marta.

"Okay, sorry Marta. I want to look after my chicken legs," Dale said.

Marta rubbed Dale Da Dude's head as he got off the bed and handed the earbuds back to her.

"It's okay, Dale, you always have to keep an eye on Danny when he's the one cooking." They all laughed.

"Okay, let's go Dale," Chuckie said.

"I'm coming, I'm coming," Dale said, and he and Chuckie left the room and headed up to the roof.

Marta eased herself off the bed, walked over to the bedroom door, and closed and locked it to keep visitors outside for now. She walked over to her mirrored dresser, removed her dress, and let it drop to the floor—revealing her naked, pregnant body. She bundled up her dreadlocks by placing a headband from the dresser around them, walked into the bathroom, turned on the water in the big open shower, and squatted on the toilet to pee. She flushed the toilet, and then said, "damn!" to herself. She forgot that in this house, flushing the toilet means a rush of hot water through the shower. So, she waited for the toilet to fill up and stop running before stepping into the shower.

Once in, she looked at her body in the mirror that was directly across from the shower. She stood with her back to the showerhead and watched the water run off her shoulders, down over her swollen breasts, and over her pregnant belly. The water ran off her belly like a waterfall and she placed a hand underneath to catch it while still looking at herself in the mirror. She loved being pregnant.

Marta already had great awareness of her body and sensuality, but even more so since becoming pregnant. She had always been told she was beautiful, ever since she was a child. She realized a lot of that time it was family members and close friends who said it. But when boys started mentioning it and then even other girls, her mindset changed, although she never let it get to her head. Her grandmother always said the cliché that, "beauty is in the eye of the beholder" and reminded her, "God gave you and all others their looks, but the beauty comes from what is extruded from within. Be humbled my child and have mercy on others who are not as fortunate." Marta took those words to heart; she was always aware of those who had much and those who had little.

She was drawn toward those who were misfits and did everything she could to make them feel comfortable and better about themselves. It was, of course, why she had the friends she had. She didn't judge them, and they didn't judge her. She was now a single mother-to-be and not one of the surfer dudes, or the Sanchez's, or even her family had said a negative word about it, including the fact that Cap wasn't around. She made it clear he had no idea of her condition; he had disappeared before she even knew herself. They all came to her aid in one way or another and they all said they owed her for helping each of them at one time or another.

Marta finished her shower, toweled herself off, and slipped on a comfortable sundress. Figuring it might be chilly on the roof deck, as the sun had already set, she decided to put on an old jean jacket as well. She started to go up the stairs, but out of the corner of her eye she saw someone sitting at the kitchen counter. It was Larson, with what looked like a couple cases of Pacifica beer. Marta reversed direction, went over to Larson, and sat down beside him.

"Hey, Larson boy! Whatcha ya doin' sittin' here all by your lonesome?" she said jokingly in a Southern drawl. Larson smiled, turned, wrapped an arm around her, and hugged her as she hugged him.

"Oh, just a thinkin' ma'am," he responded in the same accent, as they both had a chuckle.

"What is on your mind Larson?" she asked him.

Larson reached into the case of Pacifica beer, pulled out a bottle that was still cold, opened it, and gave it to Marta. Marta gave him a blank stare with her mouth wide open and leaned back to show off her very pregnant belly.

"Oh, shit! I forgot Marta. I just wanted you to taste it. You can have a taste, can't you?"

"Why do I need to taste Pacifica? I've had it many times in the past if and when I drink. You know it's my favorite."

"It's not Pacifica. I didn't have anything else to carry this in, so I went and bought two cases of Pacifica and threw them in the fridge, so I could put my beer in the cases and bring it here for you all to try out."

Marta sat up straight and placed her hands on her lower back to stretch, with a look of wonderment on her face.

"Your beer?" she questioned.

She then reached over and grabbed the bottle, slid it along the countertop, picked it up by its neck, spun it around, and saw there were no markings. She sat it back down on the counter and grabbed the bottle around its body. She picked it back up and took a couple sniffs from the top, like you would when opening a bottle of wine.

"It has an orange or citrus scent to it," she said.

"Yes, that is part of what I have in it," Larson said.

"I can't see the color, though, because of the dark bottle."

Larson got up quickly and went to the other side of the counter to the cabinets, opening a couple before finding a clear juice glass and placing it before Marta. She poured the beer it into the glass about halfway up and sat the bottle back onto the counter beside it.

"It has a nice light gold color and it's bubbly, sort of like Miller High Life," she said. "Well, Larson, I know one little taste isn't going to hurt the baby or me."

She put her index finger into the glass, stuck it in her mouth, and wrapped her lips around it. Larson stood up straight and shook his head.

"What?" Marta asked.

"Nothing, Marta. Just waiting for your response," he said with a smile, as leaned back onto the counter.

She then took the glass to her lips, slowly took a very small taste of the beer, and put down the glass on the counter. Now, Larson stood up straight and locked eyes with her, spreading his arms out wide, waiting for her response. There was silence for a moment, and then she spoke.

"That was damn good and tasty, Larson! If I wasn't pregnant, I would drink the whole glass! When in the hell did you have time to brew your own beer, what with work and business classes?"

Larson leaned back against the counter and crossed his arms.

"Well, I sort of quit school," he said.

"What the fuck, Larson! What do you mean by that?"

Just then, the side door opened and in walked Ricky on his prosthetic legs, along with a woman neither Larson nor Marta had met before.

"Ricky, my sweet!" Marta shouted.

Marta opened her arms to Ricky as he slowly and awkwardly walked over to her with a big grin on his face, and they hugged each other. The woman slowly closed the door behind her and followed Ricky over to Marta.

"Marta," said Ricky. "This is my wife, Ronelle."

Marta went to stand up, but when Ronelle saw she was pregnant, she said, "you just stay put."

Ronelle walked over to Marta and they hugged.

"I'm Marta."

"Ricky has told me all about you, but he obviously neglected to tell me about the condition you are in," Ronelle said, as the two women chuckled.

"Well, Ricky talks about you all the time, but he neglected to say how beautiful you are."

Ronelle was a tall stunning woman of mixed race, half African American and half Vietnamese. The story as Ricky told it was that Ronelle's father, of African descent, was serving in Vietnam and at the end of the war had an affair and fell in love with a Vietnamese woman. Her mother then discovered she was pregnant with Ronelle, but they could not come over to America at the time. It took her father nearly three years before he was able to bring his soon-to- be wife and daughter back to the States. Once here, her father and mother ran into a lot of racial issues and moved to Houston. They still had the same issues there, but not as many, because a lot of Vietnamese refugees were living there working as fishermen.

Ronelle and Ricky met in junior high and dated all through high school. After graduation, much to Ronelle's objections, Ricky joined the Army. Marta always teared up when she thought of Ricky and Ronelle's love for each other. She was starting to tear up again as she thought of their story now that she had finally met his wife. Marta wiped the tears from her eyes before anybody could see, except maybe Ricky. But he kept it to himself. As both ladies looked over to Ricky, who had joined Larson on the other side of the island, Ricky introduced him.

"Honey, this is Larson."

Larson reached across the counter and softly squeezed her hand.

"Nice to meet you, Mrs. . . . Damn, Ricky, I don't think I have ever known your last name."

"It's Willis," Ronelle said, as she smiled and thanked Larson for the gesture.

"We didn't mean to interrupt anything when we came in," Ricky said.

"Well, now that you mentioned it . . ."

Marta took the partially full glass of beer and slid it across the counter to Ricky, who reached out to stop it.

"Taste that, Ricky, and tell Larson what you think."

Ricky looked a bit stunned, but slowly picked up the glass to drink. As he did, Marta shouted, "Drink it all, Ricky!" and he did.

He sat the glass back on the counter and didn't say anything. Marta and Larson looked at him and Ricky responded with, "What?"

"Well, what do you think of the beer?" Marta asked.

"It's Pacifica. I love Pacifica! It's a great tasting beer and it really tasted better than usual. Why is that?" asked Ricky.

"That's because it's not Pacifica," Marta said. "That's just the case Larson used to bring over his own home brew."

"No shit! Really, dude? Ronelle, honey, you gotta have a sip of this."

Marta grabbed the now-empty glass, took the open bottle, poured the rest of the beer into the glass, and handed it to Ronelle. She, like Marta, sniffed the aroma and then took a sip. They were all looking at her when she set down the glass, licked her lips, hesitated a bit, and then said, "That's very good."

"Dude, you have a winner! My wife doesn't drink beer and if she likes, it that's a good sign," Ricky said.

Ricky offered up a fist to Larson, who bumped it with his.

"So, Larson was about to explain to me when he had the time to do this with his school and studying and all when you guys arrived. So, Larson you got some splainin' to do." Marta said this

223

in a Spanish accent, jokingly trying to sound like Desi Arnaz in *I Love Lucy* whenever Lucy did something she was not supposed to be doing.

Larson sees that everyone's eyes are on him.

"Well, in one of my business classes, we were supposed to set up a business plan for a fictitious business and I chose microbrewing because of how popular it is around here. While researching and setting up the plan, I started to get interested in trying it myself. So, I bought a little kit and started experimenting. I was cooking up a small batch when my dad caught a whiff of it and knocked on my door. I told him what I was doing and instead of lecturing me like he usually does, he said it smelled like I had something good going, so he started to help me. Before we knew it, we were working together for the first time since he taught me how to throw a baseball. So, every night when he got home from work and I got back from school, we worked on the brew."

"What about the deal he made with you about San Diego State?" Marta said.

"Well, that changed just a bit. I proposed that if I made the Dean's List at Mira Costa, he would back me on the home brewing instead of me going back to San Diego State. Then I asked if he would be my partner, and he said yes, he would one hundred percent. So, I pulled out my semester grades and showed him my near-perfect grade point average. I don't know if he thought in the back of his mind I would be able to do it. But when he read the congratulations on making the Dean's List at the top of the page, I swear I saw a tear run down his cheek."

The girls went "ahh" and Ricky gave Larson another fist bump.

"He gave me a big hug and said, 'Congratulations, partner!'"

They all had a good laugh about that. Just as he finished, Dale Da Dude came down the stairs calling for Marta.

"Marta! Marta! Danny is not cooking the legs right for me."

"Okay, Dale my dear, we are on our way. We better get up there before things get out of hand, as we all know how Danny can get a little impatient."

"Ricky, can you grab the other case and bring it up?" Larson asked, while grabbing one case himself.

Then Larson realized he forgot that Ricky may not be able to that with his prosthetic legs, but Ricky responded immediately.

"You got it, pal!" he said.

Ricky reached over to grab the other case and followed Larson up the stairs, who was right behind Marta. Ronelle followed her husband up the stairs, close behind him. She had one hand slightly touching the small of his back as if to help his balance. But Ricky had the routine of climbing the stairs down, as if he really never had an issue and he had his real legs.

Marta and the others entered the roof deck to what seemed to be a disagreement between Danny and Ron. Danny was over by the grill keeping an eye on the chicken with Dale Da Dude nearby making sure Danny would not overcook it. Larson and Ricky set the brew on the outside bar. G immediately walked over, set his empty bottle next to one of the beer cases, reached in, grabbed a bottle, twisted off the top, and had a swig. Ricky and Larson looked at each other and smiled. Neither said a word.

Marta walked over to Dale and Danny. She placed her hand on Danny's back as a hint to calm down, as she could tell he was a bit perturbed. Ron seemed to have the floor. As soon as he mentioned Bernie, Marta got the gist as to why there was an argument. Ricky grabbed two more beers. He and Ronelle sat in the lounge chairs by the gas firepit where Ron was sitting. G was leaning with his back against the deck railing. Larson grabbed a beer and walked over next to G; they bumped fists to say hi while everyone was listening to Ron.

Ron went on about how Bernie Sanders was the best choice for the country. He stated his case on why Democratic Socialism is different than National Socialism and how that wasn't why he lost the Democratic nomination.

"I'm not going to pay for others' college education with my tax dollars!" Danny remarked.

"You wouldn't be the one paying for it, because big banks, Wall Street, and the upper one percent of earners would pay for it with their capital gains," Ron explained.

"How would Bernie be able to get a Republican-run Congress to even sign off on any such deal?" Danny asked.

"The makeup of Congress would change because of the malfunction of the current Congress, which has not done anything for the past eight years. The people are fed up," Ron responded.

Danny agreed with him on that point, but still disagreed that the "old man," as he called Bernie, would live long enough in office. Ron was getting frustrated with Danny; he stood up, walked over to the bar, and put down his empty beer before pulling another out of one of Larson's cases. He twisted off the cap, flipped it up in the air like one would do with a coin, then caught it and tossed it inside the case of beer. He walked over to the barbecue and gazed into the grill to look at the chicken in front of Danny as if to antagonize him.

"Tell me something, Ricky. How do you feel about the treatment of veterans?" Ron asked.

"Ron, let's not involve anyone else in this conversation," G pleaded.

"It's okay, G; I'd love to address that," Ricky responded. "I follow the news and I also follow the military. If you don't mind, I'd rather defer this over to my wife, Ronelle, as she speaks for both of us. She of all people is well versed on this subject."

"So, you're the mystery woman this guy is always talking about," G said as he walked over to Ronelle and shook her hand. "I'm G, this is Chuckie, and that's his brother Dale over by the grill next to Marta. I assume you already met Marta and Larson. The two outspoken members of our dysfunctional family are Danny, next to Marta, and my partner in crime, Ron." G moved back next to Chuckie and Larson, leaning against the deck railing.

"Nice to meet you all. Ricky has told me much about all of you as well," Ronelle responded, straightening her posture to the edge of the chair she was sitting on. "I want to make it clear that the treatment of veterans has been substandard for many years. This is the result of a combination of lack of funding, improper procedures along with mismanagement, and the lack of experience or knowledge of medical personnel."

Ronelle paused and looked at Ricky, who smiled back, and she went on.

"This has been the failure of both parties throughout the years. However, the continued development of technology that seems to discover and find solutions at the speed of light these days, could not only assist our current returning soldiers from war, but also our older veterans. Possibly even civilians, as well. But instead of increasing funding for our veterans, they decrease it and increase funding for our military."

Ronelle took a deep breath and looked around to see all eyes were on her, with the exception of Danny, who was tending to the grill, and Dale, who was watching him.

"This cut in funding also cuts money going toward more medical research, a lot of which is done right here in San Diego at the naval hospital. This research includes trying to find the best treatment for PTSD, and also post-medical procedures for the physically traumatized such as my man." She placed a hand on his thigh and he reached down to grab her hand.

"And all of this is because of a Republican run, 'do-nothing' Congress that seems to think fighting a war or wars is much more important than solving them," interrupted Danny. "Dale, grab the tray. The chicken is ready."

Dale grabbed it and Danny continued to speak while picking up chicken from the grill piece by piece and placing it on the tray.

"Why do we need to spend more money on what is already the best military in the world and cut back on issues like this? I know your argument and I do not disagree with you." Danny finished placing the chicken on the tray. "Dale, go ahead and set it on the table."

Marta helped Dale carry the tray. "Everyone, come, dinner is being served," Danny said. "Help yourselves."

Everyone got up from where they were sitting or standing and lined up by the bar. Marta was first, grabbing a plate for Dale and placing food on it. She went to grab a piece of chicken when Dale stopped her.

"Only legs, Marta. I'm a legs man!" he said with a smile.

Marta returned the piece of chicken she had chosen, grabbed a couple legs, and placed them on Dale's plate. Dale then went over to sit on one of the patio chairs surrounding the firepit.

Marta finished filling her plate, and one by one, the others did as well. Soon, they were all sitting or standing around the pit, eating. Ronelle and Ricky bowed their heads in a silent prayer before starting to dig in as well.

"Let me continue where I left off, if no one objects," Danny bellows to no objections. There was silence, with everyone looking up from their plates and at each other. "I've recently become a tired man. I used to have good points to argue with most of you through the years, as it was no secret I was a conservative. What I respected from you all and still do is that you," he motioned with his hand in a circle, pointing at everyone, "you all respected my view, as it was my opinion, and I respected yours as well. Have we argued through the years? Yes, but they were what I'd like to call, healthy arguments. We got into heated discussions, but there wasn't any of the name-calling and even physical confrontations we all have been experiencing and seeing on TV during this current campaign season."

"That's for sure!" responded Chuckie. Dale, as usual, replied, "What Chuck said."

The gang all smiled and laughed with Dale Da Dude. And Danny continued.

"We, as a country, have been making tremendous strides in stopping and preventing bullying, to the point where if we so as much see it on social media, we share it or report it or both so the bullies caught and made aware of their wrongdoing. We do that with anything we see that isn't right. Yet, we allow a man with a lot of money and fame to just break all those rules on TV and we see people getting spit on and slammed to the ground!"

Danny's voice starts to rise, and the others are watching; most have put their eating on hold. Danny looks at everyone and sees he has their attention.

"We let him speak to women and men who are standing next to him or across from him and belittle them without any respect. Then when confronted by the press, he says nothing was meant by it, but yet the damage was done. Verbal abuse is just as bad as physical abuse, if not worse. A bruise can heal, but words may scar forever!"

"Wow, so true!" Ronelle responds, eliciting nods from some of the others.

Danny's eyes connected with hers and he went on.

"Well, I'm here to say that I'm not going to be a part of a party that does nothing about that. I will no longer be a part of the Republican Party that does nothing, and I mean nothing, as it has the past seven years under this president who is about to leave office. I don't always agree with him, but he is our president, elected twice! Twice! By most of you and the majority of America!"

Out of the blue, Manny spoke, as he had walked out on the deck during Danny's speech, unnoticed. "Let me guess, Danny. The party of Clinton? I mean you were an anomaly, as it was, being a Republican. You ae everything the establishment is against—a gay man, a minority, and an unemployed attorney."

"Manny!" Dale Da Dude shouted, reached toward him, and fist bumped.

"Hey, Dale!" Manny responded.

The others all said hey to Manny as well. Marta got up and made her way over to him.

"Come with me, Manny. Let's get you something to eat." Marta led Manny over to the bar as Danny continued to speak.

"Well, now that you have mentioned it, I haven't decided as of yet between Clinton or Johnson. That's why I was questioning Ron. I'm trying to get a feel of which way to go."

"Honey, would you mind getting me another one of Larson's beers for me?" Ricky asked Ronelle, who got up and moved over to the bar.

"Larson's beer?" Danny questioned, looking over to Ricky.

Ricky looked at Larson, as did everyone else. When Larson does not respond right away, Marta speaks for him. She and Ronelle each pick out a bottle of beer from the case on the bar and then present them like two show models.

"Gentlemen, the beer you have been consuming was home brewed by our very own Larson!" Marta then opens her bottle and gives it to Manny.

"Anyone else want a bottle?" Ronelle asks.

Ron and Chuck ask for one, so she grabbed two more bottles and made her way back to her chair, handing them off before giving one to her husband.

"Damn, Larson! I had no idea!" Danny responded.

The others all agree. Larson responds, very humbled by his friend's compliments.

"Thanks, guys! I really do appreciate it. Hey, Danny, good chicken and the speech as well. And by the way, Bernie is the way to go!"

"Cheers!" Chuckie said, along with all the others except Danny, who notices Marta not responding, either. She is just standing by the bar between Manny and Dale. She catches Danny's eye and smiles. Then Danny speaks up.

"Marta, I don't believe I know how you feel about all of this. I don't ever remember you ever saying anything about this topic."

Marta's smile disappears as she faces the thought of having to address a subject she has always avoided. Larson chimes in.

"Come to think of it, Marta, I've never heard you express your feelings on politics, either."

Marta, not usually a person who lacked words, was now silent. As she looked around at her friends, who were dearer to her than anyone else she had known in her life, she thought about how she always avoided conflict. Manny sensed her uneasiness and spoke.

"She has the right to not have to express her views."

"I understand that, Manny, but I also have the right to ask," Danny responded.

Manny began to speak when Marta placed a hand on his forearm. He stopped and gave her space as she stepped forward to speak.

Marta looks over the group of friends and catches every one of them, eye to eye. They all respond with a smile, and she smiles back.

"I have always avoided this situation, but I knew at some point I would be in this position to have to respond. I do not know of a better time than now to do so as you," she opens her hands out toward the group, "are the closest to me in my life other than my own family, however, you are my family as well. Like a family, I have always looked out for you and sometimes, if not most of the time, that means not getting involved with some of the stuff that's going around in the world today. The main reason for this is that a lot of it is upsetting to me and I see how upsetting it is to you as well."

Marta moves over to sit down on a patio chair and continues.

"Many times, I have thought about how I miss our regular daily surfing, not so much for me," as she rubs her tummy and chuckles some, as do most of the others, "but for you all as well, as we were a lot calmer group of individuals. I mean that sincerely. None of us really had any responsibilities other than waking up each day and enjoying God's gift of nature and then going our own way to tackle the day's events, whether it was continuing with school," she points to Larson, "buying or selling homes," she points to Ron, "volunteering for community events and being an advocate of fairness to our community," she grabs Danny's hand, "or working hard to overcome barriers presented to you outside of your control," she acknowledges Ricky. "And I do mean barriers and not disabilities, as I truly believe no one has a disability, but they are just different—different in the sense of the color of your skin or your ethnicity or the type of job you have or your upbringing—different as the individual you are meant to be in God's eyes."

She looks over to Dale, as she pauses, and Dale looks at her with a big smile that puts the largest smile yet on her face this evening. As she continues to look at Dale, the others see that and listen more intently.

"Let me reiterate that we are a group of individuals. We are each unique and special. Those you may think are the brightest in the room or those you may think have the most disability may actually be totally opposite of who you're thinking about right now."

The others sit back, in awe of what Marta is saying.

"What I do not support is why we are together. It is what I do not support in life. I do not support hate, I do not support unequal fairness and by that, I mean where some are given advantages while others are discriminated against. That relates to a lot of subjects. I do not support the ambitions of some to use others and then not recognize their efforts. I most definitely do not support anyone making my healthcare choices for me. I certainly would not go into G's place of business and try to stop all tattoos or body piercings. There are warning labels on everything and thus it should be up to the individual to make such choices. It's their right. I support all humanitarian efforts of any kind. What may work for one situation may not work for another, but the important thing is that an effort is being made and not being stalled or ignored. Though I feel it is important for a person to stand out as individual, it is equally important that individuals do not stand out as being selfish, motivated for self-gain, not equalization. That, my friends—and I do not use the phrase, 'my friends' loosely in regard to this group,"—she reiterates, "That, my friends, is why I choose to be around you. Whether you realize it or not, it is also why you choose to be around me, why we choose to be around each other, and why I choose to love you all." Marta sat back into the chair and put both hands on her stomach as she felt the baby kick. "Oh my, that was a big kick there, girl!"

There was a brief silence as the group realized the power of Marta's words.

"Love you, Marta!" Dale Da Dude shouted.

"Love you too, Dale!" Marta responded with a smile.

Danny arose from his chair and moved over next to Dale, put his arm across Dale's shoulders and brought him close.

"I also love you, Dale, and I love you as well, Marta!" Danny said.

"I love you too, Danny," Dale said.

G stood up, raised his beer, and said, "To all of us loving each other!"

The others all said, "Cheers!" or "Here! Here!"

"Now I know why Ricky can't wait to see you each day," Ronelle said. "It sort of makes me jealous a bit, but I understand. He says there are things he can share with you that he can't share with me." She smiled to Marta and mouthed the words, "thank you."

Marta tilted her head to the side, smiled back at her, and gave Ricky a wink. Ricky placed his arm around Ronelle's shoulder, brought her toward him, and kissed her lips with so much passion that the guys all start giving them shit like, "Get a room!" and "Please take it to the back seat!" All the while, Ricky waved his middle, fuck you finger, around the circle at them while still kissing Ronelle.

Then fireworks begin to appear in the night sky behind them to the southeast from Sea World, a part of its nightly summer/fall ritual. They all got situated where they could see them and sat mesmerized for the next twenty minutes. When the fireworks ended, the group started to mingle while finishing up eating and drinking. They all helped in the cleanup and started making their way inside to the kitchen. They lingered there for a while, still chatting away. Then it was decided they would all head up the boardwalk to their favorite hangout to sing karaoke and dance; it was sort of a biweekly tradition.

The boardwalk at night, anytime of the week, is an event in and of itself. You never know what you are going to get between the tourists, college students, and locals. Among the latter, you have to include the regulars, consisting of street vendors as well as the homeless. Many of the homes along the boardwalk and several homes deep on both sides of the stretch of Mission Beach are second homes of many San Diegans. They rent them out as vacation rentals to those traveling from afar who wish to enjoy this warm destination and its many treasures. At night, across the city, the streets bring out many colorful people, and unfortunately, its darkest side as well—the sadness of the city.

As the group walked out of their own rental home, they immediately encountered their neighbor know as Mary Magdalene. Though her first name was Mary, Magdalene was added somewhere along the way on her path to homelessness. It was said she received the name because of her angelic-like presence and attitude, even though she lived in alleys and backyard patios along Mission Beach Boulevard throughout the years. Mary was of Asian descent. Her age was tough to determine by her appearance, as her hair was a dirty gray, but her face, though darkly tanned from the daily sun she took in, didn't reflect an elderly woman. The group had figured she was in her mid to late forties. Mary always smiled when she was greeted by anyone and her teeth were surprising brilliant white and healthy looking—providing a great contrast with the darkness of her skin. Mary always had a writing pad with her and a pen in hand. When she was not walking around the area, as she could be spotted anywhere within a five-mile radius of Crystal Pier. She could be found lying down on a lawn in the Mission Park area or on the sand, propped up against any stretch of the seawall along the beaches, writing away.

Mary most definitely was an alcoholic; when anyone in the group encountered her, she usually had the distinct odor of alcohol on her. Chuckie had said she also used it on her clothes. He and Dale had seen her sprinkle a bottle of Scotch over her clothes like bathwater. She, like Marta, had a good understanding of Dale Da Dude. Whenever she was around the house, when Dale and Chuckie were there, she and Dale would talk for hours. This night, she was quiet, most likely because of the long day of walking and talking to whichever imaginary person was speaking to her in her mind. Years of alcohol and drug abuse, along with poor physical health, trigger mental health problems in most of the homeless.

As the group came out from the side entrance of the house, one by one they acknowledged Mary, then G spoke. "I'll be right back!"

He ran back to the house, unlocked the door, went inside, and up the stairs to the kitchen. He quickly pulled a plastic container from a cabinet, opened the fridge and placed a number of the evening's leftovers in it, closed the container, and then headed back down and out the door, locking it and walking over to Mary, where she was chatting with the others.

"Mary, have you eaten today?" G asked.

Mary face was blank as G handed her the container. As she raised it to her nose, she smiled, showing her big, bright teeth.

"Thank you," she said to G and then again to each of the others as they walked by her. Ricky said goodbye and Dale Da Dude broke in and said, "Mary says never say goodbye! That's permanent! Say, see you later!"

Mary smiled at Dale, who walked up and gave her a hug.

"See you later, Mary!" Dale said.

The whole group smiled.

"You are absolutely correct, Dale!" Chuckie said. "See you later, Mary."

The others followed suit and then they all turned and began to walk down the boardwalk. Mary turned toward the beach,

walked through an opening in the seawall, and onto the beach—
facing the water. She set down all her things along the wall,
got herself comfortable in the sand, and leaned against the wall
before removing the container's lid, raising it to her nose again,
and smiling.

As the group made their way down the boardwalk, they
walked in step with Ricky, as his stride, with his prosthetics, was
not as quick as the others'. While walking toward their destination, they chatted among each other and observed the many lives
of the night along the shores of San Diego's two most eventful
beaches. The lights of the boardwalk lit up the front of the beach
homes, then faded away closer to the shoreline, where you could
only make out the whitecaps of the waves in what little light was
left. As they begin to cross in front of the businesses, the lights
of each restaurant, hotel, and shop brightened up the area with
a rainbow of colors that somehow created a living piece of art,
an eclectic array to delight the eyes. The deeper they walked into
the business section, the bigger the crowd got—mostly people,
a mix of college students and others who, like the group, were
millennials in their twenties and thirties.

Bicyclists, skateboarders, and rollerbladers still made their
way along the boardwalk, as much as they did during the day.
There were the dog owners walking with their pets; the "parrot
man" with his birds doing tricks and taking photos with tourists;
the various shops offering t-shirts and souvenirs; and the lifeguards, closing up shop for the day and posing for pictures with
tourists. Then there were the various homeless who shared the
space with the tourists and local residents. They were a mi of men
and women, varying in age from early twenties to their sixties.
The younger ones were more than likely addicted to some sort of

substance. The older were more than likely to have mental health issue like schizophrenia or PTSD. Most of the homeless were ex-military, like Cap, veterans of all the different wars America had been involved in throughout the years.

Some homeless hung out with their personal belongings all in one shopping cart, kept close as they talked to others. Some were on bicycles that they used to get around while their belongings were in a shelter or kept hidden in one of the various canyons throughout San Diego. They all did something to try and survive on the streets—from standing at an intersection with a cardboard sign, pleading for any penny drivers could give them to doing the same, but selling newspapers or washing car windows before the light turns green. Some helped out local vendors and businesses by sweeping up floors in exchange for food or drink, and even liquor, depending on the type of business.

Then there were those like the homeless couple, Nels and Vicky, Gulf War veterans who served together and are very physically fit. They lay out a blanket on a small stretch of grass along the boardwalk near the Crystal Pier and do balancing acts and various types of gymnastic moves within its small area. They amaze many observers and earn tips as people pitch coins and dollar bills onto their blanket as they perform.

There was also Donna Lee, all set up on a bench along the seawall with her makeshift easel and stacks of printing paper she wrestles up from garbage cans. She uses the backs to draw pencil sketches of the local area and all its people, even tourists, who often ask her to draw one of them. Many take advantage of her and give her only pennies after she completes their drawing.

This is the Community of Marta—the good mixed in with the bad, the survivors with the hopeful, the needy with the privileged. Marta and her band of sisters and brothers saw this every day, as they share the space with all of them. There is kindness in all walks of life, as well as the flip side—the very wealthy who try to assist those in need as well as those of wealth who would spit on them and blame them for all the problems of the world. Then there's a story of legend, of a homeless vet who happened upon a house fire in one of the many beach homes. He helped save the family that was asleep, only to be accused of being the one to set the home ablaze. He was jailed until a group of locals who heard the story paid for an attorney who got him set free, proved him innocent, and found him help—only to see him back on the streets months later because of the demons he still could not fight off. All of this, every day, Marta and the crew saw and experienced. Every day, Marta wondered about Cap, whether he was in the same situation somewhere.

The group finally arrived at the Lahaina, a real "hole in the wall" type bar that has not changed in over thirty years, while everything around it has been modernized. The large open deck is out front and the main building has windows all around it to allow the sea breeze to come through, helping cool down the large crowds it attracted every evening. They came not only for the tastiness of the food, but also for the entertainment, from bands to comedians and on this night, karaoke, part of the group's biweekly ritual that allowed them to relax, sing, and forget everything else going on in their lives and around them.

As they walked in, some of the other regulars noticed them and immediately started a chant for Marta to sing.

"Marta! Marta! Marta!" the crowd shouted, and her crew joined in as they clapped their hands.

The emcee for the night announced over the microphone, "Marta is in the house! Get that angelic voice of yours up here on stage!"

Marta humbly smiled. The others grabbed a couple tables and sat as Marta lumbered up to the stage with a little help from the emcee. He placed a chair behind her so she could sit and look at the computer monitor in front of her that listed of songs she could pick. After a brief time, she said, "Hmm, here is one that is different, and I think you might enjoy."

She pointed to which song she wanted to sing, the emcee clicked on it and handed Marta the microphone, and shortly thereafter the music began to play. As Marta began to sing, the crowd was silenced. Even the wait staff, bartender, hostess, and kitchen seemed to quiet for her—it is as if the entire world has stopped to listen.

Making her way down the sidewalk to the bar is Angie, in a rush, as she is late to join the group. As she turns to walk in, she notices a Marine in his dress blue uniform with his hat and gloves under his armpit, standing just outside the entrance, halfway between one of the pillars between the open windows of the bar. She stops, looks harder as she seems to recognize him, moves closer, and notices it is Cap. She reaches out to grab his arm to turn him toward her. As she does, she begins to speak his name, but he quickly places two fingers from his free hand over her mouth to quickly silence her.

"Shhhhhhh," he said.

"Cap, you must come in with me and see the others and Marta!" she exclaimed.

Cap grabbed her by the arm and walked her toward the edge of the curb.

"I can't Angie, not right now!" he said.

"Why?" she asked as she looked at him from head to toe. "Did you re-enlist?"

"No, I was asked to speak at a military funeral earlier today of a Marine I served with. Angie, I cannot see Marta or the others right now. It's not part of the plan yet!" Cap explained as he turned to glance one more time into the club to get a look at Marta.

"Angie, you must promise me not to mention you saw me! Promise me!" he demanded of her.

"Sure, Cap, I promise," she hesitantly responded.

He took in a deep breath, reached over and kissed Angie on the cheek, and walked into the street and away from Angie and the club.

"But you must see Marta, Cap!" Angie said, her words softly fading as she says them, knowing Cap will not hear them.

She watched him disappear into the crowd, then turned to enter the bar and made her way over to the rest of group. They all hugged her and kissed her on the cheek as she sat and made eye contact with Marta. They smiled at one another, just as Marta wrapped up singing the song. Marta got a round of applause, thanked the crowd, and then Dale Da Dude shouted for her to sing another song. Marta smiled at Dale.

"I have a song just for my friends, buddies, and pals out there, and you as well, Dale." She scanned the monitor in front of her. "Ah, here it is. It may be corny, but it's appropriate."

The emcee pressed the button on song list and the music began to play, "You've Got a Friend in Me." She continued to sing, and the others wrapped their arms around each other's waists or shoulders as they were sitting around the table. Marta finished the song, got up from the chair, and was helped over to the table as the house applauds her. Then other patrons as well as some of the others in the group took turns singing as the night goes on.

Cap continued walking down the boardwalk away from the bar and through the crowd until he found himself in front of the Crystal Pier. People dodged him as he stopped in the middle of the walkway. Cap turned, moved to the stairs leading to the beach, and made his way down. As his feet hit the sand, he looked down at them. He saw that his military-issue shoes that were all slick and shiny with black polish were now partially covered in the sand. The feeling kicked in a memory of his days oversees in Iraq and Afghanistan, standing on desert sand.

The sound of the crashing waves hitting the pylons of the pier brought his mind back to the present. He began to look around as if searching for something, then walked to one of the many trash barrels lining the beach and reached inside, moving his hand through the barrel until he found what he wanted—a glass beer bottle. He held its neck and slammed it against the inside of the barrel, low enough inside it to make sure no pieces of the bottle, as it broke, dropped into the sand. He then walked out under the pier and sat down his hat and gloves in the sand. He began to remove his dress jacket, doing so without removing the bottle from his hands, and laid it down in the sand as well. He then turned and walked toward the shore and into the water with his boots and the rest of his clothes on. He continued to walk until he came across the first horizontal wooden cross brace between the pier pylons that run parallel with the beach.

He was about knee deep in the water, with waves coming in and hitting him at different heights, as he stood there looking out through the many pier pylons out into the Pacific, balancing himself after each wave hit. He could see the lights of the big ships and even the running lights of small boats. The glittering of the light shining down on the water along the sides of the pier, which reflects the pier lights above, was enough for him to be able to see. He leaned forward and placed both his hands along the horizontal cross brace. He bowed his head down toward the water, deep in thought and prayer, and began to rock himself back and forth in the water as one wave after another hit him, but he did not let them knock him down.

He lifted his head to the sky, only to see the underbelly of the pier, which included all the wiring and plumbing from the cottages built above it. He then returned his attention and focus on the cross brace in front of him. He took the broken bottle and proceeded to carve into the wood. As he carved with one hand, he balanced himself by wrapping his other arm around the cross brace to keep from falling after each wave hit him. He carved and carved into the wood to make sure what he is creating will be seen.

As he completed the task he set out to do, he stepped away from the cross board to look at it and as he did, he was hit by a wave that set him backward on his butt and completely covered him with water. He disappeared under the surf, but then recovered his balance, came to his feet, turned, and walked back to the shore to retrieve his hat, gloves, and jacket. He was drenched from head to foot. He picked up his things on his way back to the trash barrel, and as he does, he stops and looks toward the wall where the sand meets the end of the pier—where he once lived in a cardboard shack for nearly two years. He walks over to it, places his hand against it, and bows his head as a way of giving some sort of thanks for the time he spent there.

After a good minute or two, Cap walked slowly away toward the stairs, tossing the broken bottle into the barrel and slowly hiking up the stairs to the boardwalk. Water dripped from in his Marine dress uniform, his jacket was draped over his arm, and he held his hat and gloves in one hand, with the other on the railing, dragging himself slowly up each step. As he reached the top, he got a few stares. An elderly man and his wife came up to him and asked, "Are you okay, solider?" as the man put his hand on Cap's shoulder.

Cap looked at him as he placed his hat on his head and nodded.

"Yes, sir. I am! Yes, I am!" He smiled at the couple and walked away from them and the crowd, into the night, on to Mission Boulevard.

In the background, he can hear someone from the Lahaina singing "Sooner or Later" by The Grass Roots.

THE WORLD OF CAPRI

November roared throughout the country and around the world. There were protests in Europe and Brazil over economics and free trade; Australia and Ireland protested over fracking and oil pipelines; South Korea and Venezuela over elections; and Polish citizens were protesting for the right to protest. Then there was the U.S., which was involved in all these protests on its own soil, plus the topics of war and climate change that it shared with the rest of the world. December did not calm down much for those who supposedly represented "we the people." A quarter of the country still argued with a quarter of the country over the election, while a lot of people did not seem to care, with nearly half of them not even voting. There were mixed feelings—somber and ecstatic among those who did vote. Those who voted for the losers were stunned and ashamed of their fellow countrymen and women who voted the other way, and those who voted for the winner soon regretted it, as they realized promises were not going to be kept and never were intended to be carried through. But yet, for the most part, people moved forward, especially those who lived in California, as for the most part, California was doing better than the rest of the country. It was also doing better than a lot of foreign countries, including Europe . . . and so it was as well in the Community of Marta.

Marta had a large beach blanket spread out on the sand, set up like a picnic for her and her child. She sat back in her beach chair, under the attached umbrella, which was open to protect her and her child from the sun. She hunched forward as her child faced her and they rolled a small ball back and forth. Every now and then, Marta would look over to the water and watch the surfers, then go back to enjoying the time with her young child as they played with the ball or dug holes in the sand. Then one time she looked up and saw a man step out of the surf, with his board under his arm. It seemed to her that he was heading toward them. She could not make out his appearance, as the sun was behind him and all she saw was his figure. She glanced down at her child and then back up again; he was only a few strides away when he stopped and stuck his board in the sand. She still couldn't make out who he was as she watched him come over and kneel down in front of her and her child.

"And how old may this young beachcomber be?" he asked.

Marta now could only see his profile, but the voice was familiar and when he turned to look at Marta she gasped . . .

Marta awoke straight-up in bed and braced her arms behind her to prop herself up. She then scooted herself backward up against the headboard and once there, she placed both hands on on her belly and spoke to her unborn child.

"That was one hell of a kick there, baby girl! But thank you from waking me up from that dream."

Marta leaned over to the nightstand to grab a bottle of water, as her mouth was parched. When she picked it up, she found it was empty. "Damn it! All I do is drink and pee!" she said to herself. She slowly worked herself to the side of the bed, pushed herself off, and headed over to the bathroom.

When she was done, she looked at herself in the mirror. She reached up to her head and ran her hands through her hair, which was now without dreads. She still wore it long, just below her shoulders, and was trying to find a new look, but for now it was just long and straight. As it got closer and closer for her to deliver, she decided it was time for a change. She had removed all the trinkets she had collected over the years and laid out across her dresser. For now, she wrapped her hair in a bun and either used a band or hairpin to keep it up during the day, and then let it down at night. It had shocked everyone when they first saw her, but the consensus was that she was now twice as beautiful.

She turned off the bathroom light and made her way to the door of the bedroom. When she opened it, she thought she heard a noise coming from around the kitchen wall. She stood there and listened for a moment and sure enough she heard it again. It sounded to her like a moan. When she heard it again, she slowly and quietly moved her way down the open hallway to the wall that separated the kitchen from her bedroom. It was dark throughout with the exception of the evening moonlight shining through the glass window design that surrounded the exterior walls. It wasn't a full moon, but there was enough light to help someone navigate through the house if necessary to without turning on the lights. Marta thought maybe it was a burglar or even a homeless person who sought shelter. Yet it could very well be one of her housemates, just drunk and passed out on the couch. She wanted to make sure, before reacting herself, not doing anything to provoke whoever it may be and possibly put herself in danger.

When she peered around the corner, she could hear the moan more clearly and realized it was more the sound of pleasure than it was of hurt or agony. She then could make out the silhouette of two figures out beyond the kitchen into the open living room. They both had their backs to her. As she continued to slowly move out from behind the wall, she ducked down some and moved over to behind the kitchen island, peeking above the counter. She saw one person was plainly sitting on the couch and the other was somewhat sitting on top, between their legs, using their hands to balance on the other person's thighs. When she saw the top person slowly moving up and down on the other, she realized it was a couple having sex.

She wondered which of her housemates it could be. She said goodnight to G and Ron earlier and thought Danny had gone to bed long before that. She knew he had to work the weekend, with the Chargers having a game on Sunday. He was now working in public relations for the team, since the stadium deal for them to stay in San Diego was voted down. Plus, Danny didn't have a significant other, that she knew of, so who could these two be?

She continued to watch, trying to squint to see if she could make out at least one of the figures. Maybe it's Manny, she thought, and a girl he picked up at the bar after they were done with karaoke. It could even be Larson, as he had keys to the house, too. Yes, she thought, it had to be one of them. She smiled and decided to spy for a little bit longer. She couldn't very well get a water right now without them hearing her, so she watched and listened as the person on top moaned each time they would sit back down on Manny or Larson, whichever one it was. But, when the voice of the person on the couch spoke, "Oh that feels damn good!" she knew it wasn't either one of them.

She knew their voices, but didn't know who they were. Now she was thrown for a loop, wondering who these two strangers could be. There was no man in the house who belonged to that voice and Marta was the only woman. Angie had stayed a few times in the past, but she would stay with her in her bed and comfort her through the pregnancy. Maybe that is who it is, she thought. Maybe Angie ended up coming back here because she could not stay at her place. But the figure Marta could make out on top was too short to be Angie, and then the person on top spoke.

"You like how that feels, do you?"

"Yes lover! It feels awesome!" responded the other person.

Marta put her hand to her mouth, closed her eyes, lowered herself, and sat against the island cabinets. Then she heard the response that confirmed she knew it was.

"It feels good to me as well."

Then there was another moan and Marta just squinted her face as she knew that voice belonged to Danny.

Marta started to crawl back to her bedroom without the bottled water. She made it around the corner of the back wall when she got a real bad cramp in her calve. She turned and sat on her ass, trying to massage it while trying not let out a peep—and then the baby kicked, and it was a good one.

Marta let out an "Oh boy!"

She knew Danny and his friend had to have heard that. Then she felt a popping sensation. It felt like a whoosh and then a large gush of fluid spilled out onto the floor.

"Oh my God!" Marta shouted.

Just as she did, Danny came around the corner and flipped on the hall light. He was dressed in just a pair of boxers. He saw Marta down on the floor sitting in a pool of fluid.

"Oh my God, Marta! What happened? Are you okay?" he shouted

Danny gingerly stepped around the fluid and over to behind Marta, kneeling down and thinking she slipped, fell, and seriously hurt herself. Then the other guy came around the corner with a shirt on, just finishing buttoning up his pants.

"Oh my God, her water broke!" the stranger said.

Marta looked at this stranger and said to herself, "Who the fuck is this guy and how does he know what happened?"

"Wait! What! Oh my God, Marta! How far apart are the contractions?" Danny asked.

Marta looked at the stranger and then at Danny with a questionable glare when she realized he remembered everything from birthing classes.

"I don't know. I wasn't really paying attention."

"I'll go get my phone and we can time them. I'll be right back," offered the stranger.

Marta turned and looked at Danny, smiling as if to say "soooooo?" Danny saw her look.

"What, Marta? What am I forgetting?" Danny asked, thinking she was testing him on what to do once the water breaks.

Marta shook her head and pointed it toward the direction of where the stranger went. Danny realized what she was asking when the stranger came back around the corner.

"Okay, let me know when you have a contraction and I'll time it," the stranger said.

Marta looked at Danny.

"Marta, this is my friend Nathan."

"Friend?" Marta questioned Danny.

"Yes, this is my friend Nathan, who is going to help me get you up," Danny answered.

Marta then had another contraction, which was big, and she yelled.

"I got it! I started the clock," Nathan yelled.

Nathan started counting out loud as a light came on and G and Ron came running down the stairs.

"Oh my God! What happened? Marta, are you all right?" Ron asked.

When Danny explained that Marta's water broke, G and Ron went into sort of a panic mode.

"Stop!" Marta yelled.

They all looked at her. She looked at Ron.

"Ron, please go get the car warmed up and ready to go. G, you call everyone on the list and make sure the doctor and Dale are first," she said firmly.

"Right," Ron said, as he and G turned around and ran back up the stairs to get dressed.

"Doctor then Dale!" Marta shouted.

"Got it, Marta!" G shouted back.

She looked at Danny.

"Danny!" she said, then she stopped. "Ooooohhhhh Boooooy!" she said, looking at Nathan, who looked at her.

"Oh, right," Nathan said as he looked at his phone. "Five minutes, twenty-three seconds! Give or take a few seconds." He smiled as he looked up.

"Oh shit!" Marta said.

"What?" Nathan said, the smile leaving his face.

"This baby is coming soon!" Danny said.

"Danny, help me back to my room so I can change into something dry," Marta said.

Danny and Nathan helped Marta up from the floor and walked her back to her room. Nathan went back into the living room, got himself presentable, picked up the rest of Danny's clothes, and went back to Marta's room. He found Danny just finishing up helping Marta change clothes. She sat down on the edge of the bed while Nathan handed Danny his shirt, pants, belt, socks, and shoes, one at a time, so Danny could get dressed. Marta broke the silence, pointing to the two of them while trying to catch her breath as she felt another contraction coming on.

"So how long has this been going on?" she asked Danny, her voice rising in pitch while the contraction deepened.

Nathan and Danny looked at each other as Marta growled, and then looked back at her.

"Marta, another time! Come on, let's get you moving!" Danny responded.

Nathan and Danny helped Marta off the bed and she grabbed hold of them tightly as they moved toward the bedroom door.

"Grab my bag, grab my bag!" she said, pointing to a bag she had ready for what seemed like months for this occasion.

Danny bent down and grabbed it as they passed through the door. When they entered the hall, Ron ran down the stairs and passed them. He went down the second flight of stairs that led to the garage, flung open the entry door while grabbing the keys off the wall, and hit the garage door button. As the garage door went up, he opened the passenger door for Marta, then jumped into the driver's seat and started the car. Just as he did, Danny came out of the stairwell first walking backwards, then Marta followed, holding his hands, with Nathan behind her. They eased her around the front of the car and into the passenger seat.

"Where is G?" Danny asked.

Ron honked the horn, startling everyone.

"Ron! What the fuck, man?" Danny said.

"Jesus, Ron! Whooooaaa!" Marta said, as she had another contraction.

"That was four minutes, fifteen seconds," Nathan said, with Marta and Danny both surprised he was still keeping track.

"Boys, you better get me there soon or I'll be damned if I'm having this baby here in the garage!"

Danny shut the passenger door and got into the back alongside Nathan, who had opened the door for G. G came running out from the entry door and nearly fell flat on his face from skipping the last step, but caught his balance when he held on to the car's side door. G hopped in and shut the door just as Ron was backing out of the garage. Ron was still a bit panicked, and he put too much foot on the gas; the car lunged out of the garage and didn't quite make the turn sharp enough in the alley before hitting the garage door across from theirs.

"Oh shit!" Ron said.

"Forget about it! I'll talk to them tomorrow! Now get focused and get going!" G said.

Ron put the car in drive and down the alley and onto Mission Boulevard they went. Being early morning, the street was dead quiet, so, they cruised until they got onto the freeway and headed to the hospital.

"G, have you called Dale and Chuckie?" Marta asked.

"Yes, Marta, they are on their way, and I'm texting Manny and Larson right now. I left a message for Angie as well." G set down his phone after finishing the text, took a deep breath, and then softly said, "Fuck!"

"What?" Danny asked, as he and Nathan looked at G.

G looked at them both and mouthed, "I forgot to call the doctor," as he started belatedly doing so.

"What's wrong, G?" Marta asked.

G ignored her, as he was waiting for the doctor to answer, and Danny changed the subject.

"For about two months now, Marta," Danny said, as he and G locked eyes.

Then G looked at Danny as if to say, "Who is this guy sitting between us?"

"Nathan, this is G, that's Ron driving, and well, you have already met our sister, Marta!"

"Oh, you never told me you had brothers and a sister," Nathan responded.

"Figuratively speaking, we all are!" Ron said.

"Ah, well it's nice to meet you all."

"You haven't met them all yet!" Marta said, as she moaned with each word being higher in pitch.

"Hang on, Marta, we're almost there," Ron said.

Then Marta released the side lever of the seat and flipped backward—first onto Danny's forehead, and then as he leaned back, onto his chest, as he let out a "son of a bitch!"

"I'm so sorry, Danny!" Marta said. "But that'll teach ya for keeping secrets from me!"

Danny's jaw dropped open as he looked over to G. G shook his head as if to say, "ignore it!" so he did.

"The doctor is already at the hospital, and Mama and Papa Alfaro and Uncle Pietro are on their way. Angie just texted me and she's leaving soon," G said.

"Everything is fine, Marta. And there's the hospital," Ron said as they passed it on the freeway and took the next exit.

As they approached every intersection, Nathan mumbled, "green light, green light, green light."

And sure as hell, every light turned green for them. Ron pulled up to the emergency entrance and Ron, G, and Nathan hopped out of the car. Nathan went running in to get some help while Ron and G went around and helped Marta out of the car. Danny couldn't get his arm up to open the door because the front seat was still jammed on top of him. As G and Ron started to walk Marta away, Danny yelled. When Ron saw some of the hospital staff coming out with a wheelchair, he left Marta to G and the staff, turned back to the car, reached down, and released the lever to the front seat—which flipped back to the up position, allowing Danny to get free. Danny then hopped out of the car.

"I'm going to park the car. Text me where you guys all end up at, okay?" Ron said.

"Yep, will do!" Danny responded as he turned and followed Marta in with the others.

Ron hopped in the car and drove off to the parking structure. Marta was being wheeled in by a couple orderlies while Danny, G, and Nathan followed. They went down one hall then another and through a set of doors and came upon an elevator. While waiting for it, Marta let out another big yell. As the door opened, they all went in. While sitting in the wheelchair on the way up, Marta was breathing irregularly; Danny noticed this and remembered the game plan from birthing classes.

"Marta, grab my hand."

As she did, Danny and G started counting together, "1 . . . 2 . . . 3 breathe!"

Soon, Marta was in a rhythm with the boys. The elevator bell signaled they arrived at the right floor and when the doors opened, there was a big empty waiting room in front of them with the exception of Chuckie and Dale Da Dude. The two of them were the first thing Marta saw when the door opened, and she smiled. When they all got out of the elevator, Chuckie and Dale followed the rest of them.

"Are you okay, Marta?" Dale asked.

Marta responded right when another contraction came. "Yeeesssss, Dale!" she screamed, which startled Dale some.

"She's okay, Dale. The yelling is all part of the process," G said.

The orderlies pushed her through another set of doors, down another hall and then another, to finally what they called a birthing room.

"Is this it? Where it's all going to happen?" Dale asked.

"Yes," an orderly answered.

"I was beginning to wonder, as it seemed like it took longer to get to this room than it did to get to the hospital," Nathan commented to the others' chuckles.

The orderlies helped Marta onto the bed as one of the floor nurses came into the room and started taking down all Marta's information. The nurse did the typical questions—address, phone number, insurance, etc.—and the guys all pitched in to help answer while Marta tried to get comfortable.

"Which one of you is the father?" the nurse asked.

There was silence as they all looked at Marta; she looked at them, smiled, and said, "Well, they all are!"

The nurse shook her head and smiled. "Well that's a first for me. But I need one name for the record, miss."

"Can I give it to you later?" Marta asked.

"Sure, no problem."

Just then, Mama, Papa, Uncle Pietro, and Angie walked in as the nurses starting prepping Marta. Mama walked over by her granddaughter's side and leaned over to kiss her as she grabbed her hand and Papa followed. Uncle Pietro raised his thumb up in the air for Marta to see. The doctor arrived and saw the crowded room. She was short in stature and of Asian background, but spoke English perfectly. She had been Marta's doctor from the first day Marta found out she was pregnant. Marta loved her frankness and sense of humor.

"Okay, what game are we all watching that so many people are here to cheer?" the doctor asked. Everyone laughed.

"Hi, Doc!" Marta said, laughing.

"Hi, Marta. If I had known you were bringing in this many people, I would have brought in bleacher seating." Everyone laughed again.

"This is my family," Marta said.

"Except Larson and Manny are not here yet!" Dale said.

"They'll be here soon Dale, I'm sure," Chuckie said.

Nathan started to sneak out of the room, as he felt that this wasn't the place for him at this time, when Marta called him out.

"Where are you going, Nathan?" she sternly said. Nathan was caught by surprise. Marta looked at Danny and Danny nodded his head yes. "You are part of the reason I went into labor, so now you're a part of the family."

Laughter filled the room again. Angie, being confused, looked at G.

"I'll explain it later," G said.

"Well, okay then Marta," the doctor said. "What do you say we get this show on the road and get everyone where you want them."

As the doctor sat down on a stool and put on a pair of latex gloves, Marta asked Mama and Angie to be on one side, and as planned, Danny on the other with Dale close by and everyone else behind them.

"You guys can take pictures and video, but none of my hu-hu! You got that!" Marta emphasized.

"Oh geez, Marta!" Ron said.

"Ewwww, ewwww!" Uncle Pietro and Papa said in unison.

Nathan and Ron stepped back from the others, more toward a corner of the room, where they could still see what was happening but did not have a front row seat. The nurses prepped Marta, getting her feet in the stirrups of the birthing bed, and the doctor reached between her legs to check for her dilation.

"This baby is sitting in good position in the womb and is coming very soon, Marta, but not quite yet," the doctor said as she took off her latex gloves. "We will continue to monitor you and if you wish, we can give you an epidural to take away the pain for now."

"I wasn't going to, but I think I'll take you up on that epidural, doc!" Marta said.

The doctor looked at the nurse, who was already setting up an IV. "Got that?" she asked.

"Yes, doctor," the nurse replied.

"Try to relax, Marta. Don't worry if you fall asleep. We'll wake to up, so you won't miss anything," the doctor said, smiling, as the others smiled as well. "We should see you shortly. Hopefully within the next hour or so."

"Thanks, doc," Marta responded.

The doctor smiled at Marta and the others, turned, and walked away. There were a couple chairs in the room and a small couch. Another nurse brought in a couple more stools, so everyone was sitting except Mama, Angie, and Dale Da Dude, who were still standing around Marta and talking with her. An hour went by and Marta fell asleep. Mama, Papa, and Angie went on into the waiting room, where they all fell asleep. Two hours went by, and Nathan, Danny, G, and Ron went down to the cafeteria. Uncle Pietro was sitting in the corner of the room on the floor, propped up against the wall, fast asleep and softly snoring. Chuckie, who wasn't far from him, was also asleep.

Then there was Dale Da Dude, who remained by the bed, but was now sitting on a stool. He was looking straight ahead and occasionally would get up when a nurse would enter the room to check on Marta. The nurse would mouth to him that everything was okay, and Dale would sit back down on the stool. He was Marta's living guardian angel, her knight, there to protect her from any and all noise or disturbances. Then Larson and Manny walked in and Dale jumped from his stool and put his index finger to his lips.

"Shhhh! Marta's asleep!"

Larson brought his index finger to his lips and nodded in agreement as Manny gave a thumbs up; they walked over to Dale and gave him a hug. They glanced at Marta, who was peacefully asleep, and then stepped away to share a chair as Dale sat back down on the stool. The room was quiet with exception to the monitor, which was beeping according to Marta's heart rate.

Marta had been asleep for a couple hours when she rolled to one side and then to the other. She started to get uncomfortable and she was in and out of consciousness. Dale stood up as he heard her moan. Then the monitor beeped more steadily, and Larson got up to get a nurse, but was met by one by the time he opened the door, as she had obviously been alerted to Marta's condition at the nurses' station. Manny, Larson, and Dale observed the nurse as she went over to Marta, grabbed her wrist, looked at her watch, and timed Marta's heart rate. The nurse then pressed a button on the side of the bed that raised it up. Marta was moaning again, and the nurse softly asked her how she was doing. Marta just moaned some more. The nurse pressed another button as she checked the IV drip. Manny, Larson, and Dale just stood there observing it all when the doctor came in along with another nurse. The doctor grabbed a stool and scooted on up to the foot of the bed.

"Marta, can you hear me dear?" the doctor calmly asked.

Marta rolled and moaned softly. "Yes."

"I need you to lie still now on your back, as we are going to set your legs back up and check you."

"Okay," Marta said.

The nurses set Marta's feet back in the stirrups. The doctor then checked her.

"Marta, the baby's ready."

Marta opened her eyes upon hearing the doctor and saw Dale. "Dale, honey, can you go get Mama and Angie, please?"

"Yes Marta," Dale said as he left the room.

Marta then saw Larson and Manny. "Nice to see you could make it, guys," she said with a smile.

"You know me Marta, better late than never," Larson said.

"I'm only late because I happened to be with Larson," Manny said with a smile.

Then Marta let out a loud moan that woke Uncle Pietro and Chuckie. When they saw the doctor at the foot of the bed, they both stood up against the wall. It wasn't long that Mama and

Angie came in, and Dale, Papa, and the others followed. Mama, Angie, Danny, and Dale all got into position. Marta grabbed a hold of both Danny's and Mama's hands while Angie held onto the side of the bed. All the others were standing near the head of the bed behind Marta and along the wall as the doctor spoke.

"Okay, Marta, here we go! Push!" the doctor directed. Marta let out a loud groan and a nurse alongside the foot of the bed who was watching the monitor encouraged her to push more. "That's it! That's it! Okay, stop and breathe."

Danny started counting, as did the nurse. "Okay, Marta. Again, push!" Marta again let out a loud groan and pushed. "That's excellent, Marta!" the doctor said.

Now the whole group was getting into it as if they were all at a ballgame, as every time the nurse or doctor told Marta to push, they were encouraging her as well.

"Come on, Marta!"

"You got this, Marta!"

Uncle Pietro was in the back shaking his head, while Papa was silently praying. Mama and Angie were busy telling her she's doing great as Mama kept softly petting Marta's head.

"Okay, Marta! You're doing great Marta. The head is crowning Marta," the nurse said. "Push again and really give it a good one this time, Marta."

Marta let out the loudest scream yet. "Ah, fucking eh!" she yelled.

"Yes! Yes! Marta! That's great!" the doctor said.

"Almost done honey," Angie said, as she could see the baby was nearly halfway out.

"One more time, Marta!" the doctor said.

Everyone was standing on edge and then G grabbed his cell phone and put it up over everyone's head, as did Ron, Nathan, and Chuckie. Uncle Pietro continued to shake his head in disbelief and Papa's praying seemed to speed up in pace. Marta took one larger deep breath in, at the same time squeezing hard on Danny and her grandmother's hands. She let out a large scream as all the others encouraged her to stay with the push, and then there was silence. Marta placed her head back on the pillow, opened her eyes, and saw everyone staring forward, with their jaws either opened or smiling. She was feeling a large sense of relief going through her body as she tilted her head forward and looked down between her legs to see the doctor holding her baby and looking at her.

"It's a girl, Marta!" Angie said, as did the others.

"Oh, she's so beautiful, Marta!" Mama said.

Everyone else was still on their toes, snapping pictures, and now Uncle Pietro and Papa were in the crowd. The nurse asked who was to cut the umbilical cord. Marta looked to Dale.

"Go on Dale, just like we practiced."

Chuckie grabbed Dale and brought him around to the baby. The doctor held the baby as the nurse grabbed the scissors and placed them in Dale's hand. Dale looked hesitantly at Marta.

"It's okay, Dale," Marta said as she smiled.

Dale turned, looked at the baby, and said, "She's so tiny, Marta!"

The nurse guided Dale's hand, assisted with opening the scissors and placing the cord between the shears, and then helped him squeeze the scissors. There was a snap as the cord released from the shears. Dale stood there as the nurse removed the scissors from his hand and the doctor handed the baby over to another nurse, who placed the baby on a side table, cleared her throat, wiped her face, and cleaned her up. The group all watched intently, wondering when she was going to cry. As soon as the nurses had cleaned her airways, she let out a small whimper then a full-on cry and everyone was relieved. One nurse took the baby's vitals while the other cleaned up Marta and got her comfortable. All of this was going on while the others were still carefully watching.

"Eight pounds three ounces and twenty-two inches long," announced one of the nurses.

"Wow," Angie said. "She's going to be a tall one, Marta. I was twenty-one inches and look how tall I am."

The nurse wrapped up the baby and brought her over to Marta to hold for the first time. Now everyone had gathered around the bed completely to observe the joining of mother and child. Marta, now sitting up, took the baby in her arms and cradled her. Marta looked at her baby all scrunched up still with her eyes closed. She smiled, leaned into her newborn daughter, and gave her a kiss on her forehead. She looked up at the faces of all her family and friends. They were all smiling. Both Mama and Papa had tears running down their eyes, as did Uncle Pietro, though he wouldn't admit it later.

She could see that each and every one of her boys, even Nathan, had tears in their eyes as well, but all were smiling—especially Dale Da Dude, who was so touched by the whole thing that he didn't have much to say, which for him was unusual. Marta took it all in. She also could see on wonderment on their faces. She knew she had never spoken about names with any of them, even when they all at one time or another brought up the subject. Even Dale would come to her with a list of names every day, but she would never say anything other than it will come to me when it is time. Now it was time, so as she smiled, she said, "Everyone, I'd like you to meet Capri Alfaro-Marinello."

There was a brief silence.

"Awesome! Awesome! What a cool name!" Dale shouted, as he started clapping.

"That is a cool name!" Larson said.

"Yes, very cool!" the others chimed in.

"Mucho asi mi sobrina nieta mucho asi!" (Very much so my grandniece, very much so), Uncle Pietro said. "Puedo crecer con el orgullo de su madre!" (May she grow with the pride of her mother.)

"Si! Si!" Papa said as he squeezed Marta's leg.

"Okay, out! Everyone out!" Mama Alfaro said quietly. "Let these two get their rest."

One by one, everyone filed out until it was just Marta, Capri, and Mama Alfaro.

Mama held Marta's hand and squeezed it. "You rest up now, my dear child." As she turned to leave, Marta squeezed Mama's hand even tighter and drew Mama back to her.

"Mama!" she said softly, with tears slowly draining from her eyes down her cheeks.

Mama could tell by the tears that they were tears of fear. Papa Alfaro called it a special talent of hers. A gift, that she could tell by the size of one's tears whether they were tears of joy, tears of sorrow, tears of love, or tears of fear.

"Oh, Marta, what is it that you fear?" she asked.

"Mama, I have so much going on in my mind right now. I, I, I feel alone. I, I fear for my child. I fear her not ever knowing her father. Like I never knew my parents. I fear for her future that I may fail her as a mother by possibly raising her alone."

"Oh Marta, Marta my dear. That is only natural, my child," Mama said. "But your faith will shine through for you and you find that no child of this family has ever had to worry about being alone or raised alone. Marta, my dear. You have had so much love surrounding you through from birth to your now young adult life—that same love that has protected you all these years. With your Papa and me, your Uncle Pietro, your Papa and Mama Marinello, Angie, and all these wonderful young men who were here today by your side, this child will have the same love and protection throughout her life as you did and will continue to have. Something also tells me that this child will also have her father in her life, always. The words he left behind for you were words of a man who is very much in love with you. They are words of a future that you should have no need to fear. Have faith, my dear."

Mama reached over and kissed Marta on her cheek, wiped her hand over her forehead, and then used her thumb to wipe away the tears on each of Marta's cheeks. She then leaned over to kiss the baby.

"Now you two get some rest, my sweet Marta. I know of at least two angels who are watching over you. They always have been."

Mama began to leave the room.

"Love you, Mama."

Mama turned, smiled, placed two fingers to her lips to threw out a kiss to Marta, then left the room. Marta turned and looked at her baby sleeping on her chest. Marta listened to her breathing until the rhythm of Capri's breath put her to sleep as well. On this day, the world was not as lost as they all thought it had been.

AS THE SUN SETS,
SO DOES THE HORIZON

Cap knelt to one knee next to the small firepit, grabbed a log, and placed it on the fire he already had going. When the log hit the charred wood, he watched as ashes shot up in the air, swirling in a circle, until they disappeared not far from above his head. He reached again to his side two more times and placed logs strategically on the fire so they would catch a flame and burn. He then got to his feet, turned, stepped back to his camping chair, and sat down. He kicked his legs out so the soles of his shoes faced the fire, then crossed his legs and folded his arms together with each hand under an armpit as he settled into the chair.

He watched the flames and listened to the crackling of the wood burning. He watched as all the smaller flames fed into one larger one in the center that shot up into the air about two or three feet above the pit. He saw where the flames turned into grey smoke that continued up until it disappeared into the blackness of the night. Above all that blackness was the most beautiful star-lit sky on Earth! It was his opinion that there was nothing better than Joshua Tree on a clear evening, any time of the year.

This was his third trip to Joshua Tree in the past seven months and his eighth in the last three years since returning from the Middle East. Not one of them was a planned camping outing. No, they were for duty, instead. Most of the men who served with him throughout his three tours were stationed, like he was, at Twenty-Nine Palms Marine Corp Base near Palm Springs. It was where they had most of their basic training as part of the Marine Corp's Air-Ground Units. Whenever the men were given leave, a lot them took to hiking and camping in Joshua Tree, as if all the hiking and training as a Marine was not enough. Cap was one of them.

It was different than training camp. It was more relaxing and there was a real calm that seemed to sweep over him and his buddies when they entered the park. Joshua Tree has had that effect on many throughout the years. Cap described it to Suzanne, in one of their counseling sessions, as being a spiritual connection of one's inner soul with their inner mind. Freedom was the one word that could best describe it. He had already learned some about Joshua Tree while growing up from his parents. They were products of the sixties and seventies who played Eagles and Linda Ronstadt albums, and Joshua Tree was where they wrote many of their songs. He was also told of the story of Gram Parsons, who was an artist as well. His manager kidnapped Parson's corpse and tried to cremate him in the park at his request, but against his family's wishes. The legend was known to all who were stationed at the base and all who lived around the area or visited. Joshua Tree was the home away from home for a lot of artists in the music and film world, as well as thousands of photographers. The landscape is hauntingly beautiful no matter where you are in the park or what time of day or night. It rejuvenated their creative juices.

It was in the Middle East, after his team's first encounter of warfare, that reality set into the group. For the first time, a number of them thought of death and not the GI Bill that would cover the education their parents could not afford. It was why a lot of them signed up in the first place. So, they all began writing their wills during their downtime. Cap's group all agreed that they didn't mind having a military-type funeral service, but they didn't want a military funeral in a military cemetery, like Arlington; they wished to be cremated. They all agreed that whoever made it back and was the highest ranking would spread their ashes in Joshua Tree, at the location of their favorite spot. They all signed and dated each other's wills and kept them secured in their footlockers on base while they were out on maneuvers.

Cap ended up being the highest ranking survivor. Once home, he was immediately put into duty to honor three of his men's requests. These men died overseas, and their families had no problem with their requests. The only issue was that the park didn't allow cremains to be spread on its grounds. He knew, like hundreds of others throughout the many years of the park's existence, that the park rangers did not really enforce this rule, as it was pretty hard to cover nearly twelve hundred square miles of terrain.

Cap had finished hiking back into camp shortly before he settled down in front of the campfire. He had completed another one of his squad member's requests. The only thing he took issue with was that now, more of his men had died while here, at home on American soil, than had died overseas. This last one hurt more than the others, even though they were all important, as this last soldier took his own life, in Joshua Tree. It was just a little too close to home and sort of pierced him like a knife. It was very frustrating that his men, and many other men and women who served, were not able to find the solace he was finding through the help he was getting. Whenever he would learn of one of his men having issues, he would talk to them and sometimes even go to them in person to offer Suzanne's services, but there was no response. He saw in their faces what Suzanne had spoken about, that every person is different and deals with things differently, thus not all the solutions available will work. He understood this, but it still hurt—a hurt that should have been avoidable if not for the greed of war.

Cap sat there in the early evening, when it was already dark since it was winter. He slowly closed his eyes and then tried to lose thought as he went into mediation. Transcendental meditation was recommended by Suzanne. She had sent him to her teacher, as she wasn't certified herself, but she practiced it, as did her daughter, Kathleen. When he went to his first informational meeting about it, he thought, what a farce. As he thought that, the instructor said almost everyone who searched for information about it initially thought it was a farce, but he asked to just give it a chance. So, he did—twenty minutes, twice a day, of sitting still and trying to release your mind of all thought. He gave himself two weeks to see if there would be any kind of results.

At first, he found no value in it, other than he would fall asleep while doing it. It was very hard to try and maintain even fifteen minutes. When he fell asleep, it would be for hours, and when he did not fall asleep, he would always have thoughts running through his head. He would open his eyes either after only a few minutes, or ten minutes at the most. But he didn't stop going to the classes. Finally, he recognized even though he was still having thoughts and the goal was to clear them, the thoughts were all positive. No negative thought had entered his head during any of the meditations. Though they would be there at times, soon the thoughts would thin out. He was finding that the twenty minutes was being naturally built into his system and by the time he closed his eyes then opened them, the twenty minutes had passed in a flash. He found himself with more energy and his mind was clearer in daily thought. His nightmares soon were diminishing and the headaches decreasing. The energy thing was the biggest plus to him, as he found himself surfing again, regularly, for the third time in his life.

Cap grew up surfing, but he grew up surfing in the Midwest in a little tiny town of Mosel, Wisconsin. It was only a few miles from the shores of Lake Michigan, not far from the city of Sheboygan, which was halfway between Milwaukee and Green Bay. His mother was a teacher in the Sheboygan school district and his father was a surfboard shaper. His dad started his own business after learning to surf the waves off Sheboygan as a youth. He found that many other kids wanted to surf, so with his knowledge of carpentry, taught to him by his own father, he taught himself about board shaping and started his own business instead of going off to college.

He and his wife were high school sweethearts who married after she graduated from college. Cap was their only child. His dad was an innovator of his time; back then, almost all Lake Michigan surfers came to him to get a personally shaped board. As soon as he was old enough, Cap learned the skill as well. During the summers, when his mother didn't have to teach, they would take a couple weeks for family vacations to both the East and West Coasts, where his dad would pick up more tricks of the trade. This continued until Cap signed up for the Marines. As far as he knew, the last time he had communicated with his family, his mom was still teaching and his dad was still shaping.

The second time Cap picked up surfing was when he became "Keeper of the Board" for Marta. Every day, after Marta and her

crew were done for the day, Cap headed out to the waves, where
he would spend a good deal of his time, sometimes until sunset.
When he didn't feel like surfing, he would just paddle her board
out far enough where the swells were not too bad. He could just
lie down on the board and look off into the blue sky. If there were
clouds, he would try and find the ones that looked like animals
or faces or shapes of some sort, and follow them until they disappeared. Occasionally, he would be joined by a school of dolphins
or one or two sea lions, and once he was even far out enough that
a whale breached not more than 100 feet in front of him. It was
during this period of time that he felt meeting Marta had saved
his life. Then, when he became intimate with Marta, the surfing
had to stop. That was something that was between him and no
one else, his business only—something he owned that no one else
could take away from him. That attitude was changing now with
the help of Suzanne and meditation, so he began to surf again.

Cap decided it was time to walk away from the military as
a representative of the Marines at funerals. He and a few others
would attend and present the members of the family with the
flag that had been draped over their casket, now folded into the
traditional triangle. It was becoming mentally exhausting and
taking away from his recovery. So, he got himself some side jobs
as a handyman while he took the California Contractors License
course. This would allow him to work legitimately and get jobs
that were big enough to pay the bills so he could live on his own
off base. It was a slow process, but he did it. He lived not far from
Pacific Beach in a converted garage guesthouse, walking distance
from the beach at Tourmaline and from Crystal Pier. He even
grew his beard back, but kept it groomed and let his hair grow
long, down to his shoulders. He actually blended in with all the

others who were surfing and kept to himself. He had worked it out to surf toward the early evening till sunset, thinking he would be safe from running into Marta or any of the others, as he felt he wasn't ready to—or so he thought.

Cap had finished up a project early one night, headed home, changed into his wetsuit, and headed for Tourmaline. He walked down the concrete steps off the cul-de-sac where Loring Street ended and up to the shoreline. He stuck his board in the sand, slipped the sleeves of his wetsuit over his arms, grabbed his board, and went into the water. This would be an evening of surfing he would not forget. His very first wave was one to be remembered in his own mind for a really long time.

Not far behind him, Larson, Manny, and Angie had pulled up and parked in a vacant spot on the cul-de-sac and unloaded their boards. They had been up on the street overlooking the beach and checking out the surf. They saw a wave come up that they weren't sure they could even handle, but they watched to see who, if anyone, would attempt it. Several did, but only one came out of it on top. They watched as he worked every bit of it up and down with turns every which way. Larson said, "He must be a pro!" Manny followed with, "Has to be!"

It wasn't unusual for pros to be spotted around by the locals, testing out San Diego's surf every now and then or trying out a local shaper's board. Some even had sponsors based out of San Diego, even though the competitive surf was known to be up the coast in Huntington Beach. Larson and Manny watched in amazement as this guy took and used every advantage of this wave. When he finished, he got a bunch of shout-outs from those in the water, and from others such as Larson, Manny, and Angie who were on the shore.

When Cap finished, he sat and straddled his board, and said to himself, "Wow!" Others near him were giving him all sorts of compliments and he was very appreciative as he turned and paddled back out. Now, Larson, Manny, and Angie were on their way across the beach. Angie made herself comfortable on the sand as Manny and Larson plunged into the water, paddling out to join the many other surfers waiting for the next good wave. While on their way out to the surf, Cap had turned and caught another wave in. He surfed it just as well or better than the first, finishing again to rounds of cheers. He straddled his board, catching his breath but feeling great.

"Damn!" he said.

He was surprised at himself, but he was pumped up and his adrenaline was high. He took in some good long deep breaths and slowly let them out as he relaxed and started paddling back out again. By this time, Larson and Manny had tried a couple times to catch a wave, but ended up bailing each time. This time, Cap decide to wait a bit before going again, so he paddled out a bit farther, where the swells had died some, and just sat there straddling his board, taking a rest.

Larson and Manny kept trying and they got some good rides, but not like Cap's. But then again, nobody did that evening. While Cap sat out there, he watched the sunlight hit the water, making it look like sparkling gold. He observed the occasional seagull or two flying low along the water and from a distance a few dolphins were playing about. Toward shore, he could see the many bodies of surfers and their boards not too far in front of him. Farther toward land, he saw some who were already leaving for the day and many who were lining up to watch the sunset.

Many tourists and locals watched every day along the coast, as San Diego sunsets were some of the most beautiful around.

After clearing the saltwater out of his nose, he laid down on his board and paddled inland to get in line with the anticipated start of the incoming swells when they turned to waves. When he got there, he sat up and straddled his board again. While waiting there with the other surfers, he noticed Larson and Manny. He had eye contact with both of them, but was hoping they had not recognized him. He quickly turned his head and looked for the next wave.

Cap decided he was taking whatever wave that came, good or bad, and he was going to ride this one as far into shore as possible. He started paddling and he caught it. It was a good one, but not as good as the previous two. He popped and rode it in without incident. Instead of turning back out, he kept the board heading straight for the shore, and then jumped off into the knee-deep water. He unhooked his ankle strap and tucked his board under his arm, heading up the beach without looking behind him, even when he heard a couple guys shouting at him.

"Hey!" one shouted.

"Cap!" the other yelled.

He hesitated, and he knew that was a mistake. He should have ignored the calls and kept on walking and they would never had known a thing. But then he heard Manny shout, "Cap! It is you, isn't it?"

Angie heard the boys shout Cap's name as she looked at the surfer coming out of the surf and heading almost toward her. She arose from the sand, brushed off herself, and lightly jogged over in front of the man, stopping him in his tracks.

Cap looked at Angie and with both hands lifted up his board and jammed it hard into the sand so it was standing straight up on its own. He let go of the board, turned around, and saw Manny and Larson had stopped about twenty yards away from him and were looking at him curiously.

"It is you isn't it, Cap?" Larson asked.

Cap turned backed around toward Angie, who was looking into Cap's famous piercing blues eyes, and then nodded her head yes to the boys.

Both of them began to move slowly toward him. Larson and Manny did not know what to expect, as they remembered some of the violent memories Marta had discussed with them. Cap was unsure where this would go as well, thinking maybe they were going to be upset with him abandoning Marta like he did. Larson and Manny continued their deliberate, slow approach as he stood there with his hands on his hips. He occasionally glanced off to the side as the sun was beginning its descent and the glare off the water happened to be hitting him on his face.

"It is you!" Manny said, as they both stopped about ten feet from him.

"Hey, Cap, how are ya doing?" Larson asked, extending his hand to him.

Cap looked down at his hand, took it, and grabbed it firm at first. He shook it, loosened up, and let his hand go limp, which is when Larson let go. Manny then extended his hand. Cap did the same with his grip with Manny.

"Hi, Cap!" Manny said.

Cap stood and looked at all three of them, as Angie moved around to join Manny and Larson.

"Hi, Larson, Manny, . . . Angie!"

"How have you been, Cap?" Larson asked.

"Yea Cap, how have you been doing?" repeated Manny.

Cap recognized that they were being sincere, thus the tension he was feeling through his body was releasing. The meditation was definitely helping with that, as he looked at everything differently since starting it. He noticed the change in his temperament especially. Though it was still awkward to him, he responded.

"Doing fine guys! Doing pretty good, actually!"

The four of them stood there, all feeling awkward, with Angie being unusually quiet.

"Cap, we had no idea that you surfed, and damn can you surf!" Manny said.

Cap smiled. "Ah Manny, the stars just happened to be in alignment today."

Larson noticed Cap's uneasiness and then spoke. "What ya doing right now? I mean, you have any plans for dinner? Let us take you out for a couple of drinks."

"Yea, that's a great idea, Cap! Come with us for an hour or two. On us!" Manny said.

"I don't know guys," Cap said hesitantly.

"Come on, Cap. We'll just get caught up on some things. Just between us. Marta doesn't have to know," Larson said. Angie dipped her shoulder into Larson's back after he said that.

Cap stood there as the sun was nearing the horizon and shining in his face. He turned toward it, placed his hand above his forehead, and watched it for a minute, thinking about the guys' offer. He did not feel bad or weird about it and his stomach did not feel funny; in fact, he was not getting any ill feelings about the situation.

"Hell, why the fuck not!" Cap said as he turned, pulled his board out of the sand, and started walking back toward the stairs leading up to the cul-de-sac.

"Alrighty then!" said Larson said.

"Cool!" Manny said, as the three of them looked at each other and hustled up to catch up with Cap until they were on each side of him, all walking in stride.

Larson and Manny fastened the surfboards to the roof rack of their car as Cap stood there looking and Angie got into the backseat.

"Hey, um, I walked here guys, so I don't have anything to change into," Cap said.

"Don't worry about it, Cap. We're not going anywhere special," Larson said. "I do have an extra sweatshirt in the car you can wear if you want. There's a basket of clean laundry there in the backseat. Help yourself."

Cap got into the car and closed the door. He and Angie's eyes connected. Cap then looked away and into the basket of clothing, fishing through the pile of folded clothes until he came across a couple sweatshirts. He pulled the top one out and proceeded to pull it on over his head as the other two got in the car. Larson started up the car and pulled away from the curb. He headed east on Loring Street.

"What have you been up to, Cap?" Larson asked.

Cap was looking out the window observing all the street lights. They seemed to be lighting up about the same time they were driving by them. He thought it must be the sensors reacting to the sun having just set and darkness coming upon them.

"Oh, I've been doing this and that, carpentry work mostly," Cap responded.

"Really! How interesting," Larson said while glancing at Manny and then back onto the road ahead.

They then turned south on Fanuel Street until the car reached the traffic light at Garnett.

"How long have you been doing that?" Manny asked.

"Oh, just a few months now. Got my license just recently, but I really sort of grew up doing it, working with my father," Cap said.

When the light turned green, they crossed Garnett and Larson turned right into an alley. He drove up behind an older brick building and into a parking spot.

"Well, here we are."

Larson parked the car and the four of them got out. Larson took the keys he had in his hand, unlocked the building's back door, and opened it. Manny went in and immediately turned on some light switches.

"Go on in, Cap. After you," Larson said.

Cap looked at Larson and then through the door as he walked in. Immediately, he saw some large copper vats standing on each side of the large room. As he walked forward, he saw tools and other equipment lying around on the floor and leaning up against the vats and walls. Manny had gone to the front of the building to turn on more lights. When they came on, Cap noticed there were two large black canvases hanging down over the front windows to the street on each side of the front entry. Larson went to a small side fridge and pulled out four bottles of beer. He handed one to Angie, Cap, and Manny; opened his own; and tossed the bottlecap over to the corner, where there was a pile of trash.

"So, welcome to my new microbrewery," said Larson said.

"Really!" Cap replied.

"Yes. Well, I should say my dad's and mine. It was going to be someone else's brewery, as they had started it, but then some strange things happened, and they put the place back on the market," Larson explained. "Manny is going in with me and my dad as a partner. Angie and Marta have been helping with the design aspect."

Cap looked over to Angie.

"Well, both you ladies have good taste, so I'm sure it will look great. What about the shipyards, Manny?" Cap asked.

"I'm still going to be doing that until this gets off the ground. Sort of a security blanket so to speak. I'll be busy for sure." Cap nodded his head as to approve. "You caught my curiosity when you said you were a carpenter," Manny continued. "I'm wondering if you'd be interested in helping us get her ready for a soft opening in about two or three months?"

"Boy, I don't know guys; I have a lot going on in my mind right now," Cap said. "Seeing you three just got my head spinning about Marta and I don't know if I'm ready to see her yet."

Manny and Larson looked at each other, then at Angie, and it clicked to both of them that Marta and Angie had told them Cap did not even know he was the father of a new baby girl.

"Marta won't have to know Cap. Marta never comes here. In fact, . . ." Just then, Angie interrupted Larson.

"Marta works from home. We meet with her there and then I come here with the ideas and share them with the guys—although they could use someone to help them comprehend it all." Angie looked at Manny and Larson as she finished.

"We could use the help, Cap. If we can help in any way by offering you some work, well, we'd like to do that," Manny said.

"Please don't take it the wrong way. What Manny just said. We mean real work! Real money, as you can see by looking around you," Larson added.

Cap stood there with the beer bottle still in his hand; he hadn't even taken a sip of the beer yet. He looked around the room, then at Larson and Manny, and then down at the beer. He stared at the bottle for the longest time and Larson realized he was reading the label.

"Is this the beer Larson?" Cap asked, as he raised the bottle.

"Yes, Cap! That's our light ale!"

Cap twisted off the cap. He brought the bottle up to his nose to take a whiff of the brewed aroma. He then lowered it to his lips, tilted the bottle to his mouth, and let the beer flow in. He swallowed a couple times and lowered the bottle. Larson and Manny were looking at him intently and he sensed this. Angie was waiting to see how he would respond before she would chime in. He looked at the three of them and raised his bottle to them.

"Well, fellas . . . sure, I'll help you out."

Larson and Manny were ecstatic as they brought their beer bottles up to Cap's and toasted. They spent the rest of the evening and on into the early morning going over plans and directions— sharing ideas on how to get the place to reflect Larson's vision and working over some numbers to create a budget.

"Oh shit!" Larson said, when he looked at his phone and then up at Cap.

"Everything okay?" Cap asked.

Larson looked again at his phone.

"Manny, I just got a text from my dad. He says we need to get to the house to help unload the shipment of barley and hops."

"Yea, that's the text I just received as well. We better go, as that's a lot for your old man to deal with alone," Manny said

"Hey, you guys go, get out of here. I don't live that far that I can't walk home," Cap said.

The four of them headed back to the alley, where Manny un-hooked Cap's board from the top of the car while Larson locked up the place.

"Thanks, Cap!" Larson said.

"Yea, thanks, Cap!" Manny said.

Larson handed Cap his business card with all his info on it. "Call me over the weekend and we'll set things up."

"Will do," Cap said.

With that, Manny and Larson got in the car and sped off, leaving Angie and Cap standing in the alley with his surfboard.

"Well, Angie, it was good to see you again," Cap said. "I need you tell the boys that I won't be able to oblige them right now in working on the brewery with you all. I'm just not ready to see Marta yet."

Angie backed away from Cap a step, almost in shock, and then held back her angst and stepped toward Cap, placing her arm around his.

"Cap, would you mind walking me to my car before you head off?" she asked.

"Sure, Angie."

Angie didn't know how she was going to go about it, but she decided right then and there she was going to tell Cap he was a father. She knew she would have to go about it differently then she had outside the Lahaina, the first time she tried to tell him.

"Um, which way?" Cap asked. At that moment, Angie got an idea.

"Down the street near the thrift shop," she answered.

They started walking down the sidewalk toward the thrift shop. There was nothing but silence for the first block until they reached the street corner and had to wait for the light to change before crossing. As they stood there, Cap could tell by Angie's fidgeting with her purse handle that she was troubled, and he thought he knew pretty much what it was about.

"Okay, Angie, the answer is no."

Angie, startled, looked up from her purse and right into Cap's big blue eyes. It was the very first time she really saw his eyes so clearly. Even while they worked together at the thrift shop and earlier at the beach, she really never saw them stand out so . . . so. It was then that she understood Marta's description of how hypnotizing they could be, even though all of Marta's conversations were about her intimacy experiences looking into his eyes. This wasn't an intimate situation, but they sure as hell stood out to her, so she knew he was being serious.

The traffic light then turned green, and the crosswalk voice started counting down the seconds for them to walk, so Angie took advantage of that to not respond to Cap. She started to cross the street and Cap followed. When they got to the other side, they turned up the block until they reached the front of the thrift shop. Angie stopped, turned, and looked down at the street. Cap stopped alongside her.

"Look Angie, I can't work there at the brewery and see Marta as of yet . . ." Cap started to say when Angie interrupted him.

"This is where it all started," she said.

"You mean Marta introducing me to you?"

"Marta getting sick. Right there in the street between two cars."

"Marta getting sick? Is there something wrong with Marta, Angie? Tell me what's wrong with Marta?" Cap asked in desperation.

"She came into the store asking for you that morning you dropped off the note. I gave it to her as you asked. She read it. The next thing I see is her running out of the store to the street, throwing up between two cars. I followed her out to see if she was okay. She ran from me, heading toward the beach, dropping the note behind her. I picked it up and read it. I immediately followed her."

Cap stood there listening intently as Angie went on.

"She ran all the way down to under the pier, thinking for some reason you would be there. I followed her, stopping at the end of the stairs and sitting down to give her some space. She fell to her knees to the sand. She cried . . . for the longest time, then called out your name several times."

As Cap stood there listening, tears starting to come down his face. Angie continued.

"Then she threw up again. At that moment, I had never seen my beautiful, talented, independently strong Marta seem so afraid . . . vulnerable . . . and pregnant."

Cap grabbed Angie's hand to turn her toward him. Angie looked up into Cap's eyes and saw the question on his face. Angie squeezed his hand.

Cap leaned his surfboard against the bicycle rack on the curb in front of the thrift shop.

"How can that be?" he asked.

"I can't explain it other than some things happen for a reason. That, and I believe somebody up there likes you both and wants you two together. It's for you and Marta to come to some sort of conclusion."

Angie continued.

"Cap, Marta and I are to meet on Monday at the brewery to go over some things, but before that she will be down under the pier earlier, before noon . . . with . . . with your daughter."

Angie saw the tears keep flowing from Cap's eyes. She reached up and wiped them off his cheeks. She leaned in and kissed him on a cheek, released his hand, and turned to start walking back toward the brewery. Cap watched her for a bit before shouting, "Angie, your car!"

Angie turned around, walking backward.

"It's parked out front of the brewery!" she said, laughing.

She turned back around and continued to walk to her car. Cap smiled, shaking his head in disbelief, squatted down on the sidewalk with one knee to the pavement, put his hands to his to his face before moving them through his hair and placing them on his knees, then stood up and looked straight up into the sky. There was a three-quarter moon as bright as can be with a light evening marine layer slowly passing by it. It painted a beautiful picture in his head.

"Thank you," he whispered.

When Cap came out of his meditation, he looked at his cell phone and he was at twenty-one minutes. He felt refreshed and proceeded to make himself a meal and set up for the night in the back of his pickup. He sat there in peace with very little to disturb him. There were other campers in the vicinity, but all were pretty friendly and respectful of the others' presence. He had a nice little setup in the back of the pickup—an air mattress and sleeping bag designed for the temperatures that could vary in Joshua Tree overnight. When he was done eating, he got in bed of the pickup and laid back on the air mattress. He looked up at the millions of stars that shone so brightly in the clear sky—like he had done so many times before with his friends and buddies from the service. It was understandable why anyone would want to have their ashes spread around here, as it was most definitely the closest to God a person could feel. He paused for a moment to take it all in, then he thought about starting the work on Larson and Manny's microbrewery that coming Monday. He thought how it would be nice to be with the guys again. More importantly, it would actually be like taking baby steps to work on getting back to Marta and meeting his daughter—if she would even take him back. Thinking about how to go about it was harder than deciding how to attack the enemy in combat . . . or was it? Maybe he was over-thinking it. Maybe he should just respond on instinct. Once he decided what he was going to do, his mind finally calmed down enough to watch the remains of his fire curl up into the air and slowly diminish with the quiet crackling of coal. Then, Cap feel into a deep sleep.

CHALLENGING THE FUTURE

The guys, at first, were disappointed that Marta and the baby weren't staying at the house near the boardwalk. Then after Marta stayed a few times, when Capri was being fussy and disruptive throughout the night, they were fine with her not being around as much. Angie let them have it one evening regarding that; they then all felt bad and welcomed Marta to stay anytime. Marta understood. This was all new to them as well and they had been very accommodating to her for a long time.

The baby was now about six months old and summer was around the corner. Marta had not been down to the beach the whole time, other than right outside of the house on the boardwalk. Soon she would go back to work, so she wanted to get down there with Capri a few times before she felt she would not have the time to do so. Capri was a great baby; Dale Da Dude said so all the time, almost daily when Marta would stay at the house by the beach. Dale was always disappointed when Marta stayed with her grandparents, but Marta assured him there would be plenty of time for him to spend with Capri once she started back to work. So, on this day, Marta woke up and went through the usual routine with Capri. She looked at her calendar and saw that later today was the soft opening of the microbrewery. When she saw the weather was going to be beautiful, she decided it was a perfect time to take Capri to the beach and then up to the microbrewery with Angie. She called Danny and when he didn't answer, she left a voicemail. She told him she was coming by later with Capri after going to the beach and would most likely stay the night. Then she texted Chuckie to see if he could drop Dale off at the beach in about an hour. She packed a bag for herself and Capri. She then informed Papa, Mama, and Uncle Pietro that she'd be staying at the beach for the night, so not to worry, and kissed them all on the cheek on her way out of the house.

Marta drove to the beach house, parked in the garage, got Capri out of the backseat, and went up to her room behind the kitchen. She laid Capri in the middle of the bed and then set down her bag on the floor. She removed her clothes, slipped on her bathing suit, and wrapped herself with a sarong. After changing Capri's diaper, she dressed her in a cute little one-piece swimsuit. She got their beach bag packed with extra diapers, a blanket, and a couple beach toys when she heard the doorbell. She swung the beach bag over her shoulder, and picked up Capri with both hands, and sat her on the inside of her elbow.

When she opened the front door, she found Dale all smiles. Marta stepped out of the house and closed the door behind her. She handed Dale the beach bag and the two of them headed down the boardwalk, just past the Crystal Pier. They went down the steps onto the beach, over where she use to sit in the sand when she was pregnant, thinking of Cap and writing.

"Right here is good Dale. Can you lay out the blanket for me while I hold Capri, honey?"

"Sure thing, Marta!"

Dale set down the bag, pulled out the large blanket, and spread it out over the sand. Marta then put Capri down on the edge of blanket and Dale sat down alongside her. Marta pulled out the beach toys, placed them in front of Capri and sat down on the other side of her. Together, Dale and Marta began to play with Capri in the sand. Marta would occasionally look up and out over the beach and onto the water.

Memories started flowing of the time where the only responsibility she had was herself. She missed the surfing, but as she looked at Capri, she knew she would be back at it again soon. She hoped Capri would eventually enjoy it as much as her, but she would not push her into anything. If she didn't care for it, that was okay. As Dale continued playing with Capri, Marta turned her head back toward the seawall under the pier, where Cap's cardboard shack use to be. The city or the lifeguards had now put up No Camping or Loitering signs on the wall in several places under the pier. She turned back again toward Capri, smiled at Dale, and watched their interaction. Dale had so much patience, she thought, not only with Capri, but with the adults in the group who sometimes could be so childish—and she threw herself into that mix. She thought about how lucky he was as she wondered who really had the handicap, Dale or her and the rest of the group.

She tinkered with some of the toys, trying to get Capri to shovel some sand, when she looked up and out under the pier; the main cross timber caught her eye—the same one she used to use as a focal point while she thought of lyrics for her music. She noticed a bunch of kelp hanging over parts of it, but she also noticed what looked like to be carvings on it. She slowly got up and bent over to Dale and Capri.

"Dale, honey, would you mind keeping an eye on Capri for a moment while I go just right over there to check something out?" she asked, as she pointed over to the cross timber about twenty yards in front of them.

"Go ahead, Marta. I gotcha covered," Dale responded.

"Thank you, honey!" Marta turned and walked over to the cross timber.

While Dale was playing with Capri, he looked up toward the shoreline and saw a surfer walking toward him with a board under his arm. He watched as the surfer stopped and with both hands, took the board and stuck it into the sand. The surfer turned, looked at Dale, and started walking toward him. As the surfer got closer, Dale recognized him, and when the surfer realized it, he placed his index finger to his mouth to indicate to be quiet. When the surfer got to the blanket, Dale had already picked up Capri and was holding her.

"Who might this little one be?" the surfer asked.

"Her name is Capri. She was named after you," Dale said.

"Seriously? She's mine?" Cap asked.

"Yes, sir! She is!" Dale responded.

Cap reached out to grab Capri and Dale handed her over to him. Cap took her into his arms, looked at her in the eyes, and Capri smiled.

"Look she smiled!" Dale said. "She smiled, Cap!"

"Yes, she did, didn't she, Dale?" Cap responded.

Dale saw the tears running down Cap's face even though he was smiling as well.

When Marta got up to the cross timber, she first tried to push the kelp to the side, so she could read what was carved. That didn't work, so she had to painstakingly remove it, break it off the timber, and toss it aside. When she was done, the words she saw jumped out at her. She stepped back and dropped to her knees, cupped her hands to her mouth, and started to tear up. She wondered how long they had been there. She had not been to the beach since the day before Capri was born. She then sat back on her calves, shaking her head. When Cap saw this, he handed Capri back over to Dale.

"Give us a moment, Dale, will ya?"

"Sure, Cap," Dale said.

Cap then walked over to Marta from behind until he was only a couple yards away. She was bent over her knees, weeping quietly, when he spoke.

"I wrote that few months back after I saw you singing kara-oke at the Lahaina."

Marta lifted up her head, thinking she was hearing things. She didn't dare turn around yet, for fear it was just the wind playing tricks on her or she was dreaming again.

"I wasn't in any shape to see you then, but I felt I was in some sort of shape for you to hear from me, so I carved those words into the timber." There was a bit of silence before he continued. "Little did I know you wouldn't see it until today." He hesitated again before he went on. "But hey, what a beautiful day it is, don't ya think? Quite a contrast to the last time we met under here." Cap stood there silently, looking at Marta, waiting for a reaction of some sort.

Marta knew now it wasn't the wind speaking or a dream; she slowly started to get up, but avoided looking at him while doing so, staying focus on the cross timber. He moved a little closer and tried to peek at her when she slowly turned and looked. She stepped backward when she saw it really was him. She brought both her hands to her mouth as she saw Cap standing there with his long hair and beard, bare chested, wearing a pair of swimming trunks—almost no different than the day she met him, except this time he looked healthy and was groomed. She then dropped her hands, took two giant steps toward Cap, jumped into his arms, wrapped her legs around his waist and her arms around his neck, and just cried. Cap stood there, caught her, and wrapped his arms around her, rocking her gently side to side as she continued to cry.

After a brief time, she lifted her head off his shoulder. She looked at him and took one hand to wipe the tears that were flowing from his eyes and he did the same with hers. They both laughed, then she leaned in and kissed him, and they kissed long and hard until she could hear Capri being fussy in the background. She broke away from their kiss and saw Dale was walking toward them. She looked at Cap, kissed him once again briefly, and then jumped down from his arms.

"Um, I have something to tell you," she said.

Cap turned around as he saw she was looking behind him and he could hear Capri as well.

"Oh, you mean Capri. We have already met," he said, as he reached over and grabbed his daughter from Dale's arms. Capri had the toy shovel in her hand, waving it back and forth, and she started smiling again once she was in Cap's arms. "Cool name, by the way," he said.

"Great name!" Dale shouted.

"Yes indeed!" Marta said.

Cap reached around with his free hand and ran it through Marta's hair. Marta looked at him.

"Do you like it?" she asked.

"I love it, but it means we need a Christmas tree to hang those ornaments on this year!" he said, laughing.

Marta punched him in the shoulder, smiled and grabbed his hand, bringing it down to her waist while leaning her head on his shoulder. They started walking back to the blanket when Capri dropped the toy shovel.

"Oh, oh," Dale said.

He stopped and turned to pick up the shovel. When he did, he saw the words carved on the cross timber Marta had been looking at and mouthed them out loud. "Love you, darlin'." He stood there and thought for a moment, and then it was like a lightbulb went on and he smiled. He turned and caught up with Cap and Marta at the beach blanket. He helped them get everything in the bag, which she threw over her shoulder, and the three of them started to walk off. They got close to the stairs when Cap remembered the surfboard. Dale ran back, got it, and caught up with Cap and Marta at the foot of the stairs. Cap and Marta looked at each other again and smiled. She placed her hand on Cap's cheek and gave him a kiss. Cap then let her walk up the steps in front of him and Capri. Dale had the surfboard tucked under his arm and followed, across to Garnett Street. They walked past the restaurants, bars, and tattoo parlors. Past the hookah joints, health clubs, thrift stores, and many other shops until they reached the Curl Gurl Brewery.

Finis

COMMUNITY OF MARTA II

(The story will continue—here's a peek)

Gary awakened from the sound of the park maintenance man emptying the trash barrels along the South Shore Parkway path of Mission Bay. He was lying cuddled next to his bicycle, using the front tire as a pillow, and the only covering he had was that of the dirty clothes he was wearing. He slowly arose, sitting up on the hard pavement he had slept on all night. He and the maintenance man briefly locked eyes. The maintenance man shook his head and continued with his work.

Gary took his dirty hands, wiped his eyes clean from the night's sleep, and pinched his nose clean of drippings. He reached into a small plastic bucket that sat inside a small milk crate alongside his bike. Sticking out of each of the three voids created in the corners of the square crate he had three small fishing poles, along with a few other items inside the bucket. From the bucket, he pulled out a plastic bottle of water, twisted off the cap, and chugged the bottle empty, tapping the bottom to get every drop. He then twisted the cap back on and placed it carefully back inside the bucket.

He slowly eased himself up until he was standing. Gary, a man of dark black skin, stood at about six foot three, maybe a bit taller with his black and gray hair matted down. Gary shuffled a few steps over to the edge of the concrete walk to a row of neatly trimmed bushes. He unbuttoned and unzipped his jeans, letting them fall to his knees, baring his ass, and began to piss into the bushes. When he finished, he pulled up his pants and turned to see the park maintenance man looking at him again, shaking his head. Gary acted as if he was not even there and walked back to his bike, reaching down to pick it up. He put down the kickstand with his foot, letting the bike stand by itself. He then reached down for the milk crate and placed it on the rear fender carrier. He pulled a bungy cord out of the bucket to tie the cord around the crate and onto the fender carrier. He adjusted his fishing poles accordingly, then grabbed the bike's handlebars, put up the kickstand, and threw one leg over the bike, placing both feet firmly on the pavement. He looked up at the morning sun, squinting his eyes at first, and then closing them. He stood there letting the warmth of the sun flow through his face and down his body. After a few moments, he smiled and ran his hands through his disheveled hair, then placed them back on the handlebars, placing his feet upon the pedals, and slowly and awkwardly started to peddle down the concrete courtyard.

ACKNOWLEDGMENTS

There are many people to thank, but those noted below are the ones who most helped me shape the book.

To Julie Wild, for your tremendous help in making sure I had the military terms and usage correct and encouraging me to get this book done because the story was wonderful.

To Lisa Miley, for encouraging me and recommending I attend the La Jolla Writers Conference, where I could find all the help I needed to work toward getting the book completed and published.

To Gene Riehl, my mentor, and his wife, Diane, my cheerleader, for your constructive criticism and suggestions during the process and constant encouragement to finish what you thought was a wonderful love story with the potential to teach others some valuable lessons. My love for your friendship and kindness will never cease to exist; it's proof that people come into your life for a reason.

To my classmates and instructors at the La Jolla Writers Conference, who not only helped a fellow with a broken foot in a boot get from lecture to lecture, but also led me along the right path to take with my storytelling to a new level. There was never an ounce of negativity, just thousands of ounces of encouragement and high praise to not only me, but to other writers as well. No one's dream was ever put down or discouraged and that's the single biggest reason why this conference is arguably the best around.

To the beta readers and many others who received my manuscript to critique. Your valuable feedback and constructive criticism were invaluable.

To my cover models, O'Ryan and Brittany Novick, for representing my vision.

To Adrienne Moch, for your wonderful editing and making this rookie's work read much better.

To Marni Freedman and Carlos de los Rios, whose coaching and critique of my writing were invaluable in helping me find "my voice." Your teamwork and encouragement, along with your enthusiasm in believing the book was a sound piece of literature to be shared, made it easier to get through all the re-writes necessary to get it to the publishing stage. In addition, the connections with others I made as a result of your guidance will be forever appreciated.

To Jeniffer Thompson and your team at Monkey C Media, for all the hard work and effort put into shaping this book into what it appears today. Your enthusiasm in believing the story needed to be something that could be held physically in the palms of others to read and the craftmanship you all put into it has done nothing but put a grin on my face from ear to ear—and hopefully on many others' as well.

To Paulo Coelho and his book, *The Alchemist*, which changed my life.

To anyone and everyone through the years who I've come across in my life's journey who has helped me learn the worst of myself and the best of myself and taught me lessons I hope will assist others in learning from the past. If we first look at the good in everyone, maybe, just maybe, we can change the world.

A percentage of every sale of each book will be donated to
Waves of Water in honor of those whom have
left us much to soon in life!